Not Guilty

BISCAYNE BAY SERIES

BOOK 2

DEBORAH BROWN

This book is a work of fiction. Names, characters, places and incidents are either the product of the author's imagination or used fictitiously. Any resemblance to actual persons, living or dead, or to actual events or locales is entirely coincidental. The author has represented and warranted full ownership and/or legal right to publish all materials in this book.

This book may not be reproduced, transmitted, or stored in whole or in part by any means, including graphic, electronic, or mechanical without the express written permission of the author except in the case of brief quotations embodied in critical articles and reviews.

NOT GUILTY
All Rights Reserved
Copyright © 2021 Deborah Brown

Cover: Natasha Brown

ISBN-13: 978-1-7334807-7-2

PRINTED IN THE UNITED STATES OF AMERICA

NOT GUILTY

Chapter One

"Avery English, when are you going to start locking your door?" Seven demanded in a grouchy tone as he kicked open the door and crossed the threshold, a paper cup in each hand.

I wiped the smirk off my face as I turned and faced the blond-haired, blue-eyed hottie dressed in jeans and a dress shirt. Little did Seven Donnelly know, but his latest acquisition—a black Escalade with tinted windows—had caught my attention when it passed by on the large security monitor that sat on the corner of my desk. I'd tracked the car as it curved around the back of the building and pulled into the underground garage. He also didn't need to know that I knew exactly how long it would take him to climb the stairs to the second floor.

"Would you believe that a client just left?" I took off my oversized cat-shaped glasses and tossed them in the drawer, knowing that he didn't like them. I didn't actually need glasses, but they lent credence to the nerdy persona I liked to project. He claimed they blocked his ability to see my "beautiful" eyes.

With a shove, Seven slammed the door shut

and strutted over to my desk like he owned the place. He set down a cup of coffee right under my nose like he did every morning on the way to his third-floor office.

I'd really begun to look forward to these visits.

The previous occupant of the third floor and owner of the property had recently retired and now spent most of his time with cronies on the golf course, showing up on occasion to make sure the building was still standing. Seven had partnered with his longtime friend Grey Walker, both ex-cops, in their newly formed security firm, WD Consulting, which had moved into the space vacated by the owner.

"I think you just made that up so you don't have to listen to another safety lecture." He gave me a piercing stare, one hand reaching out and pushing back a couple stray locks of my sun-streaked hair that had come loose from the messy twist I'd fashioned earlier. He stepped back, claimed one of the two chairs in front of my desk, and stretched his legs out. Settling back, he raised his cup and winked. "I happen to know you're obsessive about detail, so were you by chance expecting me?" He cut off my response with a wave of his hand. "I know what's coming next—you're going to tell me that another client's about to walk through the door. Do I have that right? No answer needed, as I know how accommodating you are to your clients—meeting most of them on their turf—hence only a handful grace these premises. Good excuse, though. Save it for someone who doesn't know you."

"Did you hear that?" I tilted my head, staring up at the ceiling. "Grey's yelling for you to get upstairs and get some work done."

Stupid grin on his face, Seven rolled his eyes. "With this building's layers of concrete, we could have a bloody free-for-all going on up there and you'd never hear a thing."

"That's all we need." I air-boxed.

"How about dinner? Say yes. I promise you won't regret it."

"I don't date." Rarely anyway. I'd done my share of casual encounters and friend fix-ups, and they'd turned out okay, but nothing special. After a lot of stilted conversations where I'd done my best to dumb it down, they always ended on an awkward note with my date as eager for the evening to come to an end as I was.

"That's a new excuse. You're usually busy, with some client demanding your attention." He gave me an exaggerated frown.

It was hard not to laugh, and it just slipped out. I'd done my best to discourage him, hadn't I? He was just so damn cute, but I wasn't going to go into all the ways that we were better off being casual friends. "The truth is, I don't date clients." Actually, I liked the friendly banter and didn't want it to change.

"When it comes to WD's finances, you deal primarily with Grey. You're thinking too hard."

Seven's feet hit the floor, and he leaned forward. "One dinner, no expectations." He crooked his head to the side and stared at the security monitor. "We need a couple of these upstairs. In the meantime, something's going on…"

My eyes shot to the monitor. "What's happening?"

Seven and I watched as another Miami-Dade police car followed the first one into the parking lot and both parked in front of the building. The officers got out, checked out the building and exchanged a few words, then headed to the entrance.

"They buzzed me." I eyed the intercom pad at the door. "Wonder if they just started pushing buttons to see who might answer."

"This probably isn't a social call." Seven stood. "I'll go down and find out what's going on."

I ignored the shiver that raced up my spine. Or tried to, anyway. "Be careful. I know you used to be one of them, but you never know."

"I knew you liked me." He grinned and raised his shirt, showing off impeccable abs as well as the gun holstered at his waist. "In case you need peace of mind, I've got backup on the off chance I need it. In this case, I highly doubt it will be necessary."

I gave him a weak smile.

Seven crossed to the door and double-checked the lock, then turned back to me. "Keep it locked until I get back."

"You don't have to tell me twice." I saluted as he shut the door. I thought of Hugo's cleaning service on the first floor and hoped that none of the guys that worked for him were in any kind of trouble.

Chapter Two

From the second-floor office of AE Financial, I stared out the window at the towering high-rise office buildings on the other side of the freeway overpass. The first time I turned into the parking lot of the square four-story white stucco building, I knew that I'd found the perfect office space. I'd caught my best friend—Harper Finn, the owner's daughter—off guard when I presented her with a lease, but she'd signed after being assured that I couldn't be talked into a swankier location. In fact, I'd included in the lease that should the building go up for sale, I'd get to make the first offer and would match any others that came in.

I watched as Seven exited the building and approached the cops, of which there were now three, as another had just pulled in and parked. The commercial neighborhood was always quiet because of the out-of-the-way location. The road below hadn't been heavily trafficked since I moved in, and I'd deduced that the area, and the nondescript building in particular, didn't attract much attention, as neither stood out in any way. It helped that there wasn't an on- or off-ramp to the freeway that ran overhead only a few hundred feet away, and maneuvering the side streets required that you were familiar with the area or using a GPS.

Judging by the clap on the back and handshake that Seven and another officer exchanged, the two were more than casually acquainted. Seven had retired early from the police force in Orlando and, wanting a change of scenery and to be closer to his family, moved south and joined his brother in the family yacht-selling business. When Grey — another cop who'd retired early — also moved down from Orlando, the two renewed their friendship and started a security consulting business.

After a short conversation with the officers, Seven opened the door, and they all filed inside. It creeped me out when they disappeared from sight, leaving me wondering what they wanted. I didn't have to wait long to find out where they were headed. After a few minutes, there was a loud knock on my office door. I got up and looked out the peephole, not surprised to see Seven and the three cops. Why did they want to talk to me? One way to find out… I opened the door.

Seven backed me into the room, leaning in and lowering his voice. "I've got your back and will be working every second behind the scenes."

One of the cops stepped around Seven. "Avery English?" I nodded. "You're under arrest for the murder of Stella Basset. You have the right to remain silent—"

"Avery, not one word until you speak to your lawyer," Seven ordered in a brisk tone. "I've got one of the best on speed dial. He'll meet you at the station and walk you through the process." He crossed his lips, a 'do you understand?' look on his face.

Once again, I nodded. "Stella's dead?" I said in confusion. When did that happen? When was the last time I talked to her? A few days ago, maybe? I'd have to check my calendar. Stella had been one of my first clients, and I'd done well with her investments, giving her a healthy return on her money. The cop motioned for me to turn, and as soon as I did, he cuffed me. I shook my head, realizing he'd talked the whole time and I'd barely heard a word. "Where are you taking me?"

"You'll be booked into the downtown jail. After that, there will be a hearing in front of a judge, where he'll read the charges, you'll enter a plea, and he'll decide on bail." The intensity of Seven's blue eyes penetrated through me.

"I didn't murder anyone," I told him, wanting him to know. "I wouldn't."

"You don't have to convince me." Seven brushed a kiss across my lips. "Now, not another word. Your lawyer, Cruz Campion, will be waiting for you at the jail or arrive soon after you do. He's got a stellar reputation, and you can trust him." He rubbed his thumb under one of my eyes and then the other.

I hadn't realized that a few tears had escaped and were now trickling down my cheeks. No time for that now. *Besides*, I reminded myself, *you're not a crier*.

The cop tugged on my arm. I turned back to Seven. "My purse is in the desk drawer, along with my keys. Will you lock up?"

"I've got it covered." Seven gave me a comforting smile, his phone in his hand. "Calling your lawyer now."

The cop led me out, the other two staying behind. My mind a muddled mess, I worried over what I couldn't control. What they were planning to do in my office? Seven followed, and the three of us rode silently down in the elevator to the first floor. The cop helped me into the back seat of one of the patrol cars and exchanged a few words with Seven before climbing behind the wheel. Seven never took his eyes off me as the cop backed out and turned onto the quiet street. At the last second, I looked over my shoulder and saw that he'd gone back into the building.

"No talking," I whispered to myself and instead tried to lean back, except the cuffs poked me uncomfortably in the lower back. If I'd needed a reminder that life could change on a dime and for the worse, this was it. Would I ever see freedom again?

I watched as the streets blended into one

another, usually packed with cars and a tangle of traffic. This guy cut around it all, which made the ride to police headquarters shorter than I would've liked. He cruised into the station and around the back, parked, and helped me out, leading me through an unmarked door.

"Seven believes in your innocence, and he's a good judge of character." The cop smiled encouragingly. "I'm hoping this all gets straightened out and ends well for the two of you. My advice: Follow the rules and mind your own business."

I nodded, and he led me down a hallway to a small room, pointing to a chair. I sat and waited until I was called to be fingerprinted and have my mugshot taken. Then came a change of clothing—an orange jumpsuit.

They told me I had the right to make a phone call. But to whom? *Hi, this is Avery; I've been arrested for murder.* Who'd believe that? They'd think it was a bad joke, as I'd never been in trouble before. A female officer grabbed my arm and led me farther down the hall, coming to a metal door that she opened with a key. One cell after another ran the length of one wall. She came to a stop, unlocked the door, and led me inside, removing the cuffs. The door clanged shut behind me, the finality of the noise unnerving, but not as much as the woman on the top bunk, snoring loud enough to wake the dead. Apparently, nothing interrupted her sleep. I inched my way forward, giving the mattress on the lower bunk a suspicious once-over. I didn't want to sit on it, but it was either that or the floor. I sat gingerly and scooted back against the wall, then curled into a ball and buried my face against my knees.

It was hard to tell the passage of time, or whether it was even day or night. Barely a shadow came through the miniscule window at the top of the wall, almost at the ceiling. The woman above me hadn't moved and continued to snore; I wondered if she was drunk.

A guard showed up, this time a man, and unlocked the door. "Your lawyer is here to see you." He motioned for me to get up and turn around, then handcuffed me. We went back down the hall, and he stopped in front of an unmarked door and ushered me into a small room. The grey walls were blank, and an old oblong table sat in the middle of the floor along with two chairs. The guard undid my cuffs, which surprised me, and pointed to the only empty chair. He left, closing the door behind him.

The dark-haired, good-looking man sitting across from me cocked his head, his brown eyes looking through me, ferreting out every secret I'd ever had. He extended his hand. "Cruz Campion, your lawyer. Call me Cruz."

"Avery English. Thank you for showing up on such short notice. Frankly, I was skeptical that

Seven could pull it off." His stare unnerved me, but I managed to maintain eye contact, knowing it was important if I wanted to be believed.

Cruz chuckled. "Seven has my cell number, so that tells you we're longtime friends. He's helped me out a time or two, so it's my turn to step up." He reached out and patted my hand. "Don't think for a moment that Seven sent over someone incompetent. You're in good hands. I'm one of the best criminal attorneys in the state; I'd say the whole country, but that would be boastful. I don't like to lose and have an impeccable record as a result." His smirky smile oozed a cockiness that conveyed it really was "the whole country."

"Just get me out of here, the sooner the better." I clasped my hands together to keep them from shaking.

Cruz shot one question after another at me. I answered with directness and continued to make eye contact.

There was one question he hadn't asked, so I went ahead and answered it. "I didn't murder Stella Basset. In fact, the first that I heard she'd passed on was when the police officer told me."

"You thought I missed that question, but I never ask." Cruz smiled reassuringly. "What's going to happen next is you're going to go before a judge via video feed, and when asked, you'll enter a plea of 'not guilty.' At that point, I'll ask to have a bail hearing set, which will take a few days. Seven is arranging for a bondsman so the cash can be posted quickly, and once the hearing is over, you'll be brought back here to be processed."

"I'm surprised they let suspected murderers out on bail."

"It won't be cheap. The court wants to be assured that you're going to show up for trial and they won't have to track you down." Cruz thumbed through the paperwork in front of him. "I'm going to pull some strings and get you a jail visit with Seven tomorrow. Be aware that conversations are taped during the visitation, so don't discuss the case."

I nodded.

"Once you've been released, you'll come to my office, and we'll go over everything in detail. Then I'll put together a case that will have the jury bringing back an acquittal."

"To do that, don't you have to find the real murderer?"

"My job is not to prove that another person committed the crime, but that the evidence presented isn't enough to prove your guilt. To do that, I'll be picking apart everything the district attorney presents. When the jury comes back with a verdict of not guilty, you'll be able to go on with your life."

Cruz inspired confidence. But once I got home—or rather *if*—I'd be checking him out. "I just want out of here and will do whatever you tell me."

"That's what I like, a cooperative client."

I knew our meeting was coming to a close, but I didn't know how to keep him talking to delay having to make the walk back to that dank cell.

Chapter Three

Jail sucked. And it was scary. At night when the lights went out, there were unidentifiable sounds and cries. Out of exhaustion, I finally lay down, rigid with fear, and eventually closed my eyes.

My cellmate, Lula Blank, had been a guest of this establishment a time or six on a variety of charges. "A person can't hang out anymore without being accused of prostitution." She wiggled around in her jumpsuit, her voluptuous figure pushing at the seams, and moaned on and on about the unfairness of life. The strip club she'd been working at was sold and then bulldozed, apartments going up in its place. What was a girl to do? I half-listened, and it apparently didn't register with her that my only comment was "uh-huh," in a feeble attempt to show that I was listening or interested or... But when she started repeating herself, I got lost in my own thoughts, trying not to feel sorry for myself and losing the battle.

I'd survived the night of strange sounds. Breakfast was another matter, and I picked at it with a suspicious eye despite my grumbling stomach.

A guard walked up. So far, the same one hadn't shown up twice. "You have a visitor."

I followed her down the aisle, and she pointed to a separate area off the main unit. I had yet to check out the amenities, not venturing from the cell except when ordered to and keeping to myself. I walked into a large room with glass along the far wall lined with cubicles separated by plexiglass, each with a chair. Seven waved to me through the glass, and I sat in front of him. He motioned to the red phone on the wall and picked up his.

"You hanging in there?" He smiled reassuringly.

I nodded. "I want out of here, but I'm not sure what I can do to make that happen from in here." I noticed a row of cubicles behind him, all occupied by men and women busy talking on the phone. "I didn't think to ask Cruz more questions about what happens next."

"Your bail hearing has been set for the end of the week," Seven said with a faint smile. "Cruz will be showing up for another in-person visit, which should be later today. He'll talk you through the process so you'll know what to expect when you get before the judge."

I took a deep breath to calm my nerves.

"I promise you, Avery, there's a lot going on behind the scenes on your behalf. Your two besties aren't happy that I got the first visit. I'm under explicit orders to repeat every word of what we say when I get back to them later."

For the first time since all this started, I smiled, albeit weakly. "Rella and Harper are the best."

Rella Cabot, Harper Finn, and I met at the University of Miami, and we'd been friends ever since. Even now, we lived on the same floor of a high-rise condo owned by Rella. It didn't surprise me that they had my back, but murder was asking a lot.

"Rella's already been in contact with a bail bondsman, and I'm to admonish you that you're not to say one word about her intervening."

"Rella knows a bondsman?" The woman was amazing in her ability to deal with any obstacle. She was the CEO of the Cabot Family Foundation, which funded various charities, mostly having to do with women and children.

"I'd already spoken to a bondsman that Grey and I know, and I referred Rella to him when she was done firing one question after another at me." Seven pouted, then chuckled. "At one point, she laughed at my annoyance when I told her I was on top of everything, saying, 'I'm sure you won't mind if I speak to this friend of yours? Avery is, after all, one of my best friends.'"

"I can't thank you all enough."

"Harper wants you to know that she's staying on top of everything related to your case. And she's ordering cheesecake for the day you're released."

Harper owned a social media business; it

wouldn't take her long to set up alerts on anything that hit the internet that included my name.

Seven reached out and pressed his fingers to the glass. "I know I'm asking the impossible, but try not to worry. Cruz is a great lawyer—the best, just ask him. If he hasn't boasted his superstar status, just check out his billboards; they'll scream it at you."

"Cruz's confidence was reassuring. He made me believe that he had everything under control, and if not, it wouldn't take him but a minute to get it that way."

"Some brag on themselves and are full of it, but Cruz's numbers speak for themselves. I know how that will appeal to your analytical mind."

"I haven't thanked you for not bailing on me. I wouldn't blame you if you did. I mean…" *murder*, I mouthed.

"Trying to getting rid of me?" Seven winked.

Another one absolutely sure of himself. I wanted to siphon off some of his assurance for myself.

"The light just blinked—" He pointed. "—meaning our time is coming to an end. We have two minutes before the line goes dead. Any good gossip?"

"The food is ick."

"So when you're out of here, that's a yes to dinner?"

"As long as we can sit outside and enjoy fresh

air and even better food."

"I'm holding you to it," Seven said with a wag of his finger and a smile.

"My cellmate snores. Really loud. I'm thinking she could splinter glass."

Seven made a face that had me smiling.

I took a deep breath and let it out slowly.

"We're running out of time here. Just know that there are several of us working to get you out of here. I put money in your commissary account, so you can fill up on junk food and pass on the ick. I worked my own magic and got another visit with you tomorrow, and I'll get one for every day you're in here, which won't be long."

"Your visits will be very welcome."

The line went dead. No additional warning.

Seven kissed the tip of his finger and pressed it to the glass.

I pressed my finger to his. I couldn't bear to watch him walk away, so with a wave, I left.

Chapter Four

It was a long week, but the day of the bond hearing was finally here. I was taken from my cell and got to change into the dress I arrived in. I hoped with everything in me that I wouldn't be coming back.

Cruz met me in the holding room and informed me that the district attorney had finally agreed to a bond of one million dollars, which included additional stipulations. I gasped.

"Breathe," he said, gently patting my back. "We wouldn't be here if I didn't have everything covered." He escorted me into the courtroom, and sitting in the first row were Rella, Harper, and Seven.

The three waved. Teary-eyed, I waved back. After sitting, I turned slightly to Rella and mouthed, *Thank you*. I knew she'd posted the bail and, I'd guess, hadn't flinched at the amount.

It was a fast hearing. The judge went over the terms and asked if I understood. I responded with an unequivocal yes. Another court date was set, and I was free to leave.

To my surprise, shock actually, Cruz walked me through the process of getting released. It wasn't his first time escorting a client, as he greeted everyone we encountered by name.

"Don't you have another client to save?" I was appreciative for the company but didn't want to keep him from someone who might not be getting out today. "You don't have to hold my hand." *Except that I'd really like it if you did.*

"A certain someone threatened me with bodily harm if I did otherwise." Cruz chuckled. "I haven't seen Seven this enamored with someone in a long time, and it looks good on him. Your boyfriend has been manic behind the scenes." He lowered his voice. "He called in a few favors on your behalf, and one, I know nothing about." He nodded like he expected the same from me.

"Seven's... he's uh..." I stopped at Cruz's smirk.

Seven had visited me every day, which kept me sane, and I knew that was unusual from comments Lula made. I'd lied and said, "Mr. Donnelly works for the law office that represents me, and we've been going over my case."

At last, I was shown the door to freedom. Seven stood waiting, a big grin on his face. Without a thought, I walked into his arms for a hard hug and was reluctant to back away. The only reason I did was I wanted to go home. "Thank you seems inadequate, but seriously," I murmured.

He looped his arm around me and held me close, steering me out the exit.

The first thing I did when I crossed the threshold to freedom was suck in a huge breath of fresh air.

"I'm taking you home. I imagine you want a shower, a change of clothes, and some edible food." Seven opened the door to his SUV, helping me into the passenger seat. "If you're wondering why Rella and Harper aren't here, they're waiting at your condo. They're planning a welcome home party, which includes food and drink."

"Another thank you for the deposit to my commissary fund. It saved me from starving," I said as he slid behind the wheel.

As Seven pulled out of the parking lot, he reached over and squeezed my hand. "We're going to figure out who killed Stella Basset and why. Leave everything to Grey and I, and as soon as you're feeling up to answering questions, we'll schedule a meeting."

"The first I'd heard about the murder was when I was being read my rights. Cruz told me that she was shot in the chest at close range and died instantly. If she couldn't be saved, I'm relieved that at least she didn't suffer." I pointed to a bottled water. "Is that for me?"

Seven picked it out of the cup holder and handed it to me. "There's more in the back."

I took a long satisfying drink. "There was an eyewitness who supposedly saw me fleeing Stella's house, which was probably why my appearance was mandatory at two lineups. They never said if the person on the other side of the blacked-out window picked me out."

"Cruz told me that it was an older woman who waffled and finally said that she couldn't be certain, which is good for your case."

"I'd like to go to my office, but since my friends are waiting, I'll do it tomorrow. I keep an accurate record of my time and will hopefully be able to detail my whereabouts for the night Stella died. Cruz and I already had this conversation, and I told him as much as I could remember but that I'd email him a copy of my notes." I heaved a big sigh. "I'm used to structure and order. I don't like being out of my element and not knowing what to expect next."

Seven easily maneuvered through traffic and over to the Causeway, which would take us out to the tip of Miami Beach. As we approached, the sun sparkling off the blue waters of Biscayne Bay had a relaxing effect on me, and I knew we were close to home.

"You need to be prepared. The cops—"

I groaned. "How bad is it?" Cruz had informed me that the cops had gotten search warrants for both my home and office, and I knew that they'd removed electronics and files.

"You don't have to worry that they tore anything up; they were very respectful of your property. Having heard from a friend still on the force that they were about to head over, I arranged to meet them and let them in so you wouldn't have to replace the door."

"Their investigators are going to find that I run a legitimate investment business and keep detailed records. The numbers fiend in me won't allow anything less." I turned away for another glimpse of the water and to reassure myself that we were minutes from home. "I'm going to be needing a laptop." I had a backup, if it hadn't been found, but didn't want to share that tidbit just yet.

"Got it covered. There's a new one, same brand, still in the box, sitting on the island in the kitchen."

"You're just a little too perfect." His chuckle pleased me. "Seriously, you should've run for the hills… or the water anyway. Instead, you've been here for me, and before I even know what to ask, you've got it covered."

"That's what boyfriends do." Seven smirked.

"I heard that from Cruz, and it caught me off guard. Not knowing what to say, I stuttered through a half-denial that only made him laugh." I felt my cheeks heat up at his amusement. "You do know that boyfriends, and people in general, don't like other people's messy lives spilling over on them." I'd be finding out how accurate that was when I got hot on the phone tomorrow and found out which clients would take my calls.

Seven arrived at the beach, and I took one last glimpse of the water lapping the sand before he pulled into the driveway. The gate rolled back, and he entered the underground garage, parking next to my Porsche. Another surprise to see it parked in its usual space.

He had a security fob? "How did you...? I don't know why I'm asking, since you've proven yourself to be a man of many talents." I took a car count, and my friends were all home. "Cruz made an interesting comment—that you'd called in a few favors, but one in particular, he didn't want to know anything about and didn't want me bringing up. Fine with me, since I didn't have a clue what he was talking about."

Seven reached out and turned my face to his. "Nothing illegal, I assure you. I just made sure that the right person heard what a great person you are and gave my word you wouldn't be jumping bail."

"I would never do that to Rella," I assured him. "I'll be paying her back in the next couple of days, but still... I wouldn't smear her reputation."

"Rella already turned that offer down. Because she had the ability to post a cash bond, it'll be fully refunded when the case is over. Annoyed our bail friend, since it cut him out of a commission, but he can make it up somewhere else." I nodded, and he got out and walked around. I had the door open and was getting out.

"Now I know how you have access to the building." I pointed to my keys in his hand.

He took my hand and deposited the keys into it, folding my fingers around them. "No worries; I made a copy."

Of course he did. And he wasn't the slightest bit embarrassed.

"All your personal items are upstairs, and that includes your purse. Since your phone was confiscated, I got you another one, which is on the charger upstairs. Too bad—I'd have liked to look at your pictures."

"And my texts? You wouldn't have found anything very interesting."

Chapter Five

We rode straight up to the forty-second floor, which had its own elevator, no waiting. Rella owned the building, which she never publicly disclosed, and still occupied the same unit as when her parents were alive. She sold the other two units on the floor to Harper and myself, with the stipulation that if we ever wanted to sell, it would be back to her corporation.

"I'm sure you'll be happy to get back to your real life," I said as he unlocked my door.

Seven's growly laugh had me turning to him. "We need to talk about that."

What was he talking about? I continued to stare. The man was a force. To hold my own with him, I'd need a full night's sleep, devoid of odd noises in the dark that sent spikes of fear up my spine. Not to mention the snoring.

Seven opened my door, ushering me into the wide-open space made up of the living room, dining room, and kitchen. All the rooms had views of Biscayne Bay.

My friends, who were sitting around the island, all waved, expectant smiles on their faces. Harper and her boyfriend, Grey, had met when she accepted a contract to kill him. Long story. Rella was at the far end. The women jumped off their stools and we group-hugged.

"I want to hear all about life in the clink." Harper couldn't contain her excitement.

Rella rolled her cool blue eyes at Harper and shook her head. "What's important is that you look great, all things considered. One night this week, we'll get our drunk on, and then you can share the grisly details. You just need to catch your breath first." She sent Harper a faux-glare.

Harper laughed at her. "Admit it—you want to know just as much as I do."

"I'm so happy to see you two." The three of us hugged again.

"We're here for you, whatever it takes," Harper assured me.

Rella nodded.

The two led me down the hallway and into the last door on the right—the master bedroom.

"You take a shower and wash off the jail cooties." Harper pointed to the bathroom.

"I'll pick out something I know you like that's comfortable and leave it on the bed." Rella reached out and brushed away my tears. "None of that. We're going to fix this."

I will not cry. I nodded and went into the bathroom, eager to scrub off those cooties. As much as I wanted to, I didn't stay under the showerhead until the hot water was gone. True to her word, Rella'd picked out a pair of crop cotton pants and a matching top, which I pulled on, then went barefoot in search of food.

No one had left; they were all still sitting around the island.

"Drink?" Seven asked, pointing to an empty stool.

"A shot of whiskey."

"I knew we were fated." Seven poured the drink and sat next to me.

"Sip," Rella ordered. "You don't want to get sauced on an empty stomach."

"We ordered your favorites from Luigi's." Harper winked at me and tossed an oven glove at Grey. He got up and removed several containers from the oven, setting them in the middle of the island, which had been set with plates and silverware.

The food smelled heavenly. Rella had taken over as hostess, putting a spoonful of everything on a plate and setting it in front of me. Conversation swirled about me. I only half-listened but managed to catch up on what everyone had been doing.

We lingered over the food, and once we were finished, Grey and Seven stacked the dishwasher.

"Let's go out to the deck. The view is not to be ignored." Rella motioned to us. One of the many things that the three of us had in common was a love of the water.

I slid off my stool and refilled my whiskey

glass, my last drink of the night, managing to refrain from grabbing the whole bottle and disappearing off into a corner by myself. As tempting as that was, I needed to be proactive tomorrow, and not with a hangover.

We settled in chairs with oversized cushions, each with its own side table, which had been arranged in a circle so we all faced one another. On the other end of the deck was a dining table and chairs.

"Seven told me that the two of you will be investigating my case." As had Cruz. I stared at Seven, who sat next to me, then Grey, next to him. "Thanks to Seven—" I smiled at him. "—I'll have my new laptop programmed tonight and be able to help with any reports you need." Their eyebrows going up didn't escape my notice. "Before you blow me off, you know I'm good and fast. Another plus is that I'm available to get started immediately—after I get in touch with my family and clients to assure them that I'm not a killer. Since I'm under court order not to handle anyone's finances, I'll be turning my files over to—hopefully—Dixon, who I also need to contact. That way, I can supervise without violating the terms of my release."

"I talked to your parents every day," Rella said. "After telling Seven to keep us informed on his visits with you or risk limb damage, I relayed everything he shared. They were eager for the information, and I thought it was cute that they each got on a phone and talked at once."

"I can't thank you enough for that. Since they know and like you, you were the perfect one to relay the news." Truth was, they were more comfortable with her than me. My high IQ had always intimidated them. I realized early on that it made for awkward moments and I did my best to downplay my achievements, but the more I excelled, the more uncomfortable they got.

"They took the news of your arrest better than I'd expected, and naturally, they were Team Avery from the beginning. They didn't believe that the charges held a kernel of truth and knew you'd be vindicated." Rella smiled. "They'll be expecting you at a family dinner ASAP so they can hug and love on you."

"I'll call them once we've finished eating." I was happy to hear that they knew some of what'd happened. "Back to my helping investigate my own case… I have an appointment with Cruz in the morning. I'll make the rest of my calls when I get back, and then I'll be available."

"I'll drive you," Seven said.

"Are you going to make the announcement?" I challenged him and could easily tell he had no clue what I was talking about. I tapped my glass against Seven's to get everyone's attention. "I'd like you to meet my boyfriend." I flourished my hand towards Seven, who grabbed it and kissed the back.

"I knew it was only a matter of time," Harper crowed. "Seven's not bad. He's not Grey, but then, there's only one of him." She winked at the man, who responded with a big smile.

"How long has this been going on? And I didn't know?" Rella asked, suspicion in her tone.

"You need to ask him." I pointed to Seven. "I wouldn't have known if my lawyer hadn't told me while I was in the process of being sprung."

When the chuckles had subsided, Grey said, "Back to your case, I told Cruz we'd investigate anything he needs. Even though he already has someone on payroll, he complains they're slow. I'm fairly caught up on your case, but stop by the office after your appointment and we'll go over anything new."

"In return, tell me anything I can do for you, and it's done," I said.

"No thanks needed. Ever since you took over our investments, they've been making money. That's payment enough."

Friends are the best. They fed me, cleaned my kitchen, and slipped out the door as I started to nod off, too tired to feel guilty. Seven carried me to the bedroom and laid me on the bed, and I was out.

Chapter Six

The next morning, I woke to light filtering through the shutters and, without looking at the clock, knew it was early. I rolled out of bed and groaned, sitting on the edge. It hadn't seemed like a lot of whiskey, but my head said differently. I took a quick shower, wondering when I wouldn't feel the need to disinfect my skin.

Even though I had a backup laptop that hadn't been discovered, I left it in its hiding place, eager to set up the new one. At the end of the long hallway, I skidded to a stop. One of Seven's long legs hung over the back of the couch, a pillow over his face. I stared for the longest time, then tiptoed into the kitchen.

I ran my hand over the box that held my new laptop, noting that it was the exact same model as my old one. It wouldn't take long to have it up and running, as I had all my files backed up to a drive that I went to grab out of my safe. It didn't surprise me that the cops hadn't found it, as I didn't go for the usual place—behind a picture frame or some other obvious location. Instead, I'd had it installed behind a full-length mirror in my closet. The drives wouldn't have raised eyebrows, but I'd have had to account for the cash.

But first, coffee. With a side of aspirin. I grabbed the bottle from the cupboard and set it on the counter. Instead of my usual single cup, I brewed up a pot. If Seven wanted breakfast? Well, there were stale Cheerios in the pantry.

I slid onto a stool, a brimming mug of coffee within reach. It didn't take long to get the laptop up and running. I started by checking email. More than a few people, some casual acquaintances, had forwarded articles along the lines of "Murderer takes advantage of elderly clients." One reporter had printed a story about another of my clients who'd died two months ago and said it was being reinvestigated. He failed to mention that she was in her eighties and her death had been ruled "natural causes." There were four emails from attorneys firing me on behalf of their clients. Not that I didn't expect it, but it still caught me off guard.

"Good morning," a way-too-cheerful Harper yelled as she burst through the front door, banging it behind her.

I focused on the big box in her hands.

Seven jerked up off the couch, tipping sideways, but caught himself before making contact with the floor. "I didn't hear you knock."

"Please. We all have keys to each other's units." Harper blew by him and came into the kitchen, lifting the lid on the box and waving it under my nose.

Yeah, sure. We did have each other's keys, but Harper likely used her lockpick. She had many interesting talents, and she'd yet to teach them all to me. Seven would probably flip, so he didn't need to know. "Donuts." I licked my lips. "You got my favorite." I grabbed the French one before anyone else could.

"I knew you two would get together," Harper whispered conspiratorially.

"We're not." I shook my head. "We're... I don't know. He's made up his mind that he wants to try us out. But... there's a lot he doesn't know about me. My nerdy little habits, for one, which have turned off more than one man in the past."

"I have a few of my own 'habits.'" Harper made air quotes. "Grey snapped me up anyway." At my raised eyebrows, she amended, "Okay, I did the snapping, but he came around."

The door opened again, and Rella flew in. My eyes darted to the couch, expecting another grouchy comment. No Seven. He'd gone... somewhere.

"I knew there were donuts in that box." Rella got down a coffee mug. "You better have saved me half of one."

Rella must have been at her desk and saw Harper getting off the elevator. I'd gotten monitors for each of us, which were connected to the security camera feed and allowed us to snoop around the building.

"Your trainer is going to be shocked at the carbs you're consuming." I rounded my mouth in exaggerated shock. "I'm sure it'll take you two minutes to work it off, considering you're already in top shape."

Rella filled her mug and chose a whole donut, cutting it in half and wrapping the rest in a paper towel to take home. She came up behind me, hanging her head over my shoulder and reading the screen. "You need to stop Googling your name." She closed the lid.

Harper refilled my coffee.

"I'm losing clients," I lamented. "I need to liquidate a few accounts, and I'll have the bail money back to you in a couple of days."

"No, you won't, and not another word. I'll get it back when the trial is over. End of story." Rella slapped her manicured hand on the island.

I hoped her billionaire parents weren't going to have a conniption from the afterlife about their daughter posting bail.

"Not all your clients are ditching you," Harper said with a smile. "Rella and I aren't going anywhere, and none of my family members are stupid enough to cancel your services when I know for a fact that you've made us all money. If we hadn't, we'd've said 'sayonara' at the first sign of the numbers dropping into the red."

"Morning, ladies." Seven walked into the

kitchen, dropping a kiss on my cheek. That had Rella and Harper staring. "What did I miss? I have it on good authority that the three of you are always up to something." He poured a cup of coffee and sat next to me.

"You spent the night?" Rella scrutinized him closely.

Harper nodded with a smirk.

"On the couch," Seven said evenly.

"Harper brought donuts." I pointed to the box.

"Hmm…" Seven eyed us each individually, as though we were planning something and covering it up with the offer of sugar.

Time for a subject change. "I was surprised that my place wasn't a mess after the search warrant thing."

"It wasn't bad," Rella said. "I had it cleaned. Harper was going to check on your office, but when she mentioned it, Seven said he'd taken care of it. If not…" She turned a steely stare on him. "Let me know."

"You guys are the best."

Chapter Seven

My nerves were a bit frayed, anticipating the meeting with my lawyer. It didn't help that I didn't have any idea what to expect. At least I'd liked Cruz upon meeting him, and he'd won me over with his competence. I chose a black skirt and jacket, with a white dress shirt and heels, wanting to present a professional look. I made a mental note to ask about courtroom attire.

It surprised me, when we met up in the living room, to see that Seven had changed into dress pants and a button-down shirt. I assumed he hadn't just snapped his fingers, but with him, one never knew.

Seven whistled and gave me a once-over.

I felt my cheeks warm up. "You know..." I knew he wanted to accompany me and didn't want him to change his mind, so instead of giving him an easy out... "I'm taking you to lunch, since donuts aren't really breakfast."

"They'll do in a pinch." Seven held out his arm. I linked mine through his and walked us to the elevator.

It was a short drive to Cruz's office in Miami Beach.

Seven held out his hand and helped me out of the car. "Take a deep breath. Picture Cruz in something inappropriate, and that will calm your nerves. Just don't laugh in his face. Then you'd have to explain, and that would be awkward."

"Thanks for making me laugh."

We rode the elevator to the top floor, then stepped into the lobby. The sign behind the receptionist covered the entire wall, showing that he didn't share the floor with any other businesses, and the view of the blue waters of the Atlantic Ocean was breathtaking.

Seven approached the receptionist, who made a call, and almost immediately, an older woman made an appearance. "Seven." She nodded to him, then introduced herself to me. "Susie, Mr. Campion's assistant."

Cruz was king in his massive office, complete with huge desk, oversized chair, and the same amazing view. He and Seven exchanged smirks, along with some silent dude code that I ignored as I sat down. Keeping up with those two would give anyone a headache.

"Good to see that you survived your jail experience," Cruz said. "I had no doubt."

"I took the arresting cop's advice to lie low—something close to that, anyway—and kept to myself as much as I could."

"How did you meet Stella Basset?" Cruz asked.

I blinked at the abrupt switch into interrogation. "I was invited to give a talk about finances at an upscale retirement community, Morningside at the Beach. Afterwards, several residents and their guests came up and asked about my services. They didn't all request appointments, but Stella was one who did. I've done a few of these—I do a short presentation, take questions, and no hard sell." I screwed up my nose at that thought. "That's not me. I do give my business card to anyone who wants to follow up."

"How did you and Stella get along?"

"Our meetings were always about managing her finances. I got to know her a little bit, as I do all my clients." I wished I'd taken the beverage Susie offered. "We rarely talked about anything personal, unless it was a casual reference. I do know that she had two children, as I referred her to an attorney to update her will." Seven squeezed my hand, which caught Cruz's attention—I'd bet the man never missed anything. "Stella was one of my clients who liked to come to my office. Most prefer video conferencing or meeting anywhere food's involved."

Cruz grinned. "Sounds good to me."

"The downside is when one of them gets drunk and you need to make sure they get home okay. Sometimes it's a bit of a struggle when they think they can drive and they can't."

Cruz grimaced, and I knew that if he'd given the idea of meeting clients at a restaurant a minute's thought, it was now off the table. "I had a meeting with the district attorney." He flipped over a page of his legal pad, scribbling some notes. "He seems to think he's got a slam-dunk case, but then he always thinks that. The eyewitness who claimed to see you fleeing the scene turned out to be Stella's neighbor, and she couldn't ID you in a lineup, so that's in our favor. After seeing your picture in the news, she'll probably want a do-over but too late."

"Eyewitnesses have been known to be unreliable," Seven grouched.

"True, as in our case."

"What motive is the DA working on?" Seven asked.

"Greed," Cruz said, matter-of-fact. "According to the records found strewn across Stella's desk, money had been siphoned out of her largest accounts—small amounts that grew in size with each withdrawal. The night of her death, one account was cleaned out, and there was an attempt on another account that didn't clear."

"Why would I do that?" I asked, shaking my head. "That sounds sloppily done, and anyone with my background would know that it would generate red flags." I scanned the paperwork he handed me and noticed at a glance that the numbers didn't add up. "As good a lawyer as you are, you have to admit this is obviously a beginner, thinking they're more talented than they are."

Seven grinned at Cruz, who'd raised his eyebrows. "Wonder who told her you were a good lawyer?"

"You did," I whispered to Seven, though both men heard me.

"I could go on about my greatness, but I'm certain you want to get out of here." Cruz grinned. "Do you own a gun? I noticed that there wasn't one listed on the search warrant."

I shook my head. "I do not. I've got a friend who wants to take me to a shooting range, but I haven't taken her up on the offer."

"Has the murder weapon been recovered?" Seven demanded.

Cruz ignored him. "The DA planned to have another client of yours, Valerie Arnold, exhumed. The coroner saved him from getting a court order, informing him that he'd ruled it heart failure with no signs of foul play."

"I had very little one-on-one interaction with Ms. Arnold, as she didn't care to come to the office and we met virtually. Her funeral was private, and I sent flowers."

"Put together a timeline of your activities the day Stella died and email it over. Don't worry — I'm feeling good about your case." Cruz downed whatever was in the bottle sitting on his desk. "I've got a couple of off-topic questions," he said, then went on to ask about the stock market.

We discussed that for several minutes, and it was a great reprieve from all things legal.

Eventually, Cruz stole a glance at Seven, who looked bored, and snickered. "Unless something comes up, our next meeting will be at your next court hearing." He stood. "Don't get so much as a speeding ticket."

"No worries there. I won't even jaywalk."

"This has been fun," Seven said, not meaning a word.

I didn't run out the door but wanted to. Seven forced me to slow by hooking his arm around me. I waved at Susie, who raised her eyebrows at me. Maybe that wasn't office etiquette. Either that or she was prickly.

Riding down in the elevator, I croaked, "I need fresh air." One thing was for certain—I couldn't go back to jail. I wouldn't run... or would I? I refused to allow my thoughts to go there, reminding myself that Cruz had been encouraging—no doom and gloom, "get your affairs in order" spiel.

Seven opened the door to his SUV. Turning me around, he put his hands on both sides of my head. "I know it's difficult not to run through all the what-ifs, but you'll drive yourself crazy. I've got a good feeling about this." He gave me a cheeky grin, which made me smile.

"I may need that pep talk again."

"You're on." He walked around and slid behind the wheel. "That didn't go so bad. I could've used another cup of coffee, but I made that mistake once and it tasted like swill."

"That surprises me. Cruz seems like the kind of guy who wants everything top of the line."

"Normally, he doesn't want clients getting comfortable and forgetting to jet out the door. In your case, he found out you were a numbers whiz, and you answered his questions with a high level of competence. You can expect he'll have more in the future." Seven pulled out of the parking lot.

"It worked in that I relaxed for a moment. But when the meeting was over, I'd have run all the way back to the car if not for you."

Chapter Eight

"We've got time before lunch, so I thought we'd stop by the office. You take care of what you need to do, and I'll update Grey." Seven maneuvered the side streets, more familiar with the area than I was. I was just happy he knew where we were going because I didn't know this route.

"Since by court order, I'm not allowed to handle other people's money, I'll need to hand my client files over to someone else but would like to be available for consultation for those clients that haven't ditched me." It had been hard to get the "termination of services" notices after the long hours I'd put into building the business. "I left a message for Dixon this morning. It's my plan to bring him on board, since we've worked together before. If he won't go for it, I'll have to refer my clients to another company." Putting myself out of business would be painful. "Whatever happens, I need to keep busy. I know you and Grey were lukewarm about my offering to help with my case, but who better than me?"

"Noticed you didn't mention this great idea of yours to Cruz." Seven tilted his head. "I'm telling you now that he'd advise against it in the strongest possible terms."

He pulled into the parking lot of the office building, which had not a single car parked in front, and curved around and into the underground garage. We got in the elevator, and he stabbed the button for the second floor.

When the doors opened, I said, "As soon as I'm done taking inventory, I'll come upstairs."

Seven nodded and waved as the door closed.

I took a deep breath and unlocked the door, not knowing what to expect. I stepped inside and took a quick glance around, relieved to see that nothing looked out of place except for the lack of electronics. Once again happy that I was obsessive about triple backups, I settled behind my desk, kicked back in my chair, and stared at my cleared desk. I opened the drawers, and they were empty. The cops didn't find much in the way of hard copies, as I loathed paper clutter.

My phone rang, Dixon's face popping up on the screen. "Thanks for returning my call," I said on answering.

"Sorry to hear about—"

I cut him off, not wanting to talk about my jail stint. "I've got a job offer." I told him about the court order, that I wanted him to take over my client files, and that I'd be available to answer any questions that might come up.

"I'm happy to. Just to let you know, I've got a couple of my own clients. If you wouldn't mind,

I could coordinate everything out of your office."

"That's perfect. It would make it easy for us to meet when needed. How about we meet to talk terms, and I'll give you back the door key?"

Dixon laughed. "It's going to be good working together again."

I knew that he'd recently quit a job at an accounting firm, complaining, "they treat me like a numbnut and pile on the grunt work with no end in sight," even though he'd proven himself better at the job than anyone else in the office. He wanted flexible hours and to grow his own clientele. It didn't take him long to acquire some clients.

We set up a time for the next day.

I hung up, thinking, *One thing off my list, now what?* Realizing that every day would be like this... for a while anyway, I sighed, then locked up and climbed the stairs.

The sign on the door said WD Consulting. I turned the knob, and it opened. If I had to keep my door locked, why didn't they? When I pushed open the door, both men were on their cellphones and glanced up with a quick wave. The phone on the empty receptionist's desk started ringing. Last I heard, they still hadn't managed to hire one.

Seven jabbed his finger in its direction and covered his own phone. "Will you get a number and tell whoever it is that Grey will call them back?"

In their partnership, Grey did most of the schmoozing, enjoying the chase of finding new clients. Seven made the in-person visits, giving recommendations about needed services.

I grabbed the phone and circled the receptionist's desk, taking a seat. "WD Consulting," I answered.

"I'm in need of some help," an older-sounding man choked out, then started to wheeze and cough. "Don't hang up," he managed to get out.

"Take as long as you need; no need to choke to death." I opened the top drawer and pulled out a lone sticky notepad and pen. "I'm still here. When you're ready to talk, just let me know."

It took him a couple of minutes to catch a steady breath. "I'm in need of... I don't know what the hell."

"Before you start at the beginning, I'm Avery English, and you are?"

"Names would be good, wouldn't they?" He coughed. "Gregory Anders. But call me Anders, almost everyone does."

"I want you to know that whatever you tell me stays confidential." I didn't know if that was the policy, but it must be something close.

"I've been married six months now, and the wife cleaned out my bank accounts and took off. She tried to transfer the deed to my property out from under me, but thankfully, I managed to get it stopped." Anders went into another coughing fit.

"I'm assuming you'd like to hire WD Consulting to get your money back?"

"If you do that kind of work. I looked you up online, which probably isn't the best way, but I don't know who I could ask for a referral without having to spill my business."

"WD has the ability to trace the money. Is it recoverable, though? There's not an easy yes or no answer to that. It would depend on your wife's skills and what kind of money trail she left." Grey sat on the corner of the desk in time to hear what I'd said. He quirked his finger, wanting the phone. I shook my head and waved him off.

"I don't have a lot of money left," Anders said candidly. "Sissy—that would be my wife—would be damn mad to know that she left a couple of small accounts untouched. Neither had as much money as the ones she cleaned out, but it's better than being penniless. I don't take kindly to getting fleeced because I was thinking with my dick."

"On the positive side, you've realized your mistake and won't be doing it again. Correct?" Grey, who'd moved to the chair in front of the desk, scowled but listened with interest.

"You got that, sister."

I clicked on the cheap pen and, after much scribbling, tossed it in the trash, then snapped my fingers and drew in the air. Grey glared. I held up the notepad and shrugged, pointing at the phone. He reached in his pocket and handed me a pen. I eyed it, determining that it was a good one, expensive actually, and worked. "Mr. Anders, I'm sorry to meet under such unpleasant circumstances, but hopefully, WD can turn your situation around. I want to assure you that there will be no charge for the initial consultation." I ignored Grey shaking his head, annoyance on his face.

Now off the phone, Seven decided to join the party. He and Grey exchanged a few words, and Seven took the chair Grey vacated. No motion for the phone.

"Did you say Sissy is your wife's name?"

"Sissy Anders."

"If you don't mind my asking, how old are you and Sissy?" I asked. Seven was shaking his head. *This is my conversation, buddy.*

"I'm seventy-three, and she's twenty-five." Followed by more coughing.

I waited until Mr. Anders caught his breath. "I'm not lecturing, but I've got a couple of suggestions, since you've admitted that dick-thinking got you into this situation." I guess I should have rephrased that, since Seven covered his mouth to laugh. "Next time, try for someone closer to your own age, although that's not a sure bet. Also, before getting serious, call WD, and we'll do a background check. Gratis, of course." Seven had leaned forward, his hand out, then stopped and grinned. I took that as a good sign.

"You sound like a nice young lady." I nodded, which he couldn't see. "What's this going to cost me?"

"I strongly suggest that you come into the office so you can go over the case with the partners. At that time, they'll be able to detail fees. I also suggest that you do it as soon as possible, as you don't want to give Sissy any more time than she's already had to move your money around." Anders grunted, which I took as a yes. "If she is moving it, the more often she does that, the harder it is to follow."

"Tomorrow, first thing?"

"Tomorrow?" I mouthed to Seven and pointed to my watch. He held up his fingers. "How's nine o'clock?" I asked.

"Works good for me, as I'm an early riser."

"Do you have the address?"

"I got it right here." He read it out to me.

"Excellent. I look forward to meeting you. One other thing—bring your financial records, and we'll go over everything. And don't worry, you're in good hands."

We hung up.

"Grey handles new clients, and you should've checked his schedule," Seven admonished, the twinkle in his eye infuriating me for some reason.

"Look, dickhead." I covered my mouth. "Oops, that slipped out."

"Sure it did."

"I checked with you, and if you needed big

boy's okay, you should've asked."

"I'll do that next time." The corners of his mouth turned up.

"You busy tomorrow morning?" I yelled across the room to Grey. "I may have gotten a little overenthusiastic on that call."

Grey grunted.

"It's okay if you don't have time, as I do, and I'd be good at this job. Besides, Mr. Anders is probably expecting to meet me, and it would be less awkward if I were at least here."

"You getting involved, anything more than an introduction, isn't a good idea." Grey motioned me over to his desk. "You don't want to do anything that will interfere with your own case."

"I can introduce you and then sit right here in case the phone rings."

Seeing that Grey was about to snap, Seven cut in. "How about sharing the details of the call?"

I repeated everything Anders had shared. "Since the man sounds like he needs a lung transplant, I told him there'd be no charge for the initial consultation. Maybe throw in a discount if you can't recover the money. If that's not copasetic and for some reason you can't locate it—" *We know that won't happen* in my tone. "— then send the bill to me."

"I have a forensic accountant I use for these kinds of cases. He's good but can be slow," Grey said. "Unless Mrs. Anders is a computer hacker or in league with someone who has those talents, we'll find the money. My guy loves these kinds of puzzles."

I didn't want to hear about Mr. Other Guy. "I'm assuming that you have no objection to my showing up?"

"Anytime you want to speak up, dude," Grey said to Seven in a grouchy tone.

I guess he didn't want to be the party-killer. Too late.

"What could it hurt? Unless you're worried that Avery will show you up." Seven grinned at Grey.

"You're an ass."

"Avery and I will get here early, and I'll get the coffee made," Seven said.

"I guess you've forgotten while trying to show off that you push one button on that machine over there and done." An eyeroll in Grey's tone.

"That makes it easier, now doesn't it?" Seven grinned.

"Now that that's settled, what about my case?" I asked.

"The money was transferred from Mrs. Basset's account into one with your name on it. It landed in a bank in New Mexico and then transferred again. The accountant that I mentioned is tracking it now."

The phone rang again.

"I'll get it," I said.

"No you won't, since I couldn't wrestle the last call away. I'll get it," Grey said, grabbing the phone before I could answer.

"You know," I said, tapping my cheek. "Since I have practically nothing to do, I could fill in as the receptionist you've never hired. That would give you and Grey a break from the phones—more time to be out schmoozing."

"That's one way for me to keep my eye on you."

"If you're worried that I'm going to skate off and dodge the police the rest of my life… not yet anyway. But I'm leaving it open as an option." I flinched at the idea.

"If you need to go on the run, I'll help. No one will find you unless you want to be found. In the meantime, I've appointed myself as your bodyguard, and I take my responsibilities seriously." Seven eyed me up and down with a smile. "I'll keep you out of trouble, or try anyway, and be your alibi should you need one." He reached out and pulled me to my feet. "Let's get out of here."

Chapter Nine

Turned out that Seven took his bodyguarding duties seriously, and when we got back to my condo, he informed me that he'd be staying. "Hear me out. Since you're neither a thief nor a murderer but someone wants people, namely law enforcement, to think you are, when they get wind that we're finally onto them, they could get desperate."

We were sitting out on the deck, and I stared out at the water, caught off guard, not sure why, and surprised that his high-handedness didn't annoy me. Truth was, I didn't want to be by myself.

"The guest bedroom is all yours. You'll be the first to stay in it." I gave him a flinty stare, which he met with a challenge in his eyes. I'd never had this kind of unrelenting attention from a man. I had no clue what he wanted in a woman, but I couldn't imagine that it was one who could be found digesting financial reports in her free time.

And just like that, it was decided.

I was always an early riser, awake before daylight. It was a good time to get things done with no interruptions. This morning, I wanted to make sure I didn't get left out of the meeting with Anders with the flimsy excuse that "you weren't ready," though I could always drive myself. I chose a short-sleeve swing dress for my two morning meetings—Dixon's was just a matter of giving him the keys; he was already familiar with my clients, having worked for me in his last year of college. But I really wanted to hear what Grey proposed for recouping Mr. Anders' money. Always barefoot in the house, I hooked my shoes over my finger and dropped them by the entry.

I made coffee and poured a cup, taking it and my laptop out to the deck to enjoy the morning breeze. With the sliders open behind me, I could hear Seven moving around once he cleared the hallway. I tracked his footsteps into the kitchen—coffee, I assumed—and then he came outside and sat next to me.

Seven nodded to my laptop. "I couldn't remember if it was part of the terms of your bail that you couldn't use electronics."

I shook my head. "Happy that they didn't put that restriction on me. To be on the safe side, though, I registered this one to you. But no worries, I'm not planning on doing anything illegal. On this one." I fully expected Seven to flip and was surprised when he only nodded.

"I'm assuming you have another one that law enforcement didn't find, in the event you want to walk that grey line… or just tumble over?" He gave me a flinty stare.

"Maybe." I wasn't giving up the hiding place just yet.

"Have you had enough time to start working on something that you shouldn't?"

"Ran a background check on Mr. Anders—nothing exciting. Then ran the wife, who also has a clean record. Be interesting to learn how she got access to his accounts."

"Show Grey the reports you worked up on Anders; I know he won't have any yet. To be honest, our guy could be a lot faster."

"I forwarded a copy to you and Grey this morning." I winked at him. "I'm good at this."

"No doubt about that. So tell me, what did you find out about Avery English?"

"Oh, her. I didn't need to run a background check, though I'm certain hers now includes an arrest record. I did find out that my bank accounts have been frozen." Okay, not all of them. I had two accounts that no one would ever know about if I had my way.

"You need money—"

"I've got cash, which is how I'll pay for everything for the time being. I'm not planning on any big purchases. Out of curiosity, what do people do if they don't have money stashed away?"

"Go back to court and ask the judge to release funds, which the DA would probably fight. It wouldn't be resolved quickly." He scrutinized me a little closely, which I tried to ignore. "I know you're feeling restless, so how about coming along on one of my jobs? Observe the master at work."

"I'm not sure how much help I'd be and wouldn't want to be in the way." I wrinkled my nose. "I've taken a self-defense class, but I'm not the ass-kicker Harper is. If you want company, I can go on a coffee run while you're hanging out somewhere."

"That sounds like a stakeout, and I try to assign those to someone else, as they're boring as hell. I'm WD's expert on security systems. Our newest client just bought a mansion out on Fisher Island and wants the latest system installed before they move in. It will take me a couple of hours to check out the place, inside and out, and get back to them with a report."

A ride-along—I could do that. "Swanky. I'm saying yes because I want to go on the boat ride and get a look around the private island." They had an adamant rule preventing lookie-loos.

Seven picked up his mug and mine and took them to the kitchen while I grabbed our briefcases.

Chapter Ten

When Seven and I walked into the WD offices, Gregory Anders was seated in front of Grey's desk. The older man turned, a serious expression on his face. "You must be Avery?" He smiled, looking relieved.

I thrust my purse at Seven and walked over, hand out. "Nice to meet you in person. Sorry about the circumstances." I patted his shoulder. "Did you want coffee? Tea maybe?"

"They were all so fancy." Anders shrugged. "Didn't appear to be a plain flavor on that rack."

"Give me a minute. I know which one you'll like." I hustled to the strip kitchen, chose the plainest brew of the bunch, and crossed my fingers that he'd like it. One thing about the machine, it didn't take long to fill up a mug.

Seven, who'd stashed my purse who knows where, introduced himself and sat down. Where was I going to sit? I decided I'd lean up against Grey's desk until he told me to scram. Harper had sent an email of laughing faces at the fits I gave the man by not handing over the phone during yesterday's call. Wait until she heard what I was about to do.

I set the coffee in front of Mr. Anders, and it surprised me when he grabbed my hand. "I brought the paperwork you requested." He handed me a file, which had been resting next to his leg, and looked around. "Is there another chair?"

Seven stood with a wink and gave me his, dragging another one over for himself.

I didn't have the nerve to make eye contact with Grey. He didn't react in words, but the huff he expelled let me know I'd overstepped. I flicked through the paperwork and noticed that Mr. Anders' investments were handled by a well-known company. "How did your wife get her hands on the money in this account? I only see your name."

"That would be with this paper." Anders pulled one out of the stack and handed it to me. "Sissy forged my signature. It's not even close." He pulled his wallet out of his shirt pocket and handed me his driver's license.

Not even close, all right. "I'm surprised that your account representative didn't verify this with you before adding her to the account. You do know that they possess a certain liability in this?"

Anders grimaced. "Charles, my account rep—his grandmother is my neighbor, which is the reason I called you first. I don't want him getting fired, and it's hard to know what trickery Sissy used."

Grey cleared his throat and held out his hand. I handed over the file. I'd held back one report and noticed that Grey's brows went up. "We're happy to start looking into this today," was all he said.

"I realize that, as a partner, you oversee all your employees, but I'm happy to continue with Avery." Anders reached out and patted my hand.

"Avery is not a licensed investigator," Grey gritted out.

Awkward. I pasted on a friendly smile. "Grey's right about my lack of licensing, but I do know numbers and I'm happy to contribute in any way I can. Just so you don't think I'm trying to pull one over on you, though, I feel compelled to tell you that I'm currently out on bail on a murder charge. Probably not the best time to be poking my nose around, some would say, but I'm game if you are." I easily identified the loud groan without having to turn my head to investigate.

"I'm betting you're not guilty." Anders gave me a toothy smile.

I beamed at him. "In addition to the promise I already wangled out of you, I suggest you think about getting better financial management. I can give you a couple of recommendations, so when you get your money back, it can be better invested while still remaining relatively safe."

"I'd have to tell Charles I'm moving my

account." He worried his lip over that one.

"Actually, that can be dealt with on your behalf, so you wouldn't have to deal with Charles. I highly doubt he'd be telling his grandmother about a screw-up like this anyway." I didn't say that he'd be lucky to keep his job, which would depend on the company's investigation and what they found.

Anders nodded but seemed uncertain.

"These guys are the best, and they will find Sissy," I assured him. "You have to prepare yourself for the chance that she's already spent the money."

"Sissy's a shopper, all right. But she also has a frugal streak and would want to make sure she didn't have to worry about money in the future. Funny thing is, she had that security with me. Not certain why she stole the money when it would've been hers eventually… most of it anyway. My son's in the will too, of course." Anders finished off his coffee and set the cup on the desk. "That wasn't bad."

"It's hard to know why Sissy would take such a drastic step, but maybe she'll answer that question when she's found. Will you be pressing charges?" I asked.

"Not sure I have the stomach for it." Anders shook his head. "I just want to go back a few days to when I thought I had a loving wife. Now I'll be happy to get the divorce papers signed."

"I think I've got all the information I need to

get started," Grey said. "I'll be keeping you updated so you know where we are in the investigation."

I stood along with the men, and they shook hands. Anders grabbed my left hand. "No husband?"

"Avery's married." Seven stepped to my side. "She keeps leaving her ring on the bathroom counter," he said, making a tsking noise.

"Him?" Anders tossed his head in Seven's direction.

"Seven's not always so grouchy." I shot the man a phony smile. "The kids zapped his patience last night. And then they were awake early and woke us up, and he needs more coffee."

"I remember those days," Anders said wistfully. "I'm happy that you're able to give my case immediate attention. I'd like it if you could include Avery; that way when I call, she can keep me in the loop," he added, letting the men know that's what he preferred.

I handed the financial report I'd been holding to Grey. "I'll walk you to the elevator," I said to Anders.

Seven anchored himself to my side and walked with us.

"Don't worry, we'll find Sissy, and when we do, it will be your decision as to how we proceed," I said.

Anders got in the elevator, and we both

waved as the doors closed.

"That randy old man was hot for you," Seven grouched.

"With you and all those kids of ours, I don't have time to be thinking about another man." I smirked at him.

Seven looped his arm around me, and we walked back to his office.

"What's the name on the door?" Grey yelled as we crossed the threshold.

"Don't you know?" I looked up at Seven, who laughed, which only further irritated Grey.

"You're not employed here, despite what Anders thinks. And when he finds out?" Grey grumbled.

"Calm your shorts. It's not like anyone's going to tell him. The upside is that I'm free help."

Seven continued to laugh.

"I'm wearing jeans, if you hadn't noticed," Grey snapped.

"Not fitting quite right today?" I said, cutting off what was sure to be a tirade about how I'd overstepped. Old news. "You can't be mad that I charmed one of your clients. Anders is happy; you should be less grouchy." I needed to quit with the hard sell. "I do have a few talents that you could easily utilize. The same ones that I used on your behalf every time Harper—your girlfriend, in case you forgot—needed information to find one person or another who wanted you dead. I delivered. Didn't hear you grouching then."

Grey stared at me for a solid minute, his jaw clenching, then said, "You're in luck; after looking at these financial reports, I need someone to decipher them for me. It's easy to tell he's worth plenty—or was, anyway—but anything else?" Grey waved a hand at a chair in front of his desk. "Don't let this go to your head, but you're better and faster than my regular guy."

"Sissy zeroed out one account, and it surprises me that didn't raise a red flag." I sat in the same chair as before. "Be interesting to know how she got the account authorization past the rep. Surely the guy overseeing the account has a boss who'd have gotten notification and asked a few questions, but it appears no one asked anything. With another, she drained it off, only leaving a few bucks, but at some point, the account would've automatically closed due to the miniscule balance. As for the others, it seems she wasn't able to gain access or she'd have helped herself. But you can't be certain of that until you do more digging. Was the rep in on it or did she seduce him into failing to pay attention? That's the approach she used with her husband. I was able to get a picture of her, and she's got the trashy sort of sex appeal that men drop their pants for."

"I just remembered that you're not supposed to be using a computer," Grey said.

"No, the court only stipulated that I wasn't to

handle anyone's finances. I'm turning over the files of current clients to a man I've worked with in the past, but I'll be hanging over his shoulder."

"At the rapid pace we're growing, we will need someone to run the office, and you've shown me that it's something we should give some thought to," Grey said.

Seven's watch beeped an alert. "I've got to head out on that job on Fisher; the client's expecting a call when I'm done with my walk-through." He stood and walked over to his desk, grabbing my purse and handing it to me.

"I emailed a contract to Dixon this morning. He agreed to the terms and should be here by now, so I need to hop downstairs and make sure he got the key I left."

"You left the door unlocked *again*?" Seven growled.

"The last time, I promise." I held up my right hand.

"I was surprised to hear you two have kids and I haven't met them yet. Wait until Harper finds out." Grey laughed.

"I was afraid to ask how many." Seven smirked. "Figured why not be surprised?"

Grey shook his head.

"Don't start. Not considering how you hooked up with Harper," Seven reminded him.

Chapter Eleven

Seven maneuvered through the streets and headed towards the Causeway.

"I'm hungry." I rubbed my grumbling stomach. "If you could veer through Hank's Burgers, that would be very swell of you."

"Wouldn't want my honey to starve."

He bypassed the busy main street, opting instead for side streets, and pulled into the drive-thru from the back entrance.

"I'll have the protein burger, an iced tea, and some of your French fries." I didn't bother looking at the board.

"How do you know I'll share?"

"Just a couple—you won't miss them." I laughed when I heard his order. The man could eat. "You didn't have to get me my own fries."

"They're both for me. You can have a handful."

He got our food and parked under a tree.

"This would be a good time to tell me what to expect on this job of ours." I snatched up one of his fries.

"Ours?" He raised his brows. "I thought you would sit in the car and soak up the ambience of the neighborhood."

I yawned, loud and exaggerated. "What happened to keeping an eye on me? Can't do that if I'm in the car."

"There's not much to this job. I'm going to determine the type of security the client will need based on his requirement to have round-the-clock monitoring, inside and around the perimeter."

"I thought Fisher was a safe place to live, more so than anywhere around, and that they have private security guards that patrol the island."

"Yes to all of that. Even though there's a miniscule chance of security needing to be called, most of the residents prefer to have their own system in place."

We finished eating, and Seven tossed the trash.

I was happy now that my stomach was no longer growling, having wolfed down my burger. I'd exercise off the fries in the fitness center, twenty floors below my condo. I made time to run on the treadmill on the days it was too hot to run on the beach.

Seven retraced his steps and headed over to the Causeway that would take us out to Fisher Island. The island's history went back hundreds of years. These days, you had to be a resident or their visitor to get on the island. The guard checked credentials, and if you took the ferry ride thinking you'd go for a drive and check out the neighborhood, you'd be disappointed — forced to turn around and wait in line for the return ferry trip.

"I've given myself the title of associate; sounds good, don't you think? I thought it was sufficiently vague, since I don't know what's expected of me. I'm telling you now, I'm not sitting in the car," I said as we waited in line for the ferry. "I can't believe rich people wait in line to go back and forth."

"They don't." Seven pointed to a set of boat docks. "They hop on their boat and make the short trip. There's also a garage on this side where they can keep a second car."

I slurped down the last of my iced tea, not wanting to waste one drop.

"Sounds like you need a refill."

"Sarcasm isn't friendly. Nor is rolling your eyes. Back to me and my duties..."

"You've got a couple of options. We've already discussed the first one, which is my favorite. Sit in the car, if you forgot. Option two: follow me around and watch the master at work. No talking, since I'll be dictating notes and taking pictures to submit with my final report."

"Do you have gloves?" I looked into the backseat — clean as a whistle.

Seven half-laughed. "Don't make me regret asking... What for?"

"I wouldn't want to leave my fingerprints anywhere. If we stumble across a dead body, I don't want to be leaving evidence that I was even on the property."

"You're not going to be needing gloves. The reason—you will not touch anything. Got it?"

"Uh-huh." I turned and stared out the window, watching as the water rippled out from under the ferry, creating a white foamy wake.

Seven reached over and grabbed my hand, his fingers laced through mine.

"It's incredibly beautiful out here. Thanks for bringing me. It's something I've wanted to do but thought wouldn't happen, since I don't know anyone who lives out here, not even a client."

The ferry cruised up to the dock and cut the engine. We exited and curved around the main road that circled the island.

I turned my head from one side to the other, taking in everything I could. We passed the private club and got an eyeful of gated properties. I was disappointed that most of the mansions weren't visible from the street. It was a quiet area, not another car on the road.

Seven turned into a tree-lined driveway, entered a security code, and the gates rolled back. He continued down the brick drive past beautifully landscaped grounds, circled the fountain, which was dry as a bone, and parked in front of a two-story English Tudor house with a six-car garage attached to one side.

"It's really quite incredible," I said in awe, staring out the windshield.

Seven hung his head over the steering wheel. "I'm going to walk the front exterior and circle around to the back." He pointed to a side path. "Then I'll be going inside."

"If you need anything from me, whistle. Better make it loud." I ignored his snort. "I'm going to check out the water view and compare it to the one we've got at home."

I watched as Seven got out, hooking a camera around his neck and pulling out his phone. He appeared to have a set way of doing things. I left him to his note-taking and wandered down the path he'd pointed out. It meandered along the side of the mansion, with nothing blocking the way to the backyard. The focal point was the enormous pool, complete with waterfall and slide, that overlooked Biscayne Bay. There was an outside kitchen with a bar and wraparound seating for eight or ten—hard to tell, since there were no stools.

I walked out to the end of the empty dock and took in the impressive view.

Turning, I ran my eyes over the exterior, and a lump covered with beach towels caught my attention. It appeared to be on a lounge chair tucked up under the bar. From what I could see of its condition, it needed to be hauled away. I fixated on the toes hanging over the edge. There hadn't been so much as a ripple in the towel. Dead body? I squeezed my eyes shut, shaking my head. "Oh officer, I didn't kill this one either." Another glance around the backyard told me that Seven was still working in the front. Asking myself "What would Seven do?" was stupid when I knew that, whatever the answer, he wouldn't want me doing it.

Staring wasn't getting me anywhere. I sucked in a deep, deep breath and crept over, stopping a good foot away. Upon closer inspection, the toes were attached to a foot, and let's hope that wasn't all. The size and shape of the lump suggested that it was a male. What if he was still alive and needed help? A mumble-grumble would be a good sign.

"Breathe, breathe," I told myself and edged my way over. No sign of... well, anything. I stuck my foot out, toed the bottom of the foot, and hopped back. Judging by the size of the paw, it was definitely a man. *Did I hear a grunt?* I craned my neck. Then I stepped forward and toed again—harder this time. The body rolled over, arms stretching out of the top, legs coming out the sides. I leapt back as he jerked the towel off his face.

The young guy said nothing for a moment, just looked at me with fogged-over pale blue eyes. "Could you bring me a cup of fresh coffee?" He yawned.

I'm not a maid, you arrogant piece of... And even if I were, "No. Hell, no."

"I like the beans freshly ground." The barely twenty-year-old stared. I expected Mr. Arrogance to snap his fingers any moment, *Why are you still standing there?* on his face.

"You're trespassing." I figured it was a safe bet, since the new owners hadn't moved in yet. I doubted the previous ones would have left this one behind, but they'd probably have given it serious thought.

"Is that a no on the coffee?" He closed his eyes and rolled on his side.

I kicked him in the butt, hard enough that he jerked onto his back. "I'm calling the cops." I hoped that would be enough of a threat that he'd jump to his feet and make a run for it. Nope... He buried his face in the crook of his arm.

"Life just keeps squatting on me," he mumbled in a pitiful tone.

"Sounds like a sad story, but I'm not the one to share it with, as I have no patience for other people's drama." That wasn't completely truthful, as I was finding out that I did. "But finding a property worth millions to... what exactly?" He oozed a "life owes me" vibe, despite the fact that he was squatting. *Not paying off for you, is it?*

"I don't have anywhere to go." He sat up and rubbed his eyes.

"You need to take what I'm about to say seriously. Find someplace else to go and do it now. When my partner shows up, being a by-the-book kind of guy, he will have you hauled off to jail. I'm telling you now—there's nothing about the experience that you're going to like."

He pulled the beach towel over his head and sat there.

"Surely you must have family. You can sleep in their backyard legally, and maybe they'll let you inside to use the amenities."

He jerked the towel back down. "'It's time to grow up,' my father yelled as he booted me out of the house. How am I supposed to do that?" He squinted. "My trust fund doesn't kick in for another eight years and three months. What do I do until then?"

I backed up and leaned against the bar top. "What you need to do is throw yourself on Daddy's mercy and convince him that if he gives you another chance, you won't blow it."

He buried his face in his hands.

"Who are you?" Seven bellowed as he stomped across the grass.

"Avery." I waved with a cheeky grin.

Seven shook his head. "Your friend here."

"Hey, dude." The young man stuck out his head. "Ryan."

"I hate to interrupt this little lovefest, but what the hell is going on?" Seven stared between the two of us.

"Ryan and I are old friends. He just happened to stop by, and we were catching up," I said over Seven's snort, which let me know he hadn't bought one word I'd said. "Since you didn't believe that one… Ryan's squatting. I just suggested that he make a run for it before you showed up, and here you are. The path over there will take you to the street." I pointed to the one I'd come down.

"I'm going." Ryan stood and wadded up the beach towels, shoving them into a leather designer backpack he pulled out from underneath the lounger, and slid his feet into a pair of trainers.

"Are you finished with the inside?" I asked Seven.

"No changing the subject."

"I'll take that as a no." I couldn't help smiling as Seven, who'd grumped out in a second, now eased off, shaking his head at Ryan. "You finish up, and I'll deal with squatter here."

"I can resolve the situation with one phone call." Seven pulled his out of his pocket.

"I'm thinking that there's a happy ending for all to be had." Seven telegraphed that he thought I'd lost my mind. He'd have to get used to that if he was going to be around me. "There's no reason to upset your client with this story because Ryan's going to promise not to come back. Your alternative is harsh."

Seven stepped in front of me and glared down.

I patted his chest. "Just give me five minutes. I can handle this."

"Five." Seven tapped his watch, more for Ryan's benefit than mine. "I won't be taking my eyes off you, and if *you*—" He turned to Ryan and jerked up his shirt, showing off a firearm. "—try anything, I'll shoot you, and it will be justified." He didn't venture far, paying only half-attention to the pictures of the exterior he was snapping.

"Ryan, I want to be sympathetic and all, but the clock is ticking," I said.

He grimaced, still staring after Seven.

"What did you do to pee off your father that was so bad he tossed you out? I just need the overview, and while you're doing that, we'll head to the front." I motioned him to follow.

"Threw a weekend party while my parents were out of town. I will admit that more people showed up than anticipated, and someone called security." Ryan flung his backpack over his shoulder and trudged beside me. "Okay, the drinking got out of hand and most weren't fit to drive, so they camped out wherever they could find space. The patio got a bit trashed, but I thought I had that covered, slipping the housekeeper cash on the side. Apparently, it wasn't enough to buy her silence, as she reported back to my parents. She should've disclosed that up front. I got probation, and the terms were to find a job." He brushed the hair out of his face. He needed a shower. "You know how hard it is when you've never had one and aren't particularly qualified? The jobs I could get without experience…" Ryan wrinkled his nose.

"I'm a Fremont."

"Theodore Fremont?" I struggled to keep the surprise and shock out of my voice. Mr. Mega Bucks was the biggest hedge fund manager in the Miami area.

Ryan nodded.

We'd made our way back to the fountain in the front. I jerked on his arm and pointed to the bench, and we both sat. "I'm guessing the reason you were able to access this property is because your parents have a mansion on the island. You knew it was for sale and thought, why not pitch your beach towel here?"

"Maybe..." He looked down the long driveway. Nothing to see from this vantage point.

"You can't continue to hide out here." I poked his arm to make sure he was listening, and he nodded begrudgingly. "If the new owner catches you, he'll call security, and they won't let you walk. And it's likely that you'll be banned from coming back to the island, even for a family visit." If word got out that security had given him a pass, they'd be looking for new jobs.

Ryan rubbed his hands over his eyes, leaned back, hands behind his head, and let out a whistling sigh. Whatever was going through his head, he wasn't happy. He stood and jerked up his backpack. "Thanks for not calling the cops. Or... I don't know what, but it wouldn't be good. Appreciate it."

I walked down the driveway with him because I was curious to see where the heck he planned to go next. Not that I knew the area. I clapped him on the back. "Think about calling your parents with more promises, and then make an effort to keep them."

He nodded and, with a wave, walked out the front gate and sauntered up the street. Thank goodness it was a beautiful sunny day, the weather mild. I couldn't imagine being a spoiled twenty-year-old and homeless. He eventually turned into the park we'd passed on the drive here. I waited for him to reappear, and when he didn't, decided he must've found a bench to stretch out on. I pulled out my phone, found a map of the park, and discovered that Ryan had several options for exiting. I walked back to the fountain and settled on the bench, turning my face to the sunshine and closing my eyes.

Chapter Twelve

That was where Seven found me. He sat down next to me. "Why the long face?" I opened my eyes as he scanned the driveway. "You get rid of… the squatter?"

"You raise your kid, never expecting anything out of them, and one day you decide the best option is to throw them out on the street?"

"It could be a scared-straight tactic."

"Maybe." I knew I sounded doubtful.

"I'm all done here." Seven stood and pulled me to my feet, then cut around to the SUV.

Before he exited the driveway, I asked, "Could we cruise the island before we head back to the ferry? I'd like to look around, since I can't see myself coming back here for any reason." I stared out the window and paid particular attention as we cruised by the park. Not only did it appear empty, but we hadn't passed another person.

Seven was about to get in line for the ride back when I tugged on his arm. "I need a few more minutes before we make the trip back." I pulled out my phone. "It will only take a minute." I quickly went online and initiated a search.

He easily found a parking spot in an adjacent

lot. "Are you going to tell me what the urgency is?"

"Hmm…" I easily accessed a website that I'd used before and located the address I was looking for. "Do you mind one more stop here on the island before we head back?" I entered the address into my phone and clipped it into the holder on the dashboard. "It's not that far."

"Do I dare ask what you're up to?"

"You could wait and be surprised."

Seven groaned. "I don't like surprises… in fact, hate them."

"I accessed a website to get Ryan's parents' address." I glanced at the map and realized we were getting closer. "Now I'm going to… not mind my own business. At least, not without trying to contact them. In all likelihood, we'll get to this address and be greeted by security gates. Your part in all of this will be to get us inside so I can talk face-to-face with either parent. Talking with a faceless voice over a speaker isn't the way to go." I wrinkled my nose.

"I hate to be the killjoy here…" Seven pulled over and coasted next to the curb. "Spill."

"I'm going to let Ryan's parents know where he can be found. Suggest in a nice way that a second or sixteenth chance would be better than a black mark on their reputation. And that's what it would be if Ryan were found trespassing on a neighbor's property and got arrested." I pasted on a phony smile and flashed it at Seven.

"Needs work. I've seen you do friendly, and that's not it."

"I'll work on it."

"I won't even bill you for this gem I'm about to impart." Seven grinned. "When you're face-to-face with whoever, make it short and sweet, tell them where Ryan's at, and leave the rest up to them."

It surprised me to see no security gate when we got to the address, just another long driveway.

"I'm thinking that you should keep your quasi-grumpy self in the car. Engine running in case… something, anyway." I reached for the handle as soon as he parked and opened the door.

With his long legs, it didn't take long to catch up with me. "In case you need backup, I'll turn on the charm." He gave me a cheeky grin.

"Maybe stand behind me, because one look at the annoyance you're projecting, and they may not open the door." I started up the steps of the contemporary mansion.

Seven pulled me to his side and, at the top, rang the doorbell, stepping back.

I expected to have to go through the maid to talk to Mr. or Mrs. Fremont and instead got Mrs. Fremont herself. I recognized her from a picture I'd seen on social media.

"I'm Avery English, and I'm here about your son, Ryan."

First surprise, then fear showed in Mrs. Fremont's eyes.

"Ryan's fine," I assured her hurriedly. "I thought you'd want to know…" I told her how I'd met her son and where she could find him.

Mrs. Fremont continually shook her head. "I told my husband that he should wait until he calmed down, but did he listen? No."

"After talking to Ryan, I think he may be far more receptive to growing up now than before." At least I hoped.

"Thank you for coming and telling me. Most wouldn't." Mrs. Fremont reached out and shook my hand.

"He reminds me of my little brother. I had to try, and I'm happy I did." I smiled and started down the steps. Seven was already at the bottom, and Mrs. Fremont looked over my shoulder and sent him an admiring glance before hurrying back inside.

"Maybe drive slow, so I can see if she's going to reach out to her son," I said when we got back in the SUV.

Seven pulled over and parked, still in sight of the Fremont driveway. It didn't take long for a Lexus to come out of the driveway, Mrs. Fremont at the wheel. It roared past us, and Seven followed at a distance. She turned into the park area, and we continued to the ferry.

"That's more than I would've done," Seven said. "I wouldn't have called the cops, but I'd have scared him into not even thinking about coming back. Or looking for another property to camp out on."

"Hopefully, Ryan's tired of being a jerk-off."

Seven laughed.

Chapter Thirteen

"How about we go to dinner?" Seven asked, rolling off the ferry and heading home.

"I'd rather do take-out and eat out on the balcony."

We made the short drive back to Miami Beach in companionable silence. He held my hand most of the way.

"You going to share what you're worrying about? We've been together all day, so I'm thinking nothing new could've happened." Seven unlocked my door and ushered me inside, and we headed to the kitchen, both of us eager for something to drink.

"I've been thinking that I need to stay busy or I'll go a bit nuts. Since your information guy is a bit of a laggard, I could take up the slack. I would just need someone to put in a good word with the partners of WD. Do you maybe know anyone?" I batted my eyelashes, which had Seven laughing.

"I've got another security job; you're welcome to come along as my associate. That was your title, correct?"

I laughed, my cheeks getting warm. That title

was the best I could come up with at the moment.

"You handled Ryan like a pro." Seven opened the drawer with the menus, pulled them out, and spread them over the countertop.

How was it that Seven always knew where to find everything? "I know you promised someone that you'd keep an eye on me, but it's not necessary. I know you have a life. How about if I promise to give you a heads up if I get the inclination to go off half-cocked?"

"You trying to get rid of me?" Seven gave me a scrutinizing look.

"It's not that…" I liked having him around but didn't want to get used to it. "I want you to know that the promises I made… I don't renege on my word."

"You want me gone, you say the word." He pouted. "But as long as there's a murderer walking around, you need to be mindful of your safety. Who better to protect you than me?"

"I don't want to take advantage of you."

"No need to worry about that, as I've been enjoying every minute." He grinned.

"Every one of these restaurants is good. This stack are my faves." I pushed the menus across the countertop. "You pick, and I'll tell you what I want."

He chose Mexican, and I licked my lips. While he placed the order, I grabbed my laptop and went out to the patio, setting up the table and taking a seat at the opposite end.

Nothing new going on. I did get an email from Dixon—"I'm on top of everything." He went on to let me know that he'd contacted the clients and introduced himself. I knew I'd made a good choice reaching out to him.

Once Seven got off the phone, he grabbed his own laptop and came out to sit next to me. He had a report to put together for his client. I decided to follow up on Sissy Anders, even though I hadn't been asked.

I snooped through her social media accounts and was surprised to see that, as of a couple of days ago, she was posting pictures lounging on a beach in Pensacola. She must have been feeling confident that she wouldn't be found or that her husband wouldn't come looking for her. I hadn't checked for accounts under Gregory Anders, and doing so now, I didn't find anything. I emailed a report to Grey, mostly to get on his good side.

It didn't take long for the food to get delivered, and we changed seats, watching the waves lap the beach below while we ate.

Afterwards, he talked me into a movie. We sat on the couch, his arm around me. Eventually, I curled up next to him and went to sleep.

Chapter Fourteen

It was Saturday morning, and that meant meeting Rella and Harper for our weekly get-together at the Cat House Cafe. Awake earlier than usual, I got dressed and left Seven sleeping, leaving a note next to the coffee pot: "Out with the girls." I didn't want to hurt his feelings by telling him "Girls only" since Grey sometimes showed up unannounced.

It was a short drive to trendy Washington Boulevard. For once, I arrived ahead of Rella, who almost always showed up first, as one of her friends owned the restaurant and she was their chief backer. Luckily for me, a parking space had just been vacated, and I slid in ahead of another car that attempted to cut me off. I walked up the steps and maneuvered around the recently added tables and chairs on the outside deck; it'd taken months, but they'd finally gotten approval to add more outside dining. I breezed through the entrance and past the hostess with a wave, and she gave a smile of recognition. I bypassed our usual window table on the back patio—the reserved sign would hold it until the other two arrived.

The glassed-in room attached to the back patio—a playhouse for cats and kittens in need of a home—called to me today. The owner, Prissy Mayes, had sent out an email that their new additions—a momma cat and her babies—were ready for adoption. The long-haired black-and-white kitten I'd liked best from the picture was asleep alone in the corner. The oversized chairs for prospective parents were occupied, so I knelt down to scratch the kitten's ears. To my delight, he didn't run off, instead licking my fingers.

"What are you doing over here by yourself?" I picked him up and stood off to one side, running my fingers through his fur until he nodded off.

Rella knocked on the glass and motioned me to come inside. Harper was already seated at the table. I wasn't going to put the kitten back where I'd found him, knowing someone else would immediately scoop him up—he was that cute. Taking him inside was against the rules, but I'd risk getting the boot. I sat down and scooted my chair partially under the table, kitty stretched out on my lap, and to my surprise, he went back to sleep.

Prissy, the red-headed wonder, approached the table in a flowing tropical tent dress splashed with a beach scene and shell bracelets lining her arms to her elbows. Always one to wear flowers in her hair, today was no different; she'd tucked a large pink hibiscus behind one ear.

"Someone rushed up to me and whispered—conspiratorially, of course, and entirely for my benefit—that one of my customers *stole* a kitten, then just walked out. Any clue who the perp might be?" She stared right at me.

"You're not talking about Arco are you?" I asked, looking down at the ball of fur in my lap. "Cute name, don't you think? Just came up with it. If that woman on the end can have a support dog, well then, meet my support puss." I inclined my head.

"Avery and Arco—so cute." Harper grinned. "Mobster's going to be excited to have a kitty cousin," she said, talking about her gigantic black Maine Coon. Rella scratched the head of her over-one-hundred-pound St. Bernard.

Prissy flicked the back of my head. "What do you know about felines?" She didn't allow an adoption unless she'd thoroughly checked out the potential owner.

"We have instant bonding in our favor," I said. "I'm pretty sure Google can help me figure out anything I need to know. I also have two neighbors, both with pets, who won't let me screw up." I nodded to Rella and Harper, who smiled to show their support, knowing I'd be a first-time pet owner.

"Do you have everything Arco is going to need?" Prissy asked with an arched eyebrow.

"No worries about that," Harper said. "I've got extra of everything. And let's face it, cats are the easiest. It won't take long for him to be the boss."

"I'll send you home with a starter pack of food." Prissy pulled a white ribbon out of her pocket. "In case Arco wakes up and decides he wants to go for a romp."

"You're the best. But then, we all knew that." I fished out my phone to make a donation to her animal rescue.

The server approached to take our order, Seven and Grey behind her, each dragging a chair. Grey kissed Harper, who grinned up at him.

"I'm certain you won't mind us joining you." Seven plunked down next to me. "Imagine my surprise when I woke up to find that you ditched me."

"I left a note." Eyeroll in my tone.

All eyes were on us, grins on their faces. I wanted to yell, *Stop it. Whatever you're thinking, it's not happening.*

"What's that?" Seven pointed to Arco.

"Being the good mother I am, I thought it would be fun to surprise the kiddos with a pet."

"According to Seven's announcement, those two got married, and not a word to any of us," Grey announced, then went on to tell them about the scene at the office.

"Marriage and children in one day." I turned to Seven. "Did we decide how many? Would be horrible if we misplaced one of them."

Seven leaned in and kissed my forehead. "We'll leave it open, in case we need to add another one at the last minute."

The server came back and took our order. "I'll have whatever she's having," Seven told the woman.

"You won't be disappointed. There's not a single item on the menu that isn't delicious," I said once she left.

"Anything new on your case?" Rella asked.

"Cruz assures me that he's got everything under control and not to worry. It's kind of hard. He's assigned a couple of investigators to my case, both with impeccable reputations. The bad news is that the money stolen from Stella's account has been transferred a couple of times, whereabouts unknown at the moment. One of his investigators is a forensic accountant, and he's tracking the transactions." I made a face. "I've been admonished not to go near them."

"Have you told Rella and Harper that you're working at WD now?" Seven smirked.

"I think the powers that be at that office should take the idea seriously." I eyed Grey, who shook his head. "I got you one client already."

Harper laughed. "Oh boy, did I hear about that one."

Grey made a face, and she laughed again. "Anders has called twice, both times asking for you. It's annoying when the person he'd rather deal with for updates doesn't work there, no matter what she tells people."

"Have you located his money yet?" I asked, knowing that he hadn't or he'd have led with that news flash.

"Sissy wasn't very sophisticated and has, so far, left an easy-to-follow money trail," Grey said.

If it's that easy... I kept it to myself, knowing Grey wouldn't appreciate me voicing that thought.

"I don't suppose it's legal to transfer it back?" Harper nodded at me, telegraphing, *Get on it.*

"I'd think you'd need to do that before Sissy finds out you're onto her. If Mr. Anders waits for a court to decide, the money will be gone," Rella said.

"A couple of clicks." I held up my fingers, making the motion.

"I know this will surprise you ladies, but WD is on it." Grey shot a stern stare around the table.

Harper winked, which softened him up.

Our food arrived—all different variations of waffles. All talk of my and others impending legal woes was tabled.

Arco sniffed at the bit of waffle I offered, took a lick, and went back to sleep. Probably a good thing.

Harper's phone rang, and she glanced at the screen. *Gram*, she mouthed and answered. "We're just finishing our breakfast, so can I call you later?" Her eyes turned to me. "Avery did? No, I didn't know. I'm certain she has a good reason. Her life has been hectic lately, as you know." She shook her head in response to whatever Gram was saying. "She's right here." She handed me her phone.

My cheeks burned. Jean Winters had called me a couple of times, but knowing that she's a character, to put it mildly, I hadn't returned her calls. "Hello, Mrs. Winters."

"Gram, please. I've been trying to contact you. I'm sure you're about to say you were going to call me back, but no need. I'm doing it for you."

I nodded and then realized she couldn't see me. "What can I do for you? If it's about your account, I'll have to refer you to my associate, Dixon. I'll be reviewing everything he does, but I'm not allowed to be hands-on."

"I don't have one complaint about how my money is being handled; that's not what this call is about. I'm having a little family soiree to show you how much we love and support you. How does a poolside get-together sound? A great way to soak up the sunshine."

"That sounds…" I squeezed my eyes closed, which also served to block out Harper's amusement, which was encouraging me to accept when all I wanted to do was blurt out, *Not coming.* "…wonderful." That one word sounded like a death sentence. "Life is so up in the air right now, though, that I'll have to take a rain check."

"Oh, nonsense. It'll do you good to make time

for some fun and be surrounded by those that love you. I know you agree."

I shook my head at the phone, for whatever good that did. None. "How about after the case is over?" I managed to say in a conciliatory tone.

"That's not…" After a pause, she started to cry.

I turned and buried my face in Seven's shoulder. "Please don't cry." More like howling. I don't know how long it took for Gram to pull herself together. Too long. I shuddered with every sob.

She sniffed and then blew her nose. "Then you'll come for lunch? Saturday. One o'clock." She hung up.

I stared at the screen to be sure. Then met the amusement in Harper's eyes. Grey wouldn't look at me.

"Gram cried?" Harper asked in faux shock, no sympathy in her tone. "After you turned down her invite?"

I nodded.

Harper noticeably bit her lip.

"She's a wily one," Rella said. "I wondered how she was going to command your attendance. Now I know. Crying is one way to get what you want."

"You two knew what Gram was up to? And not one word? You even handed me the phone, knowing I was about to be ambushed?" I shot the questions mostly at Harper.

"She wanted it to be a surprise," Harper said with too much glee in her tone. "I couldn't break an old woman's heart."

Seven snorted.

"You've known Gram for how long?" Harper continued. "You should know by now that it's easier to just say yes. So you'll know for next time, the whole tears thing is a con job."

The guys laughed.

"This is just a lunch and nothing else?" I asked.

"I've got your back." Harper patted my hand. "I'll call her and have her cancel the live band and animal act."

I turned to Seven. "You're coming as my plus one."

"No worries, I already RSVP'd for both of you," Harper said.

"You're as conniving as your Gram."

"It's going to be fun," Rella assured me. "Harper and I are going to take you shopping for something fun to wear." Harper nodded in agreement.

Seven hugged me to his side. "Don't worry, I'll protect you."

Prissy came to the table and handed me a large shopping bag. "A few things for Arco."

I took a quick peek in the bag, then set it on the floor. "I'll send pictures so you can include them in your next newsletter."

Grey and Seven complimented the food we'd devoured.

With the check taken care of, I snuggled Arco under my arm, and we walked out together.

Chapter Fifteen

Monday again and back to work. Seven had left long before I thought about getting up. When I heard him rumbling around, I rolled over and went back to sleep.

I finally got up and got dressed for the office, even though the files I had to update would take all of five minutes. I also had to meet Dixon.

Turning into the parking lot, I saw Dixon's two-seater Jeep—an older model that had been sanded and primed, with flecks of red still showing through. He said it ran like a charm and he could park it anywhere; no one would steal it, as it wasn't given a second glance.

I cruised past and into the garage, then hiked up the stairs to the second floor. It was going to be good to have someone to share the office with again. Dixon and I worked well together—two nerds who loved numbers. I opened the door, and he looked up from the pile of paperwork spread across the desk and waved.

Dixon had recently met a woman who gave him a makeover. She got him to ditch the oversized clothes in favor of a more professional appearance—now he often wore suit pants and a button-down shirt. He still looked young, but no longer twelve years old and wearing Daddy's clothes. His dark hair flopped down over his eyes, and he also had an eyeglasses fetish but, like me, wore them less and less.

"Hope I'm not interrupting the genius at work."

He laughed, then downed his soda and sent the can flying into the trash. Direct hit. "Your client files are right there." He pointed to the corner of his desk. "I finished calling all your clients, and some remembered me from before. I updated them and assured them that AE Financial had them covered. Most wanted to gossip about you, but I kept that to a minimum."

I walked over and swept up the files, then settled behind my desk and gave them a quick scan, knowing that Dixon was as much a stickler for details as me. If I noticed any discrepancies, I'd dive right in.

We worked in companionable silence—Dixon on the financials and me back to checking Sissy Anders' social media. No new postings from her. I was impatient for this case to wind up, maybe because the missing money reminded me of my own case.

Dixon jumped up from his chair. "I've got a meeting." He flew out the door and the second it closed, it felt eerily quiet. Tapping my finger on the desk, I mentally ran through my options. It was a short list, since I had nothing pending.

That left sitting in silence, going home and playing with Arco, or... I made the trip to the third floor. Surely there was someone I could annoy at WD. The door was locked, and no one answered my insistent knocking. I ran back to my office and got a lockpick. Once I'd heard that Harper had honed the talent, I hounded her until she taught me. Fingers crossed that Seven would be the first through the door. If it was Grey, I'd... think of something. "You really should lock your door." Maybe not.

Someone had brought up the mail and dumped it on the desk, so I made myself useful, sorting it into stacks. I was tempted to ditch the junk mail, but not my call. Several times, I caught myself staring at the phone, willing it to ring.

Laughter could be heard through the door before it opened. Seven ushered in a voluptuous blonde who'd poured herself into a form-fitting dress. He quickly recovered from the surprise of seeing me. "Avery, this is our new client, Stacey Camp."

The woman never acknowledged me, turning away and pursing her red lips up at him. "I knew as soon as I met you that I'd made the right call," she cooed.

Seven led her over to his desk and pulled out a chair for her, waiting until she sat down. She crossed and uncrossed her long legs and gave her dress a slight tug, never breaking eye contact with him.

"Sometimes with referrals..." She wrinkled her nose. "I think we're going to work well together."

I waved at Seven, who looked at me with a raised eyebrow that said *Behave*.

The blonde turned in her chair to see what had drawn his attention from her, gave me a once-over, and wrinkled her nose before turning back to him. "As I told you on the phone, I'm being followed. You can't imagine the overwhelming fear that invades my body every time I leave the house."

When Ms. Camp didn't swoon, I did it for her, falling back in my chair, hand on my forehead. Seven's smirk came and went so fast, I almost missed it.

"I just know it's my ex-boyfriend. The split was... well... messy."

Seven pulled out a notepad.

I held up a pen, but he ignored me.

"Have you seen him following you? Has he confronted you?" Seven asked.

"No, no... But I'm certain I've seen an Audi following me on several occasions—I got a partial tag." She pulled her phone out of her purse and read off the numbers. "The car's been outside my house and gym."

"I take it you didn't get a look at the driver?"

"Nooo," she mewled. "Tinted windows, but then aren't they all here in Florida?" She stood and rounded the desk, leaning against the edge and staring down at Seven. "Until we catch him, I'm going to need your services 24/7, starting now."

Ms. Camp bent over, and my guess was Seven could see to her navel. I shot out of my chair and crossed the room, staking out the other end of the desk. "I'm sorry," I said, sounding anything but, "but that won't be possible. Mr. Donnelly is booked with a longtime client, and it's been on the calendar for weeks. But Floyd is available. He's one of our best men, and I'm sure you'll be happy with the level of service he provides."

If looks could kill... But I had no intention of keeling over on the floor.

"You're a secretary," Ms. Camp said in disdain.

"That's an outdated term. I'm an assistant to both partners."

Seven sat back in his chair, a smile fleeting across his face... a couple of times.

"Well then, get on the phone and arrange for this Frank person—"

"Floyd," I stopped short of snapping.

The woman continued without acknowledging that I'd spoken. "Have that man guard your other client. Problem solved."

"Look, hon," I said, and Ms. Camp and I engaged in a stare-down. "You'd think that would be doable, but when we're talking a longtime client, it isn't. WD doesn't dump a client in the middle of a job. You wouldn't like if it were done to you, now would you?" I asked with syrupy sweetness.

Death glare.

Seven cleared his throat, which got both our attention. "Why don't you go check with Floyd," he said to me, his eyes shooting to the door. "I'll finish up my appointment with Ms. Camp."

"If you're certain you won't be needing me…"

Seven nodded, amusement in his eyes. "I've got it handled."

My cue to scram and mind my own business. "I'll see if Floyd's available to meet with you." I shot Seven the stink eye before leaving. I closed the door with a click and leaned against the wall. *What got into me? Total territorial meow mode.* I groaned.

I ran down to my office and grabbed my purse, deciding I needed ice cream. The elevator doors opened, and of all people, who was coming in from the garage but the man himself—Floyd.

"Is one of them in the office?" He pointed upward.

Seven would never believe I didn't send the man, but oh well.

Chapter Sixteen

My favorite ice cream shop was a little out of the way, but I made the trip anyway. My cheeks burned all the way. What had gotten into me? When Grey heard the way I'd talked to a client, I'd probably be banned from the office for life. In addition to the caramel cone, which I got dipped in chocolate, I added two pints to go and wolfed the cone down in the car.

Thoughts of my case and Anders' missing money kept me occupied on the drive home. Better than thinking about Seven and Blondie. If it weren't for the court order, I was certain I could've located the cash already... or at least been hot on the trail.

Once I got on the Causeway, it was hard not to focus on the sun bouncing off the waters of the Atlantic, which took my mind off my antics of the morning, however briefly. For once, traffic cooperated, and I got home in record time.

I opened the door, and Arco, who'd been sacked out on the back of the couch, jumped up and stared expectantly. I picked him up and carried him into the kitchen to feed him. I went to my bedroom and changed into sweats, rolling them up, then pulled on a t-shirt and slipped into a pair of flip-flops.

"Behave yourself," I told Arco, who'd finished eating and trailed after me to the bedroom, jumping on the bed and curling up. I went into my walk-in closet, pulled the mirror away from the wall, and opened the safe. Grabbing the laptop that no one knew anything about off the top shelf, I stuffed it in my beach bag. I was tired of not being in charge of my life.

I rode down in the elevator and made my way out to the beach, pausing at a stack of chairs and grabbing one. I chose a spot away from any possibility of interested eyes, sank my toes into the sand, and opened my laptop, pulling up a connection that would be difficult to trace. The last thing I wanted was for anyone to find out that I was looking into files that were off-limits to me.

In my senior year of college, I had a lab partner who'd been hacking into systems since he was in high school. He let it slip once that that was why he had no college loan debt. I struck a deal with him—in exchange for writing his papers, he taught me what he knew. Most who knew us thought we were dating, and we'd never corrected them. I was fascinated by everything he taught me and knew there was more to learn, but it was probably best that I didn't pursue it to the degree he had. I'd run into him a couple of years ago, and we caught up over a cup of coffee; it surprised me to hear he'd gone legit. It didn't escape my notice that he added "sort of," which I ignored. He and a couple of his friends had partnered up and designed a couple of apps that had paid off. I was happy for his success. He then laughed off almost getting caught up in a sting by the Feds, which had scared him mostly straight. As much fun as the reunion was, I'd be happy not to run into him again. I'd had a ringside seat when another friend's life got derailed by pairing up with a bad guy; I could learn from other people's mistakes.

My fingers flew across the keyboard, and it didn't take me long to hack into Anders' accounts, which surprised me. Not only had the security not been tightened, but the same financial planner was still assigned to the account. The money was easy to trace, as there had only been two transfers. The thief either wasn't trying to hide what they'd done or had limited knowledge of how to cover their tracks.

Why was Grey's guy taking so long? Seemed straightforward to me. I wanted to meet this computer wizard but hadn't been able to get a name, even though I'd hinted a couple of times.

Clicking away, I found that the money had been transferred to an account in New Mexico, where it had sat for a few days before being transferred to one in Tallahassee. It surprised me that the two almost back-to-back transfers hadn't raised any red flags. A few clicks later, I transferred the money back to its rightful owner—one of Anders' accounts that Sissy had no access to. I'd have preferred to send it to a new account, but setting it up would require information from Anders that I didn't have.

How hard could it be to find Sissy since she blabbed her whereabouts on social media? I knew from her latest postings that she was only a half-day's drive away.

I caught movement out of the corner of my eye and saw Seven bearing down on me, having changed into shorts and a t-shirt. I rapidly clicked an icon, and a book popped up on the screen just as he bent down and bit my shoulder. That was close.

"Where's Blondie?" I didn't bother with a glance over my shoulder; if she were close, she'd be draped over him like an old coat.

"You know, you like me. I mean really like me." He grinned.

"Maybe."

A charged silence hung between us, broken only by the herons diving into the waves, hunting for dinner.

"I'll take it." He grabbed my hand, kissing my fingers. "You know, I was never signing on for bodyguarding duty, not with her anyway. I already have a gig. Not sure how you knew about it, but fine with me. The prince is coming to town and would flip if I foisted him off on someone else." He leaned in and pecked my cheek. "Thanks for sending Floyd."

"You're not going to believe this, but running into Floyd was a total fluke. And what prince?"

"Whenever Prince Alaman comes to town, which will be in a few hours, I bodyguard him while he parties down. He hits it hard for a week or so, then goes home with a couple of women in tow."

"I shouldn't have... well... inserted myself into your *business* discussion."

"Didn't bother me in the slightest." Seven winked. Eyeing my laptop, he leaned over my shoulder. "What are you working on?"

I briefly flashed him the screen, and at the same time, snapped it shut, sticking it in my bag.

"That looks different than the replacement one I bought." He helped me to my feet.

"You can check it out when we get back." I'd switch it out before he got a good look.

We started up the sand.

"We should come down and walk along the shore. The best time is early evening." I stared wistfully at the water. "How did you end it with whatever her name was?"

"Floyd muscled through the door, and she forgot I was sitting there. He turned on the charm, and the next thing I know, they're discussing the job and he's assuring her that whatever she wants, he's more than happy to provide."

"*Whatever?*"

"None of my business."

He opened the door to the garage, and we cut across to the elevator.

Once through my door, I went straight to my bedroom, stashed the laptop in my safe, and grabbed up the other one, in case Seven decided to give it a closer look. He'd have plenty of questions when Anders reported he got his money back.

Chapter Seventeen

I'd been dreading the weekend, and now it was here. More specifically, Gram's lunch. I still couldn't believe I'd been guilted into accepting the invitation by a torrent of tears. Seriously, what were we celebrating? That I got arrested for something I didn't do? If anyone had asked me, and they didn't, it would have been better to wait until the case was resolved. In addition, there hadn't been a word on Anders' case, and I was waiting for that shoe to drop. Though it was possible that WD's computer guy would take credit and that would be the end of it.

Seven whistled, leaning against the doorframe as I twirled in front of the mirror in a spaghetti-strap tropical print mid-calf dress. I'd pulled my hair into a high ponytail. Earlier, I'd thought about calling Gram and faking sickness. Too late now. I wouldn't put it past her to show up and check on me.

"Is there anything you want to tell me?" His blue eyes bored into mine, searching for an answer.

I wanted to look away but managed to maintain eye contact. "Could you be more specific, or did you just want to chat in general?"

"Out of the blue—" Seven snapped his fingers. "—Anders' money was returned. Not to either of the original accounts, but one of his others."

"That's great news."

"Anders thought so too and would like to express his profound thanks to you. He's certain you're the angel that got the transfer done. As it turns out, he's got a couple of other issues that he'd like your help on. It irked Grey that it was the first he was hearing of the money's miraculous return. As for his insistence on talking to you, Grey dumped it on me to figure out."

"An easy fix would've been for Grey to disabuse Anders of the notion that I had anything to do with his money showing up and give the credit to Boy Wonder."

Seven snorted. "If Mr. Wonder were responsible, he would've called as soon as the job was complete. Plus, at no time was transferring the money back something we discussed."

"Oh, brother." I shook my head. "What, pray tell, was your hot idea? Contact Sissy and tell her 'You've been caught'?" I said that in a squeaky voice, which got me a smirk. "Then boom—money gone again, and she hits the road." I suddenly realized I'd given myself away by sharing my opinion too strongly.

"Don't make me wish I hadn't promised you wouldn't get into a hint of trouble."

"That's right—that promise that we're not supposed to mention. Someone high up? How high?" I deciphered his head shake as indicating I wouldn't be getting an answer. "I thought your main job was to make sure I didn't skip town, sparking an international manhunt."

Seven handed me his phone. "Now that Anders is your client, you might want to find out what he wants."

"I should call Gram first and tell her I won't be able to make lunch."

"You'd disappoint an old woman?" Seven made a tsking noise. "Make her cry? Again."

I grabbed the phone out of his hand and backed up, sitting on the side of the bed.

Seven stalked over and sat next to me.

Anders' number was on the screen, and I pushed the call button. "It's Avery English," I said when he answered.

Seven leaned his head against mine so he could listen in on the call. I attempted to shake him off, but he just chuckled.

"I'm certain you've heard the good news," Anders said conspiratorially.

"I just heard and I'm very happy for you, but I don't deserve any of the credit."

Anders' sniff conveyed that he didn't believe me. "I have a couple of other problems I'd like to hire you to take care of that since I don't feel comfortable discussing with the partners at WD."

"I'm happy to help you with anything I can."

Grey was going to love this.

"You suggested that I move my accounts, and I'd like you to do that on my behalf. I'd rather it be a business decision than me confronting a friend."

"How about if we meet at the office on Monday? I can recommend a couple of investment firms. Once you've decided, I can have my associate, Dixon, handle the transfer for you. After that, it won't take more than a couple of days."

"There's another... well, issue." Anders faltered.

Seven nudged me, and I pushed him back. It barely took him a second to recover, and he ended up sitting closer, if that was possible.

"Okay..." I responded weakly.

"Sissy was back at the house with her suitcase yesterday, and when she figured out I wasn't home, she tried to break in." Anders huffed. "She set off the security system, which alerted the police. She told them that she lived there and we were only separated. When they asked her to provide proof of residence, she claimed not to have it at the time but said she'd come back. They warned her that if she did, she'd better have proof or they'd take her to jail. I know her well enough to know that she's getting proof together, and it won't take her long. The cops suggested that I get a court order if I don't want her moving back in."

"When you come to the office on Monday, we can talk about your options on that."

"So you know, I stayed a couple of nights with a friend, but I can't continue to do that. Truthfully, it gets lonely banging around this big house by myself."

"What are you doing today?" Seven poked me in the side. I tried pushing him away again, and he didn't budge an inch. "There's a lunch today, which would be a good opportunity for you to meet new people, have a little fun. I'll text you the address and put your name on the guest list."

"You don't have to—"

"The hostess's philosophy is there's no such thing as too many people." That was probably a stretch, but one more—especially a single man, almost anyway, who'd be fought over—would be no problem. "I'll see you then, and no talking about your problems—you're there to have fun."

We hung up, and I texted the address, then handed Seven back his phone and grabbed mine. Taking noting of his *You're crazy* look, I said, "And you haven't run out the door yet, have you?" He laughed, knowing I'd read him perfectly.

I called Gram. "You better not have some cockamamie excuse for being a no-show," she grouched.

"No, no. I'd like to add Gregory Anders to the guest list. Introduce him to the ladies; he needs perking up."

"Done," Gram said with a growly laugh.

"You're the best. I'll see you soon."

Seven pushed me back on the bed and lay next to me. "What was that all about?" he asked.

"Just being nice. Morningside is a great place for Anders to make new friends, and Gram is a good place to start. He hooks up with another hoochie bunny and brings her around, Gram will tell him he's lost his mind."

"Make sure I'm there when you update Grey, because I'd pay big to see the look on his face."

"Expect to hear a slightly different version where you get most of the credit."

Chapter Eighteen

Seven started to tickle me, and with a shriek, I managed to roll off the bed, grab my purse, and run out into the hall, skidding to a stop at the front door. He stalked after me. "I didn't get a single question answered, so I know you're up to something. I'll be keeping an eye on you."

"Are you accusing me of something specific?" I attempted to scoot around him and out the door, but he blocked me.

"Just promise me you're not snooping into your own case."

I held up my right hand and shook my head. *Not yet.*

Seven kissed me. It was only a brief kiss, but I liked it. A lot.

"Ready to go?" he asked. I nodded. He grabbed my arm and wrapped it around his elbow. "In case you thought about ditching me and getting lost on the way to the party."

We rode down in the elevator.

"You know... that's a great idea. Why don't you turn your back and I'll make a run for it? You can put in an appearance for both of us. The older ladies will like you."

Seven laughed and opened the passenger door of his SUV. "Grey assures me that Gram is a well-meaning, fun nutjob. Since it's just a small group of friends, you'll know everyone, so there shouldn't be any staring or finger-pointing."

"Since you're not hot about my great idea, how about I phrase it as a backup plan?" Before he could shoot me down, I blurted, "Eat and run." Laughter was the only response, and I deduced that meant maybe.

I leaned back against the seat as Seven cruised up the Causeway to the Interstate and headed north. Surprisingly, the cars weren't stacked up for miles, and we'd be arriving on time… close enough anyway. He exited north of Ft. Lauderdale and headed towards the water. Morningside at the Beach, a retirement community located conveniently across the highway from the beach, had every amenity. He turned in and gave our name to the guard, who checked his list before raising the arm to let us in.

"When you see a cherry red '57 Thunderbird parked in one of the driveways, we've arrived. That's Gram's way of letting people know she's home." I kept waiting to hear that it'd been stolen, but when I expressed that sentiment, Gram admonished me: "Morningside is upscale, not packed with thieves."

Seven pulled up behind Grey's SUV and Rella's Mercedes. "Appears we're the last to arrive."

We were barely out of the car when Gram rushed out the front door to meet us in a dress that swallowed up her thin frame. My eyes shot to her brimmed hat, which extended a foot in the air and was shaped like a bowling pin. The woman had a hat fetish. The same as my glasses. Today, I'd toned it down and opted for a pair of the darkest sunglasses I owned.

"You've got yourself a hottie." Gram gave Seven a once-over, even though they'd met several times. She held out her arms for a hug.

I heard Seven whisper to her, "You behave yourself."

Gram chuckled. "Not a spit's worth of fun in that." She hooked one arm around me and the other around Seven and steered us inside. "Your friend Gregory Anders arrived—he's a sweet man. I introduced him to one of the neighbors, and they headed down to the pool to join a game of cards."

Gram pushed the door open into the living space—a large living room, a dining room with its own patio, and the kitchen behind a set of louvered swinging doors. My friends were seated on the couch and chairs around the room, and everyone waved.

I relaxed considerably. This group, I could handle. I should apologize to Gram for suspecting that she was up to something. On the other hand, she didn't need to know.

"Since the guest of honor is here..." Harper

stood. "It's too beautiful a day to sit inside. Let's go down to the poolside bar. Gram has everything set up for us to eat in the restaurant down there."

Gram crossed the room and picked up a shopping bag. "So, we know you're the guest of honor..."

"Everyone knows me." I eyed the... What did she have in her hand?

Gram came up and stood in front of me, having removed a hat from the bag, and thrust it forward. It was sequined and... Before I could get a good look, she set it on my head. Harper and Rella both grinned. Gram put her hands on my shoulders and moved me over to the mirror. "It's an authentic police captain's hat... adorned, of course, and much cuter than the plain version, don't you think? And these?" She fingered the metal telescopic glasses sitting on the rim.

"You outdid yourself." I turned and hugged her.

"You're a good sport," Seven whispered in my ear after I drew back.

"Follow me," Gram bellowed and led the way to the pool. I fell into step behind her with Rella and Harper, and the guys moved up to join us.

"Nice of you to invite Anders," Grey said. "Hopefully, we'll get a few minutes to talk." His bland expression didn't give away any of what he was thinking.

"In case Anders didn't tell you, he's coming

into the office Monday morning."

Grey nodded.

"Enough business," Harper cut in. "The food is really good here. They do a buffet on weekends, and there's a wide array of choices. You won't be disappointed.

We trooped down the road that circled the complex and over to the far end of the property, where the gated pool area was off to one side. The pool itself took up half the space and had a view of the ocean, and a bar had been built half-in and half-out of the pool, so guests could be served on land or water. Complete with its own kitchen, the dining area had plenty of seating, and every table had the option of an umbrella.

"Avery!"

I turned towards someone yelling my name, waving frantically. It couldn't be.

My mom flew across the concrete, arms out, and enveloped me in a hard hug. "You're in so much trouble, young lady, avoiding your family." She laid several big kisses on my cheek. "Phone calls just aren't enough."

Dad appeared behind her and embraced us in a three-way hug. "Now, now, let our girl breathe."

Tears filled my eyes. "I didn't kill... I'm not a—"

"Stop right there," Mother admonished, then lowered her voice. "If you'd done it, you'd have been smart enough to hide the body."

Dad shook his head and hugged us again. "I agree with your mother. But enough of that kind of talk. Someone overhears and who knows what they'd make up."

"I just couldn't face your disappointment." Tears trickled down my cheeks.

"You've always been way too hard on yourself." Mom brushed tears off my cheeks, then slung her arm around my shoulders and held me to her side. "We've always been awed by you and everything you've accomplished, never, ever disappointed."

"I still say you got your smarts from my side of the family," Dad teased.

Mother elbowed him, which he dodged.

"Can anyone join this party?" My brother and sister, Weston and Eden, walked up and hugged me.

"Ugly hat." Eden wrinkled her nose.

"Ssh." I winked at her. "I had no idea you were going to be here. But I'm happy." I hugged her again.

Seven appeared at my side and looped his arm around my shoulders. All eyes zeroed in on him. "Are you going to introduce your husband to the family?"

I groaned.

"Explain yourself, young man," Dad grumped.

"Seven Donnelly," I introduced. "He's more like my bodyguard." I looked at him wide-eyed, imploring him not to go on with the husband... whatever you call it. "My mother and father, Stuart and Camille English. It's okay to ignore Seven's humor. He thinks he's funny and, well, sometimes... maybe."

Seven shook my dad's hand and kissed Mother's cheek. "It's nice to meet all of you." He nodded to my brother and sister. "I think a family dinner is in order, and soon."

"What's going on?" Mother demanded, scrutinizing him from head-to-toe. He was obviously met with her approval.

"It's such a long story. But let me tell it," I implored, unsure of how detailed Seven would get. I was happy to see Gram rushing headlong in our direction.

She slid up in front of me and grabbed my arm. "I'm stealing Avery away." Without waiting for an answer, she hauled me to the patio area, where a section was cordoned off with flamingo streamers.

Five tables had been pushed together. I rapidly counted, seeing they seated six people each and all except two tables were occupied. All eyes turned to me, and they waved and called greetings.

I knew I was sporting a deer-in-the-headlights look, which felt like the perfect reaction, as I only recognized a handful of the faces that were staring. The rest? No clue who they were.

Somehow, Harper managed to procure a tray

of shots and handed them to those standing around me who were drink-free. I caught my little sister taking a drink, doing her best not to choke, then watering a plant with the rest. I winked at her. I'd tell her later that tequila was an acquired taste.

Harper thrust a shot in my hand. "Drink."

I downed it and was tempted to shout, "Refill." But even though it had been a while since I'd put on a drunken display, today wouldn't be the day.

Gram held my arm in the air. "Avery English," she yelled.

Everyone clapped, and some whistled and hooted.

"I knew you'd be a popular draw, and when I put the word out that you'd be my guest, the phone rang off the hook," Gram crowed. "I underestimated the response or we'd have filled the area."

Harper had called her Gram wily a time or two, but that was an understatement. "Why?" I pasted on a smile and waved back when I noticed a couple of people holding up their phones.

"You're a celebrity, my dear." *No brainer* in Gram's tone. "Now don't look at me like that." She screwed up her nose. "Put on your friendly face. You don't want pictures of you sporting a demented face going up on our activity board. Take it from me, this to-do will be the talk for months and you want it to squash all talk of murder."

"You tricked me," I hissed at her. "What happened to the *small* get-together you bawled your eyes out over? You're lucky you're old enough to be my grandmother or I'd beat the smack out of you. Fair warning: I'll get even."

"I love your spunk." Gram grinned. "At least you didn't run off." She patted my cheek and pointed to a chair with a bouquet of balloons tied to the back. "For the guest of honor."

Harper and Rella appeared at my side.

"Turns out an accused murderer is quite the draw," Harper said. "People were p.o.ed when they couldn't get a seat."

"I'm giving you the same warning I gave your Gram. I'll get even. I can't believe you." I waved her off. "You may not have known the exact details, but you knew something." As evidenced by her smirk.

"Look how excited Gram is." Harper pointed.

Rella put her arm around my shoulders. "Harper and I have your back. We won't leave your side."

"I can handle a bunch of old people," I snapped, then took a calming breath. "At least, I hope."

"From personal experience, stay on guard, or the next thing you know, they'll have put one over on you and you'll have to regroup. Good example—this lunch." Harper's eyes sparkled with amusement.

"Listen up, because this is good advice." Rella pinned me with a stare. "Paste a smile on your face." She shook her head. "Not that one. A growling dog isn't friendly. Nod, a small laugh, say something non-committal." She demonstrated all three.

"Is this what you do at those fundraisers of yours?" I ran through a couple of smiles.

"That one right there." Rella pointed. "The rest will scare people, and we can't have that. You don't know who's going to be on the jury. Could be one of these folks, or friend of a friend even. That's if it goes that far."

Harper and Rella flanked me as we walked from table to table, the three of us doing exactly as Rella suggested. I nodded as the guests relayed how they'd read about the *murder*, always whispered in a tone loud enough for all to hear.

"Coverage is almost non-existent now," one complained.

My favorite was, "You don't look like a murderer."

It surprised me to see Ender Perry grinning at me from where he'd managed to ease his bulk into a chair without it collapsing to pieces. I imagined he found out about this shindig through his grandmother, who was besties with Gram. He was one of WD's first clients, and I'd run into him a time or two in the elevator.

When I got to Ender's table, I saw poker chips strewn around the table. We exchanged, *What's up?* smiles.

"You ever need anything…" He cracked his massive knuckles.

One of the women from the neighboring table gave him a moony smile.

Gregory Anders flashed me a smile and held up a fistful of cards, which I took to mean he had a winning hand.

Seven snuck up behind me, wrapping his arms around me and whispering in my ear, "The buffet has been set up and is ready for the guests to fill their plates."

I turned in his arms, facing him. "I'd rather drink." He chuckled. "Saw you and my dad in a hot discussion. I don't know whether to apologize or not."

"Have faith. I won him over, answering all his questions, including, 'What are your intentions, young man?'" I groaned. "It didn't take long for the rest of your family to join us, and I entertained them with the PG details of your life."

"Like there's any other version." I poked him lightly in the ribs. "I've talked to them every couple of days, but always went light on the details. I should've realized that more would've been better."

"Your dad and I exchanged phone numbers, and I told him to call anytime."

I wrapped my arms around his midsection and hugged him. "Let's get some food and then go with my original plan of sneaking out of here. We just have to be careful not to get caught."

Shrieking over and over at the top of her lungs, a woman came barreling through the pool gate. Several men ran over, circled her, and appeared to be calming her down as they helped her into a chair.

"I tried to place a small wager with Grey, and he wouldn't go for it," Harper said as she approached. "For those of you that don't know her, that's Marge, one of the residents, and I'm willing to bet a fiver that her bearded dragon has gone on the run again."

Several heads bobbed up and down and a couple stood for a better look, but no one was willing to put out cash.

Those that weren't drinking their lunch went back to eating. Seven and I grabbed plates and wound through the buffet. Being the guest of honor, I was seated at the head table, Seven next to me.

Not sure how, but it didn't take one man long to find the reptile. He came through the gate with it wrapped in a beach towel. Marge launched herself on the man, hugging him and the dragon.

A woman dropped down next to me, taking Gram's seat. I'd let the two women battle it out over who got to sit there. The wispy blonde leaned over, lowering her voice: "I really didn't want to wait for the question-and-answer period, so I thought you could answer while we eat. What's jail like?"

What was she talking about? These people came to ask questions? "It's not fun." I smiled lamely. It was clear she didn't like that answer. "It's just like what you see on television." Let's hope she didn't ask for a specific show, since I wasn't a watcher.

"Ohhh," she said, clearly having a couple in mind.

Seven threw out a couple of names, and the woman beamed at him.

Just then, Gram interrupted. "You're in my seat."

"Surely you don't mind."

"I do, though." Gram flicked her finger. The woman picked up her plate and utensils and sulked off.

"Can I have your keys?" I whispered to Seven. "There's an exit over by the restrooms. At least, I think so."

"That gate has a chain on it," Gram said with a pointed look.

"You won't get out of here without Gram tackling you." Seven winked at the woman. If she hadn't thought about it before, she was now. "I can wrestle you free, but you can't ditch your parents." He pushed his plate away. "You ready for the Seven Donnelly show?"

He stood and unleashed a whistle.

Conversation stopped and all eyes shot to him.

"We found out just now that you all expect Avery to answer questions. On advice of counsel…" He pointed at Ender. "Avery won't be able to answer any questions."

All eyes were now on Ender, who stayed seated and bowed. Let's hope no one asked why I'd hired someone who specialized in real estate law to represent me.

"So that none of you leave disappointed, Grey here is a licensed private investigator and has offered to answer your questions. As for your jail questions, I've been there a time or two, so I can answer any you have."

Rolling with being caught off guard, Grey laughed.

I crooked my finger at my dad behind Seven's back and whispered, "He's a retired Orlando detective."

"A lot better than what I was thinking."

The woman who'd sat next to me earlier jumped up. "Can you describe a day behind bars?"

Horrible food. Minding your own business if you know what's good for you.

My dad scooted back and over, and I did the same. "Your mom and I like Seven. Seems like a straight-up guy. Looked me in the eye and answered my questions."

"I like him too." I blew out a soft sigh. "I just don't know how to do relationships."

"I'm thinking that Seven would be happy to show you the way." Dad leaned over and wrapped his arms around me, laying a big kiss on my cheek. "Your brother threatened to kick his butt if he hurts you and I joined in."

Seven walked around the tables and made sure every question got answered. The ones that weren't cop-related, he handed off to Grey and Ender, and both men appeared to be enjoying themselves. I did wonder a couple of times if their answers were embellished, but the group was hanging on every word. They wrapped up to a rousing round of applause.

Gram came over and pulled me into her arms. "I admit there was a bit of trickery involved in getting you to come, but you were a good sport. This group is going to hang around for hours, and I know you've been wanting to sneak away. Go through those double doors—" She pointed behind me. "—and through the back kitchen, then make a right, and you'll be back on the main road to my unit."

"This was good for me." I kissed her cheek. "Forcing me to socialize more than I would normally. And Seven once again showed me what a great guy he is."

"Oh, he's a keeper." Gram winked.

I made my way over to my family, and we decided on a date for a family dinner. I voted for my dad's barbeque since it had been too long. I said good-bye to Harper and Rella, not wanting them to wonder what happened, then came up behind Seven as the women were finishing up fawning over him. I thought about asking Harper to pick Seven's pocket and give me the keys, then laughed.

Seven looked down at me and kissed the top of my head.

"I have something I want to show you." I led him across the patio to the double doors. "This is a Gram-approved exit."

Chapter Nineteen

Seven closed the bedroom door quietly, glanced over his shoulder, and jerked to a halt. He gave me a head-to-toe once-over, and I wanted to ask if he approved of my sweatpants and t-shirt. "Where do you think you're going in the middle of the night?" he demanded.

After we'd gotten back from Gram's, we'd watched a movie... or he did. I read. We'd both gone to bed early.

"I suppose I'll find out when we get there." I returned his stare.

"How did you know I was even awake? You got a camera in the bedroom?" His eyes cut into me.

Even though the answer to his question was no, I didn't answer. Let him wonder. "Give me a minute to put my shoes on, and I'll be ready to go." I glanced toward the wall where I'd left them. "Leave without me, and I'll track you down."

"You're not going," he said in a glacial tone.

"Okay, hon, whatever you say."

Seven stomped out the door.

I should've just told him that I couldn't sleep,

heard him moving around, and knew something was up, but what fun would that be? I didn't hurry, knowing that I'd have to wait for the elevator to return to the top. I tied my shoes and grabbed my backpack, which I slung over my shoulder. I had it packed and ready to go. One of the nights when I couldn't sleep, I'd put a tracker on his phone, and tonight I'd get to use it. He'd put one on mine... so turnabout and all that. I don't know why he did that, since I didn't go anywhere he didn't know about. I'd evaded him a couple of times, but he'd found me in short order. I hadn't gone far either time, just down to the beach. I ran back to my bedroom, grabbed a sweatshirt, and tied it around my waist.

"This is stupid," I told myself while riding down to the garage. The doors opened, and I was surprised to see Seven's SUV in its parking space but not the man himself. As I got closer, I realized he was sitting behind the wheel, leaned back in the seat. I bypassed my car and reached for the door handle, surprised to find it was unlocked. "You could've at least opened the door for me." I slid onto the seat.

Seven grunted and squealed into reverse.

"You going to tell me where we're going?" I asked.

"Floyd was on stakeout tonight. His sister went into labor, and he's her baby coach and is needed at the hospital. I told him to go and I'd be right over. But I was held up waiting on you."

I knew Floyd was from a large, close-knit family. I hadn't met any of them but heard plenty of stories. "It was all of a minute or two." His jaw tightened. "I've never been on a stakeout. Is there going to be a shoot-out or something fun?"

"Let's hope not. In general, they're boring. You familiar with the phrase 'Hurry up and wait'? If it's a typical case, that's how the rest of the night will go."

"Then it's good you have me to talk to." More grunting. "Just know that I can be helpful."

"You should've stayed home." He blew out an irritated sigh. "There is a miniscule chance that something will go wrong and I won't be able to protect you."

"I can't shoot anyone — not that I'd want to — but I have taken a self-defense class." I air-boxed.

Seven headed north on Highway One, turned off on a side street, and then several more turns. We passed a small grocery store, not a car in the lot, and the street became one lane each way and turned into a green jungle on both sides of the road. The storage place just up ahead was lit up like it was a twenty-four-hour operation. Across the street, a several-story building was under construction. The headlights flashed on the sign, which didn't give a clue about what was being built.

"Once it's finished, this is going to be an office building." Seven passed it, then turned left onto a dirt road and right through low-hanging branches, taking cover under the trees. "We're here to stake out the construction site. According to a tip, the electrical crew is running a side gig in the wee hours of the morning." Seven reached over the back seat, grabbing a duffle bag. He unzipped it and removed two pairs of binoculars, handing me one.

"Sounds illegal. Why not call the cops?" I'd heard of infrared binoculars, but this was the first time I'd looked through a pair. I'd be able to see anything going on across the street.

"The owner wants to know what he's reporting before he calls in a favor. He doesn't want bad publicity surrounding the project."

"Who was the tipster?" I asked.

Seven pointed diagonally. "The man who owns the storage lot, who also happens to be a friend of the owner. He claims to have witnessed activity that can't be legal."

"Since whoever it was doesn't have any legit reason to be on-site so early, you'd think they'd cover their tracks better."

"These meetings have become a regular occurrence, and they've gotten lax."

"What do you want me to do?"

"This has a camera feature." Seven tapped a button on the side of the binoculars. "I'm going to need the license plate numbers of whoever shows up."

I took a couple of pictures of the building for practice.

"So you know, this is generally the way everything unfolds—a couple of cars show up, then a panel van. The latter stays about ten minutes. An hour or so later, more cars show, and five, ten minutes later, they all pull out. The tipster tried to spy on it through a telescope but couldn't get anything concrete. Thought about hiding in the weeds but didn't want to get his ass kicked or worse if he got caught."

"They might opt to kill him rather than risk jail, even though the penalty would be life or worse." I shuddered. "You get the license numbers and then what?"

"We'll run a check on every plate, and then on the registered owners. Some more investigation, and we'll figure out what the product is that they're selling and where it originates, though I have a good idea."

"The computer investigation would be easy-peasy for me to do." I caught his eyeroll. "I'm reminding you again—faster than your regular guy."

He reached back into the bag and pulled out a camera and long lens, attaching the two.

"Did you bring snacks?"

"Remember when you're bored out of your mind that you're the one who invited yourself."

"I take it that's a super-duper model that shoots in the dark." I pointed to the camera.

"Yep." He handed me his phone. "If you get bored, you can snoop through my phone…

again. I'm certain you're familiar with all the apps, as you must've perused them while installing the tracking app."

"Guess where I got the idea? You. So I knew it was a good one." I smiled cheekily. "If you used your words instead of grunts, I'd understand you better."

It was impossible to see his expression, since we were sitting in the pitch-dark, but I'd bet on at least a half-smile.

"Get comfortable, because now we wait." Seven produced a small flashlight and fiddled with the camera.

I adjusted the seat back so I could still see out the windshield. I turned on his phone and scanned to see what apps he had loaded, since despite what he thought, I hadn't done it the first time.

"What are you doing?"

"Your pictures are boring." I scrolled through. "Nothing fun here. Headed over to your text messages next." His hand shot out to grab it back, but I was ready for him and turned away. "You don't have anything to hide, do you?" I said over my shoulder.

"It will make for short snooping, since I delete everything."

Seven was right—it took me less than five minutes to finish scrolling through his texts. "If I snooze off and something happens, wake me." I closed my eyes. "I can see why you don't like these kinds of jobs." I peeked out from under my lashes.

"Sitting around is boring. I'd rather be in the middle of the action. I suggested that I join the crew, but the client vetoed it. He doesn't want anyone finding out that he had anything to do with these folks ending up in cuffs."

"I don't blame him. Retribution could be painful or worse." I closed my eyes again.

Seven nudged me. "We've got company."

I jerked upright, realizing that I'd nodded off. Two cars followed by a van turned off the road and into the construction site, then drove inside the building, where one of the walls hadn't been finished yet.

Everything unfolded as reported, Seven and I both snapping pictures as the vehicles came and went.

"I realize that the building is still a shell, but if I were the owner, I'd have security cameras installed," I said.

"Got it covered. There was always the possibility that they'd run a check prior to their meeting, but everything went down too quickly."

I was learning a few tricks for what not to do if I were a criminal, but they'd be going to waste.

"Before we turn over any of the evidence we've collected, we want to track that van. If they're smart, it's a rental or, better yet, stolen." Seven clicked away until the last car left the property. He waited until no headlights were visible in either direction before pulling back out onto the road. "Did you have fun?" he asked, amused with himself.

"The idea was exciting, but sitting in the trees… not at all. I'll have a good story for our weekly breakfast. At least I've got time to come up with a story about how important I was to the operation to bring down criminals." Over Seven's laughter, I said, "I'll pass on the next stakeout. You can lie to me when you get back about how much fun you had."

Chapter Twenty

When Seven and I were invited to Harper and Grey's for coffee, I knew something was up. Before leaving, I stood in front of the mirror and practiced a bored face. We'd see how that worked out for me.

My meeting with Anders had been postponed. Something had come up, though he didn't say what; he just apologized. "Call me when you to want to reschedule," I told him.

Not long after, Cruz's assistant, Susie, called requesting a meeting, implying that he'd had a last-minute cancellation and could fit me in.

"What's this meeting about?" I asked.

"Don't be late."

I double-checked the screen to make certain, and sure enough, she'd hung up. For about a minute, I entertained the idea of calling back with the excuse that we'd been cut off, but I didn't want to deal with the icy tone I'd heard her treat someone else to.

Harper ushered us into the kitchen, and we sat around the island. She'd barely gotten our mugs filled and sat down across from me when Grey's blue eyes zeroed in on me.

I'd known something was up before I got there and was ready for him, staring back. The key was not to look away. Maintain eye contact, I reminded myself.

"I spoke with Mr. Anders earlier, and I want to thank you for all the help you've offered him. I know that he appreciates it, and I'm sure you'll be hearing from him. I'm certain that you've heard he got his money back, and although happy, he's been on edge, afraid that Sissy will steal from him again. I got him an appointment with a new investment firm, which I assured him is one of the best and will keep Sissy's greedy fingers off his money."

"What's the name of this stellar firm?" I barely contained my sarcasm.

"Client confidentiality."

"Whatever."

Harper grinned.

I kicked her, and to her credit, she flinched slightly, but not a sound. "All this could have been conveyed in a text message."

"It's my way of saying I appreciate what you did," Grey said. "I don't know just how helpful you've been, but one day, I'll find out."

Having barely touched my coffee, I stood. "Hate to drink and run, but when Cruz snaps his fingers..." Okay, his assistant, but invoking his name sounded better. "I won't be needing a ride," I told Seven, just short of spitting my annoyance in his direction. "I know you have a report to put together about your stakeout last night." He'd get it done faster without any interruptions.

"Neither Seven nor I want you getting into trouble while you're out on bail, especially not on our behalf," Grey said.

I bit back everything on the tip of my tongue—it all sounded gripey—and instead pasted on a smile.

"I'll walk you out." Harper hooked her arm around me.

"No need." Seven appeared at my side. "I'll be taking Avery to her appointment."

Once we were in the elevator on the way down, I said, "I'm just bored and don't know how to deal with it, and I was looking forward to helping Anders again. And I'm disappointed that my company wasn't the one recommended."

* * *

We walked into Cruz's office and took a seat.

"I wanted to update you on your case." Cruz's hand smacked down on a large file under it. I wondered if all that paperwork pertained to me. "The medical examiner has now released the full details of the autopsy." He proceeded to share them with me.

Even though I knew she'd been shot point blank, I winced at the graphic details. "How do you shoot someone and just walk away? So close, it had to be someone she knew."

"There are a lot of people wandering around with no conscience," Seven said.

"Unfortunately, the gun hasn't been recovered. If it had, it's possible that it would've given us additional information." Cruz chose a file and flicked through the papers. "My investigator checked out Mrs. Basset's background and didn't uncover any red flags." He asked me what seemed like a hundred questions about Stella and her family. I hadn't met her children and had nothing new to offer. He handed me a spreadsheet. "Do you recognize this account?"

The forensic accountant had uncovered months of cash transfers from Stella's accounts to an account in my name. In the beginning, it was minimal amounts, which gradually got larger. He'd found that the account had been opened online, but his guy had been unable to obtain a copy of the ID used. Luckily, that had been handed over as part of discovery. I examined the driver's license closely, and although it was for a female, that's where the similarities ended. This woman was older, had a few pounds on me, and appeared to be wearing a wig, as her hair didn't sit quite right on her head. She wasn't anyone I recognized. I handed it off to Seven, who'd been staring over my shoulder. "Isn't this proof I didn't do this?"

Cruz shook his head. "It doesn't prove that

you didn't set up the account. You could've been using fake ID. Plus, this woman... we ran a search and couldn't find a match."

"What about the eyewitness?" Seven demanded.

"She proved to be weak for the prosecution, but we wanted to talk to her anyway. She's been evading one of my best servers and also fired her family attorney. He wouldn't take my call once he found out why I was calling." Cruz snorted at that. "I found it unprofessional. Since I've never met the man, there's no good reason he'd evade my calls."

Cruz launched into questions that, to me, sounded like the same ones he asked at our last meeting. I gave him straightforward and truthful answers.

"The good news is that no new and incriminating evidence has popped up," he said finally.

"Is there anything I can be doing to help my case?"

Seven enveloped my hand in his and squeezed.

"You can use this free time to get caught up on other projects."

I struggled not to roll my eyes at Cruz. When you're as married to your work as I am, it precludes hobbies. However, since that sounded argumentative, I stayed silent, and the smile I'd worked on was back in place.

Cruz and Seven talked about another case of his, and I zoned out, thinking that, to me, no news wasn't good news.

Finally, the meeting was over. We all stood and shook hands. I wanted to teleport back home and out to the beach.

"Am I being mean or was that meeting unproductive?" I asked Seven, who'd looped his arm around me on the way back to the car.

"That's the way lawyers assure their clients they're hard at work on their case." Seven unlocked the car door and held it open for me, then went around and slid behind the wheel. "I can hear you thinking." He leaned over and gave me a quick peck on the lips.

"The eyewitness, did you happen to catch a name? He did let it slip that she was a neighbor." How many could there be? Though depending on how someone used the term, it could mean the whole block.

"We track her down and then what?" He cruised the streets with a familiarity that suggested he'd lived here forever.

"What we could do is casually run into the woman. Be interesting to see her reaction. Not accost her or anything," I hurriedly added at the way his brows went up.

"The legal term for what you're suggesting is intimidation of a witness. Which is what you'd be charged with if she called the cops."

"I just thought that maybe if she saw me up

close, she'd realize her mistake and change her story."

"There was talk of hauling you in for another lineup, and that's when the witness stopped communicating with the district attorney's office. As far as I know, it's a dead issue except for Cruz wanting to question her—to what end, I have no idea. My professional opinion is to forget her and move on."

"I don't want this to go to trial. I want the charges dropped for any old reason—don't care—so I can move on with my life." Even though the windows were up, I could smell that we were getting closer to the beach. "I think it's odd that she ID'd me by name to the cops when they came around asking, then fell apart at the lineup."

"You need to have a little more patience."

I nodded, since I didn't want to argue.

"Raise your right hand." He demonstrated.

I swallowed my groan and did as he asked.

"I want you to solemnly swear to take me with you should you decide to go off half-cocked. Though I want to make it clear that I'd prefer you didn't."

Putting one over on Seven was getting harder and harder. "You're turning out to be a good fake husband, taking the time to talk me down from doing anything stupid."

"You know how you could show your thanks…" He gave me a level stare. "We make it official and start dating."

"Your friends and family would be horrified that you chose an accused murderer to be seen out and about with, no matter how cute." I fluttered my eyelashes.

"When I take you home for a family dinner, they'll be warning you off me. As for what other people think, don't give a flip. Probably why more than a few have whispered 'arrogant dick' behind my back. Too pussy to say it to my face, knowing I'd rearrange theirs." Seven flexed his muscles, which I felt up.

"Calm down, tough guy. If someone is a meanie to you, tell me. I'll take care of them."

"If you're willing to beat the smoke out of someone on my behalf, that means we're official." He grinned.

"In celebration, and since I've been the one to drag my feet, dinner's on me. I'll call and see if I can get a reservation at my favorite hot dog cart down at the beach."

"You're on."

Chapter Twenty-One

The phone rang early the next morning, and Grey's name popped up on the display. I wondered if I was about to be called out on something, even though I'd stayed out of trouble... for a day or two anyway. I raised my brows at Seven over my coffee cup and turned the screen so he could see it.

"Yes sir," I answered cheekily.

Grey growled a laugh. "If only I could get Harper to respond to everything just like that."

I chuckled. Harper was a sneaky one and better at making things happen than I was. I could do with another lesson or two.

"I called to ask a favor. We're expecting a delivery at WD this morning and everyone will either be on a job or at a meeting, so I was hoping you'd agree to hold down the office and sign for the boxes."

I blew Seven a kiss, knowing he was behind the call.

"Before you answer, this comes with the stipulation that you don't turn the office upside down."

"Are you certain you don't want me

organizing your files? After I read them, of course."

Grey grumbled something I couldn't hear. "A couple of people highly recommended you. Were they wrong?"

"You'd be surprised what I can get accomplished." I ignored his groan. "I would love to, and I'll be the best fill-in office babe you've ever had." In addition, I'd be getting Harper a box of donuts in bestie appreciation.

"Seven and I both appreciate this. I understand that a key isn't necessary, so I won't have one dropped off."

My cheeks burned. "I super swear that I'll try not to do that again after today." I couldn't make out what he mumbled. We hung up, and I leaned across the island and crooked my finger at Seven, brushing his lips with mine. "You're the best. I had no clue what I was going to do with myself all day. Now I can go to your office and get in trouble." I grinned at him.

"Grey hears the word 'trouble' and he'll be barring the door so even I can't get inside. We talked it over and agreed that you were the perfect pick, since we both trust you."

It would be fun going to the office, knowing that I had something to do. Seven warned me that waiting to sign for a package wouldn't be exciting. "Don't suck the fun out before I get to my desk." I didn't bother to add, *Sometimes you have to make your own fun.*

We rode down in the elevator together, then split up, each of us taking our own car.

I drove straight to the office and hustled up the stairs, first stopping at my own office, which was quiet. No sign of Dixon. I went on up to the third floor, picked the lock, and settled behind the reception desk, unloading my laptop from my bag.

After the meeting with Cruz, I'd decided that contrary to advice of counsel, I wanted to be more proactive on my case. I didn't want to end up in jail, wishing I'd done something to help myself. It was time to investigate all the nagging questions I had, and when better than when I had free time while waiting on a delivery? On the drive over, I'd thought there was no better way to pitch myself as the best one to temporarily run the WD office than proving that I could do the job without incident.

I opened a new file and started making a list. At the top: track the money from Stella's accounts. Not that Boy Wonder didn't do a good job, he just wasn't thorough enough. Seven knew I was behind Anders getting his money back but hadn't confronted me; there was something to be said about not knowing for sure. He had no idea of the extent of my skills, and I didn't think he wanted to know. Since they were in no way legal, it was better to keep it to myself. That could be a surprise for another time.

I continued to pound away, making a list of all

the people I knew to be even remotely associated with the case. It was a short list. I closed the file, then went to the internet and searched for any mention of Stella Basset's name. No mention of an eyewitness. There had been an interview with Stella's son and daughter, which yielded nothing except that she was a good mother. Tired, I saved everything to a thumb drive and shoved it in my pocket.

A clunking of boots in the corridor followed by a banging noise alerted me that the delivery man had shown up. I jumped up and threw the door open wide so he could roll in his hand truck and motioned for him to unload the boxes in the corner. It didn't take him long, and as he turned to leave, he stepped aside for a muscular man in jeans and a dress shirt who came through the door, catching me off guard.

"Can I help you?" I asked as the thirty-something looked around the office. I was somewhat reassured by the fact that he didn't look menacing, but who knew these days.

"I'd like to speak with someone about locating an old friend," he said.

"If you'd take a seat, I can get the paperwork started." I stepped over to Seven's desk to grab a chair.

"I've got that." He brushed by me and picked it up with ease, setting it in front of the desk where I'd been sitting.

"The partners are out of the office this

morning but I can take your information so they'll have it when they speak with you." I handed him Grey's business card. "How did you hear about WD?"

"The website came up first in a search, and I co-own the gym a couple of blocks over. I took a short break to come over and check you out." He eyed the card and stuck it in his pocket. "I figured it wouldn't take long to find out how this process works. The little bit of searching I've done isn't getting me anywhere, and I'm out of ideas."

"Avery English." I extended my hand.

"Riggs Brennan." He leaned forward to take it.

I took a notepad out of my briefcase. "You said you're trying to locate someone. I'll need the name." And what else? I mentally made a list of questions from all the background checks I'd done in the past.

"Cara North."

"Is there any reason that Cara wouldn't want to be found?"

"There's a lot about this situation that I don't understand, but I can't think of a good reason for her to disappear. Cara was really angry when I told her I enlisted in the army. My father and grandfather served, and she didn't understand why I had to do it. Once I finished basic training, I was shipped overseas. After that, I received a couple of letters, and then they stopped. I assumed she moved on but hoped that wasn't the case." His brown eyes filled with sadness.

I asked a couple more questions—birthdate? last known address?—to make sure we located the right woman.

"When I got back to the states and was discharged, I went to her old address, and none of the other residents of the apartment building knew who she was, which really surprised me, as she was the kind of woman that had a friendly word for everyone. I went to the management company and was told that they couldn't give out information on any tenant. But the girl at the desk whispered, 'Cara didn't leave a forwarding,' adding that most don't."

"How long were you gone?" I asked.

"Four years."

"How will you feel if we find out that she's married? Or has a boyfriend and has basically moved on?" I asked.

"I've thought of that and wouldn't like it, but if Cara's happy…" Riggs stared down at his hands. "Here's the problem. I ran into an old friend of hers who told me that Cara found out after I deployed that she was pregnant and gave birth to a boy six months later. If I do have a son, I'd like to get to know him."

"I take it this friend didn't know where Cara moved to?"

"There was an old rivalry there that doesn't seem to have died any, and Dana appeared to enjoy blurting out the news. I had a feeling that she knew but wasn't saying." Irritation replaced sadness in Riggs' eyes. "A more disturbing story, and what motivated me to stop dragging my feet about trying to find Cara is that I looked up another of her old friends who said she recently ran into her and claims that she's homeless. This friend said that Cara and a young boy were camped out in a local park. She approached the two, and when Cara recognized her, she jerked the boy up and ran off."

"Sounds like she doesn't have anyone to go to for help." I asked questions about the two friends, thinking maybe they'd remember something if asked by someone else.

"I want you to know that it doesn't matter if he's my son or not; I want to help them."

"And if he is your son?"

"I don't want him growing up thinking his father didn't give a damn. Cara may not want to have anything to do with me, but the two of us can be good parents."

"Did this friend tell you where she saw Cara? With no resources, she wouldn't have been able to go far." I couldn't imagine what Cara was going through with no one to help her. Riggs gave me the streets, and I winced, knowing it wasn't the best area.

"I've been over to the park and surrounding streets, and the people there are suspicious of new faces. I tried asking questions and was met with hostility, so I stopped. Farther on down the road is a tent community. I showed her picture to a couple of women there; they wanted money but had no information. Paid them anyway." Riggs blew out a sigh.

"You have a picture?"

Riggs nodded. "It's old though."

"If you could forward that to us, it would be helpful." I scribbled down my cell number and shoved it across the desk.

Riggs took out his phone and sent me a text. A minute later, my phone pinged, and I checked to make sure I'd received it.

"Don't worry, we'll find her," I reassured him. "I can get this started and hand the information to the partners so they can jump right in." I did my best not to wince as I said it. I could already feel Grey's fingers around my neck.

"I just need to find her. Living on the street is no life."

I agreed.

The door opened, and Seven and Grey walked in. Seven sized up the situation with one look and smirked. Grey's brows went into his hairline, a militant look on his face. Why couldn't I have lucked out and just got Seven?

"Here they are now," I said in a cheerful tone and made the introductions. "Riggs... Mr. Brennan needs help locating his old girlfriend. I've made a few notes that I'm forwarding now, along with her picture." I'd remind Grey later that he didn't say a word about not being nice to new clients, so he could lose the stern look. To irritate the man even more, I added, "You'll probably need a woman on this job, and I'm available."

"We're certainly happy to help you," Grey said with a tight-lipped smile, motioning Riggs over to his desk.

Seven blew me a kiss behind their backs, to which I made a face. Hmm... I hadn't been invited to join the men and didn't have the guts at the moment to drag over a chair. But I wasn't about to go anywhere, since I could hear what was being said from where I sat. Opening my laptop, I started a search on Cara North, starting with the "Who's in jail?" records for Florida. Turned out she'd been arrested twice, once for shoplifting and once for assault. The latter had happened a month ago. It showed she spent a couple of days in jail and the charges were dropped. A little more digging, and I got the address where the arrest was made. No mention in the court records of the son. What did that mean? That he'd been turned over to Social Services? I shuddered at the thought he might have been left behind.

The guys wound up their meeting and shook hands.

"Nice to meet you, Avery," Riggs said on his way out the door.

After the door closed behind him, I struggled not to flinch under Grey's stare. "Before you get started, you're welcome. Aren't you happy that I was here to welcome a potential client?"

"I was about to say thank you," Grey said drily. "Riggs sang your praises. He was pleased that you were attentive to his problem and appreciated that you didn't go through the motions of listening when you weren't."

"This is the kind of case that we'd normally pass off to Floyd, but for this one, I volunteered." Seven winked at me. "As my *sidekick*, I thought you'd like to go and check out the area where Cara was last seen… that's if you have time in your schedule."

"I'd prefer partner. The other sounds…" I made a face. "Since you've elevated my status…" I told them about Cara's arrests. "Check your email."

"It's odd that there wasn't a Social Services referral in the court docs," Seven said. "Their files can't be accessed online. Legally anyway."

"I'm going to have a noncompete agreement drawn up," Grey said, "in case you get the idea to open up your own investigations firm one floor down. Wouldn't surprise me if you stood out front and waylaid our clients."

"Now there's an idea." I grinned at him.

His phone rang, and he looked relieved to be answering.

"Come on, Trouble." Seven held out his hand. "I'm taking you to lunch."

"Don't we have work to do?"

Chapter Twenty-Two

Seven put checking out the two last-known addresses for Cara on hold until the morning. I reluctantly agreed that we'd attract unwanted attention asking questions in a homeless encampment at a time when there were a lot of people milling about and all eyes would be on us. He said early morning was the best time to go and to not worry, that we'd find someone to answer our questions for a few bucks.

After lunch, Seven wanted to know my plans for the rest of the day. I was deliberately evasive, and he scrutinized me like I was under a microscope until I finally told him I was headed home, which was true.

I changed my clothes, lay down on the bed, and played with Arco until he fell asleep. Then I got up and opened my laptop, looking over the files that Dixon had forwarded me. We'd already agreed on the necessary changes to clients' portfolios, but I was always one to double-check everything. It didn't take long to give my okay and shoot them back.

Tired of not feeling in control of my life, I

oozed frustration, and it had gone through the roof after the last trip to Cruz's office. It was hard to believe that his information guy hadn't uncovered anything new, though maybe I was hoping for a miracle and that wasn't how criminal cases unfolded.

Needing fresh air, particularly the smell of the beach, I grabbed the laptop I kept in my safe and headed down to the sand, this time getting into the storage box to pull out one of the folding chairs that were there for the exclusive use of the residents. I set up the chair close to the water and in the right alignment to boost the connection I needed.

I went to work researching Stella Bassett's neighborhood, a tree-lined street in North Miami Beach. The two houses across the street were the only ones with unobstructed views of the front of Stella's house, easily able to see any comings and goings. The neighbors on either side were blocked by shrubbery and trees. The other possibility was someone walking their dog or out for a jog. Murder must've come as a shock on the quiet street.

The murder happened in the early morning hours, and the witness claimed to have seen me running across the lawn. Wonder why there was no mention of my Porsche, which would have surely stuck out, since I'd have had to park it in the driveway or on the street.

Now that I had the addresses that were the

most obvious choices... what now? Bang on the door? "Recognize me?" Terrible idea. But doing nothing was tedious.

I'd put together a file on Stella—everything I could remember from our appointments. There were only a few brief references, as I kept everything businesslike with my clients and anything personal was kept casual. I winced at the thought of the seventy-year-old woman's life ending the way it did. I'd found her to be genuinely nice and easy to work with. I opened a file and made several more notes. Next on my list—checking out who owned the two houses.

I caught movement out of the corner of my eye and turned to see Harper dragging a beach chair across the sand. I didn't bother to close my laptop, as I'd shared with her long ago that this was the best location to get a strong signal. I did back up to my drive, taking it out and shoving it in my pocket just as she sat down next to me.

"Grey and Seven were having an online meeting and making too much noise for me to concentrate. Not sure how they're able to get a clear idea of what's going on when they talk over one another. Went out on the patio, saw this little blob in the distance, and knew it was you. Knowing you're up to something, I came down to find out what it is."

"Do you know how tired I am of getting accused of being up to something?"

"But we both know it's true. So spill. Between

the two of us, we can brainstorm whatever you've come up with." Harper dug her toes in the sand with a satisfied sigh.

I pulled up the picture of Stella's street and turned my laptop around. "The so-called eyewitness claims to have seen me run across the grass here..." I drew my finger across the screen. "She's backed off, but I want to know why she fingered me in the first place."

"That would be so rude of you, considering there's a walkway from the front door to the sidewalk." Harper lifted my computer off my lap for a closer look. "Where did you park?"

"Good question. If it was ever answered, I didn't hear it, and I can hardly ask without garnering a stern stare, which I'm also tired of."

Harper handed me back my laptop. "What's your plan? Shouldn't you just be happy that the woman is no longer a witness for the prosecution?"

"For now. As to your other question, I was about to check the records to see who lives in the only two houses with a line of sight and see if their names are mentioned in a news article that I might've missed."

"When Grey had his legal trouble, I concocted a story about writing a book on the murder that I was using to launch my career, or whatever it was I said, as an excuse to interview people. I made lots of mistakes, but I don't have to repeat them. This time around, I could make my cover story more believable."

"You?" I shook my head. "Grey would kill me."

"It's not like you can go knocking on doors. Someone might recognize you from the news coverage, and then it would hit the fan. Besides, you know I'm the one with the gift for gab." Harper chuckled. "Some would have a harsher word."

"I can't ask you to do that."

"You're not; I'm volunteering, and besides, pretending to be a writer isn't a crime. We'll have to include Rella. Once she realizes there's no talking us out of this idea, she'll want to come along. She may not have the same adventurous streak we do, but she hates being left out." Harper reached out and grabbed my face. "Stop shaking your head before it falls off. That's a Gram-ism. What I'm suggesting is not illegal."

"You're the best. The three of us should get an ice cream at the beach and talk about it. Maybe one of us will talk some sense into the other two."

"You stay in the car and out of sight. I'll mic up so you can hear every word," Harper continued in an excited tone. "This will be fun. It's not a guarantee of success, but it's worth a try."

"Maybe."

Harper turned her head. "You might want to close the screen, as Seven is headed this way. He gets a whiff, and there'll be endless questions until he thinks he's wrung every bit of information out of you." She stood and waved him over, pointing to the chair. "I'll text you with a time and date for our outing."

I powered down the laptop.

Seven loomed over us, and he and Harper exchanged hellos.

"What are you two doing?" he asked, suspicion in his tone, as he sat down. "Grey assured me it would be something, as it's second nature to you three, though you're minus one at the moment."

Harper laughed and turned to me with a thumbs up. "We're on for the ice cream." She headed back up the beach.

"Take a second to enjoy this gorgeous day." I pointed to the waves breaking on the beach. "How long did it take you to find me?"

He settled back in the chair. "I'm an ex-detective."

As if that's an answer.

"You didn't answer my question." He arched his brow.

"You're the detective, you tell me." *This banter could go on forever.*

"If you think sarcasm will have me stomping off in a fit, you'd be wrong. It's a turn-on." Seven leaned over, slid my laptop out from under my hands, and opened the lid.

And here I'd thought I was getting a kiss. *Good*

luck, buddy. I smirked at him. I wasn't fool enough not to use a password on my computer. Let's see if he could hack his way in.

"I don't suppose the password is Seven?" Which he entered and was promptly rejected. He closed the lid. "It's a lot of work keeping up with you. I saw signs you were up to something and ignored them. Last time that happens. Did you get your paperwork done or was that bull?"

"I got everything on my to-do list done, and what better place? I'd move my desk down here into the sand if I thought I could get away with it and it wouldn't wash away."

"Anything else you want to tell me? You know I've got your back, and if you think otherwise, that's insulting."

"Don't get your shorts in a tear."

"It's wad."

"Correction noted. I've decided to hire a new investigation firm for my case, since Cruz's dude is moving too damn slow for my taste. And using WD is probably a conflict of something."

Seven shook his head, his expression clearly letting me know he hated the idea. "You need to be careful or you'll end up getting in more trouble."

I thought he was about to hand me back my laptop—wrong again. Instead, he turned it over and scrutinized it closer. "This isn't the one I bought you. You just happened to have another one... in the kitchen cupboard or something? It's not brand new, so splurge purchase is off the table."

"Kitchen." I snorted. "You know the police searched my condo. And being one of their brethren, you know just how thoroughly. Where could I possibly hide it that they wouldn't find it?"

"It happens. What I find interesting is that you don't have a safe. Unless you do, and it wasn't discovered."

"You're welcome to do a more thorough check."

"Don't think I won't take you up on that," Seven grouched. "Can I extract a promise that you'll share whatever this new consultant of yours digs up?"

I was fairly certain that I'd be hearing more on this subject. "Deal." I stuck out my pinkie. He looped his around mine.

"In the spirit of being upfront, our guy at WD is tracking the withdrawals from Stella's accounts. He'll also trace any IP addresses back to the owner." He handed me back my laptop, which I shoved in my bag. "Your file at WD is top priority, and anytime you have a question, just ask. I'll make sure to update you more often. We're going to get this figured out." He pulled me in for a kiss.

Chapter Twenty-Three

Seven and I were on the road early and headed to the park where Cara was seen last. I'd stayed up late and finished her background check, which I forwarded to Seven and Grey. I'd also located the birth certificate for River Brennan North, father listed as Riggs Brennan. That answered the paternity question. I called in a favor from Rella, who also had to broker a favor, and found out that Cara's son wasn't in the custody of Social Services. The biggest question now: where were mother and son?

I turned my travel mug almost upside down to get the last drop. "I was thinking..."

"I'm certain that you never stop. Give yourself a rest." Seven chuckled. "I can't wait to hear what you've come up with now."

"You need to add a woman to your team—some cases would be better served by a woman's touch—and in the meantime, I'll fill in until you find such a paragon."

"Funny you should mention it, as Grey and I just had this discussion. I might suspect you of eavesdropping, except I know you weren't even in the building. Grey wanted to put cash down that once you heard of the possibility, you'd be the first to sign up. I laughed in his face, not wanting to lose money." Seven cruised through the streets over to the Interstate, where despite the early hour, it wouldn't be long before cars were stacked up bumper-to-bumper. He exited not far from the airport.

"I've got an idea for today," I said.

"Why doesn't that surprise me?"

No groan—that was a good sign. "I pose as Cara's sister, flash her picture around. Maybe we'll get lucky and someone will recognize her. You should make yourself scarce, as your glaring mug isn't conducive to getting people to talk."

"I have no intention of leaving your side, and if you try to ditch me, I'll handcuff you."

"I'll scream."

"Anyone within hearing distance will think they're witnessing your takedown and be wondering what you did. The ones with legal issues will be hightailing it out of there." Seven turned and stopped in front of a small park located next to an apartment building. The "park" was nothing but a barren lot, weedy and brown, with spiked security fencing around the perimeter. "I'd say the cops have been here and cleaned this place out." He pointed to a "No Trespassing" sign citing an ordinance number.

I took my phone out and rolled the window down, taking pictures. "I'm happy that they're not here sleeping in the dirt."

"There's a homeless shelter not far from here. We can check that out. Maybe they'll know something." Seven pulled out his phone and entered the address. He slowly cruised to the corner, checking out the street, and turned onto a side street, and then another. This one housed a variety of businesses, all with wrought iron fencing. At one corner, a large liquor store had been boarded up, and several men were asleep on the sidewalk in front of it.

"There it is." I pointed to a two-story concrete building.

Seven slowed, but continued several blocks to the north before looping back around. Except for the occasional person asleep in a doorway, the street was deserted. The shelter had several reserved parking spaces in the front, and we lucked out and got one of them.

"Cash is a good way to get information out of people, and I'm willing to pay, so long as I'm not being conned. Sometimes it's easy to spot, and other times…"

"You're giving me grief about making plans, and it sounds like you came up with at least one of your own." I shook my head at him.

He pulled me in for a quick kiss. "We agreed that you're going to stick to my side." I nodded. "We go in there and you sell your sister story. If they think they're talking to a family member, they might be freer with information."

"A few years back, Cara had a social media

profile, and I sent this picture to my phone."

I picked up my phone, scrolled through my screen, and held it out to him. "Better than a booking photo." I squirmed.

"Remember: no wandering off."

"Since the cuff threat was just that…" I lifted the back of his shirt just to be sure, looked up, and caught his smirk. "Surprised you haven't rigged up some kind of wrist leash."

"Go ahead, give me a heart attack, and I'll be getting one of those. Probably should anyway."

I scanned both sides of the street—one nondescript building after another, most without a sign, making me wonder if they were vacant. "Don't you go worrying your pretty head; no way am I *wandering off*." In fact, I moved closer—if he turned quickly, he'd have to be careful not to knock me over.

We walked up the steps, the sign off to one side assuring us that we were in the right place. When Seven opened the door, a young woman sitting at the reception desk welcomed us with a smile. Or Seven anyway, since her attention was focused on him.

Seven." He extended his hand. "Nice to meet you… Barbara," he read off her nametag. "We're here to see Cara North." His smile, larger than normal, turned her cheeks pink.

"Our policy requires that we honor everyone's privacy. People come seeking help, and we do our best to provide it."

I was tempted to push Seven aside with my hip, laughed silently at the thought of how that would go, and opted to step between the two. "It's my fault," I said, forcing the woman to turn her attention to me. "Unfortunately, I had a few issues of my own and lost touch with my sister. I recently ran into a mutual acquaintance who mentioned that Cara and her son were homeless, and I've been looking for them ever since."

Barbara turned and looked for something in the open room behind her. Finding it empty, she turned back. She leaned in and lowered her voice. "Cara's been here a couple of times to avail herself of our services. Because she has a child, she was referred to a woman's shelter that could accommodate both of them. To my knowledge, she never went." Her focus was back on Seven.

"If you have any idea where we should look next, it would be extremely helpful," I said.

Continuing to keep her voice low, she said, "Last I heard, Cara moved into the olive-green apartment building to the north. The one on the other side of the neighborhood bar." Once again, she looked around. "They must have an in with the code department, as nothing's been done about the number of people occupying each unit. If you go there, be careful." She wrinkled her nose. "There's an onsite manager, and the stories about him... Just be careful."

"We appreciate your help." Seven put money in her hand and closed her fingers over it.

"I couldn't." She shook her head and attempted to hand it back.

"You keep that," Seven told her in a stern tone that had her blushing again.

I managed to control my eyeroll and instead smiled my thanks.

Seven grabbed my arm and led me out the door.

"Barbie would go out with you in a hot second." I sounded jealous, and judging from his grin, he noticed.

"Can't help it if I'm a chick magnet."

"And modest." I took one last look up and down the block before getting in the car—nothing had changed.

Seven turned me to face him. "You know I'm only hot for you."

"And I thought I was the weird one." I couldn't help laughing at his wounded expression, knowing it was an act.

"Listen up." He finger-wagged. "The building up the street that Barbara described sounds like a whole lot of trouble. And we need to keep an eye on the manager. Not certain how one man could keep the tenants under control." He backed up and crawled down the street. "The only reason I don't make good on my handcuff threat, which is one way to make sure you stay in the car— Go ahead and roll your eyes; you don't know that I don't have a pair in the back. But in this case, my worry is that the car will get stolen, and I sure as heck don't want you in it."

I shivered at the thought of being hauled off as part of a carjacking. "Happy that you ixnayed that plan. Put on your cop hat and come up with an alternative to going door-to-door, since I'm fairly certain you've kicked that idea to the curb."

"Going out on a call, we were always paired up, and even then, we had to grow eyes in the back of our heads."

"Good thing you have me. You bark orders, and I'll do my best."

"Since most people can't resist taking a few bucks, I say we bribe the manager and hope he doesn't want to charge a premium. If he wants to go that route, I'm not without a few hardball tactics of my own."

As Seven got closer, it wasn't hard to spot the drab three-story building surrounded by a large parking lot. It showed wear but didn't have graffiti all over it like the warehouse-style building beside it. Several men of various ages leaned against the security fencing, smoking and talking. Once again, Seven cruised the block before coming back.

"Those men are eyeing your SUV, probably wondering what you're doing in the neighborhood." I nodded. "Maybe we should come back even earlier tomorrow." The last thing I wanted to do was hike home; it would take a couple of days.

"See that kid over there?" He pointed to what appeared to be a pre-teen smoking at the far end of the warehouse. Why wasn't he in school? He had a youthful appearance but a mean as stink glint to his eyes. Seven parked in front of the kid. "I'm going to pay him to make sure my SUV's sitting right here when we're done." The kid ground what was left of his cigarette under his shoe, never breaking eye contact with Seven as he got out and approached him. An amicable deal must have been negotiated, as the two returned to the car and the kid leaned against the bumper, arms crossed.

I got out and anchored myself to Seven's side. "I'm following your lead, babe," I said as we walked up the street. I could feel several sets of eyes staring a hole through us. I didn't make eye contact.

Chapter Twenty-Four

We walked through a glass door and into a small entryway with mailboxes lining two walls. Not a name on a one of them, nor any kind of directory. Two doors were tucked under the stairwell, one marked "Manager."

I wrinkled my nose at the stench that wafted down the stairs as we passed.

Even louder than the television blaring inside, Seven's knock made it clear that cops were on site.

I nudged him with a shake of my head. *Friendly*, I mouthed.

He flashed me his signature smirk.

The sound on the television muted, and after some rustling behind the door, it flew open. A grey-haired oldster gave us a scrutinizing once-over. "What can I do for you?"

"We're looking for Cara North," Seven barked.

"Unless you have a warrant… I respect all my tenants' privacy."

Seven reached into his pocket and handed the man money, which he eyed with interest, then shook his head, conveying *not enough*.

"How about..." Seven reached in his other pocket and pulled out his badge, sticking it under the man's nose.

"You have a warrant?"

"Here's your best and final offer. Take the money and answer my question. If you don't, I'll have code out here in the next five minutes to shut this place down." Seven thrust the money under his nose.

The manager jerked it out of his hand. "301. They're quiet in that unit, so no need to expect any trouble. You'll want to use the stairs." He shut his door.

We both looked under the stairwell and spotted the elevator tucked in the corner, yellow construction tape crisscrossing the front.

The smell that I'd found offensive before only got worse as we climbed the stairs to the third floor. *Breathe through your mouth*, I reminded myself over and over. I didn't envy anyone living on the top floors and having to cart belongings up and down.

The whole floor was quiet. Seven put his ear to the door and shook his head. He knocked, this time a lot less intimidatingly. He waited and, not hearing any movement, knocked again, this time more insistently. Finally, a thirty-ish dark-haired woman opened the door, wiping the sleep from her eyes. She was wearing a faded satin robe that hung open, showing that she had nothing else on. She suspiciously eyed Seven, then me.

I stepped closer to Seven and pasted on a smile. "Sorry to disturb you, but we're looking for Cara North."

"Who wants to know?" She stepped into the doorway, attempting to close the door behind her.

"Her sister." I returned her assessing stare.

"Hmm... Funny, she never mentioned you." She turned, opening the door all the way. "Come on in, make yourself at home." She went over to one of four mattresses lined up on the floor. A quick glance showed all were occupied by barely clad women. She threw herself down on the corner one, covering her face with a towel.

As Seven moved into the center of the room, we were forced to pause so our eyes could adjust to the dimness. He kept me glued to his side, his hand in mine tugging me along. The apartment was a dank one-room hole, newspaper taped over the only window above the sink in the strip kitchen. The one door, standing wide open, was clearly the bathroom.

Once my eyes adjusted, it was easy to pick out Cara, her face turned toward us as she snored softly in the opposite corner. Seven tipped his head toward her, indicating I should be the one to wake her up. I took several steps forward and nudged her foot. She didn't so much as twitch. I tried again.

Cara grumbled and rolled onto her side, opening her eyes. "I don't know you." She blinked, then closed her eyes again.

"I'm here because..." Why hadn't I worked up what I would say? "Riggs Brennan has been discharged from the Army and is back in town. He'd like to reconnect."

Cara's eyes flew open and went wide. "Does he know about...?"

"He ran into a mutual friend, who told him he has a son," I said, my voice not as steady as I'd have liked. Seven put his hand on the small of my back, which calmed me.

"You can't tell... Riggs can't know where I am. I don't know how I would answer all the questions he must have." Cara teared up, a couple leaking down her cheeks.

"How's River doing?" I asked, seeing no clothes, no toys, no sign that he'd ever been in this room.

Now the tears flowed, and she turned her face into the pillow.

I stepped back into Seven and looked up at him, projecting, *What do we do now?*

He took a step back and reached over to the kitchen counter, grabbing a napkin off the stack someone had helped themselves to at a fast-food place. Cara took it with a nod and blew her nose.

When she pulled herself together, I asked, "Where's River?"

Seven squeezed my shoulders.

Cara covered her face with both hands. "I'd like both of you to leave. If you don't, I'll—"

I cut her off. "Did someone take River from you when you went to jail?" It surprised me — what with the crying and the three of us talking — that none of the other women had woken up.

"How did you know I was arrested?" Cara rubbed furiously at her face. "It was stupid and not my fault. I'd met this guy; we barely knew each other, but a few drinks later, we were fighting. Walking back to... it's kind of a blur. He hit me, I hit him back, though he says the opposite. Still don't know how the cops got involved, but they showed up. They didn't care who did what and cuffed us both."

"It didn't help that you were both drunk," Seven admonished.

"If River wasn't with you, then where was he?" I asked, wondering why she hadn't yet given a straight answer as to where her son was and hoping he was okay.

"River's been staying with my friend Evelyn since before that incident. I'm grateful that she's been able to provide a safe and stable home while I'm working on improving my situation."

"We're here to help you in any way we can," I said, not sure what that would entail, but I could figure it out.

Cara glanced at her watch. "I have to get ready for work. I'm dancing tonight. If you leave Riggs' number, I'll get in touch with him."

"Does Evelyn still have River?" I asked.

Cara ignored yet another question about her son, and the fear that filled her eyes when I mentioned Evelyn didn't escape my notice. "If you want to be helpful…" She sounded skeptical. "I'd like to be the one to contact Riggs before you report back. Or whatever it is you do."

"We can do that," I said, then felt a nudge in my side. *What was I supposed to say? No? Or call now?*

She inched her way off the mattress and stood, blowing her a nose a couple of times, turning the napkin into a soggy mess. "I'm running late. I've got the opening shift and could use a ride to work. It would save me time and money, not having to take the bus." When neither of us responded, she said, "I guess you're busy. That's fine." She beelined for the bathroom and closed the door.

"Now what?" I whispered to Seven.

"We take her to work, which is one more piece of information about her, and hopefully, we'll learn more there." He took my hand, and we waited by the door. "I'd suggest we move into the hall, except I haven't forgotten how bad it smells."

"Could you shut up?" one of the women yelled, barely disturbing the others. "A girl's got to get some sleep." She stumbled to her feet and over to the bathroom. Finding the door locked, she kicked it, then hobbled up and down and over to the kitchen sink, where she got sick over and over.

Seven knocked on the bathroom door. "We'll wait outside to give you that ride," he called out, then came back, grabbing my hand and steering me out of the apartment and down the stairs.

Once we were back outside and standing in front of the building, he said, "Just breathe."

"Thank you for getting us out of there. When that woman got sick, I thought I was done for."

Seven hooked his arm around my shoulders, and we walked back to the street, several sets of eyes watching our every move. But no one set foot in our direction. "You're going to wait in the car."

"I can tell by your tone that you're expecting an argument, but you're not getting one."

Seven unlocked the door and held it open. He met the young guy who'd stood guard at the bumper, not moving an inch, and more cash was exchanged. It surprised me when Seven handed him a business card as the two continued to talk.

For someone who was in a hurry, Cara was taking her sweet time. Or there was a back entrance we hadn't seen… or a fire escape. I shuddered at the latter. When, or if, she showed up… how to get her to talk? Going back to Riggs with a bunch of "I don't knows" and not being able to tell him where River was would frustrate the man and have him wondering why he hired WD.

To a chorus of catcalls and whistles, Cara exited the front gate in a miniscule dress, which wouldn't cover anything if she bent one way or the other, hooker heels, and a large bag slung over her shoulder. She looked around. Spotting Seven, she waved. He moved toward her and escorted her to the SUV, opening the back passenger door, and she climbed inside.

I asked for the address and plugged it into the GPS. I kept an eye out for a bus bench as Seven pulled away from the curb and headed up to the main highway. Not spotting a single one, I figured it had to be somewhere out on the main street. Even if it was just around the corner, she had a long walk through a seedy area to get back to her apartment. How did she do it without being accosted?

"Have you had anything to eat?" Seven asked over his shoulder.

"I'll take a hamburger if you're paying."

I wanted Seven to ask where River was—the question Cara had avoided answering when I asked. Maybe he could get a more complete answer than just with this Evelyn woman.

Seven breezed through a burger stand and told Cara, "Order whatever you want. I'm paying."

Not having gotten all the smells out of my nostrils, I ordered an iced tea.

While we waited for the order, Seven asked, "How do you get home?"

"Sometimes I get off early and it's not dark yet. Other times... I know the back streets and the neighborhoods to stay out of."

Seven grabbed the order and handed it over the back seat, setting our drinks in the cup holder—apparently I wasn't the only one not in the mood for food. Cara ripped open her bag, and I felt guilty as I watched her devour every last bite.

It was a shorter drive than I thought it would be, and it surprised me when the GPS directed Seven to turn into an alley. He cruised past the rear entrances of businesses—hard to tell what they were, since there wasn't a single sign. On one lot, new construction of a four-story building was underway. He turned into the parking lot of the strip club and came to a stop under a broad awning with "The Girl's Club" painted in red overhead.

"Is this a busy location?" I asked, wondering who thought it was a good idea to open a club nestled between two alleys and how they attracted customers.

"We have a steady stream of customers all day and night."

Seven turned in his seat and asked, "What can we tell Riggs about River?"

"I really have to get inside." Cara opened the door, one leg out. "Before I answer any more of your questions, I have a few of my own. We should maybe meet for coffee sometime soon."

"Do you have a phone?" I asked.

"It's pay-as-you-go, so I have to keep it short."

I entered the number into my phone as she recited it. "No need to answer. I'm calling so you have my number and know it's not a nuisance call." I waited until I heard a ringing sound coming from inside her bag and hung up.

Seven handed her a business card. "We really do want to help you and River. You can call this number anytime."

Cara stuffed it in her bag. "Thank you for the ride." She jumped out, just managing to remain upright, and disappeared through the double glass doors shrouded in black.

Seven reached over and patted my knee. "I know you're frustrated. You might want to relax your jaw. It's hard on the teeth."

"Who notices something like that?" I made a face.

"I notice everything." A few turns later, he made his way back to Highway One. "Cara doesn't know us, and Riggs' name wasn't enough to get her to talk — probably afraid he'll swoop in and take their son."

"I just want River to be okay. Did she willingly hand him over to this Evelyn woman?" Whoever she was. "No way to locate her without a last name."

"This is what we're going to do — it's obvious Cara hasn't been eating very much, so we offer to pick her up from work and take her to dinner."

"Since she was very wary of us, and wouldn't let her guard down for a second, I'll be surprised if she doesn't put up resistance to a meet-and-greet. Not that I can fault her, but in the same circumstances, I'd jump at the opportunity to improve my situation if I had a child."

"My guess is that she's going to try to avoid us. If that happens, I'll bring you to the Club on a date."

"I've never been to a strip club—now that would be a story for Saturday breakfast. Maybe I'll exaggerate and say I got on stage for amateur night." I felt my cheeks warm.

"I'd throw you over my shoulder, and we'd be out of there." Seven laughed. "Seriously, at some point, Cara is going to have to talk to Riggs; she won't be able to hold him off indefinitely. If it were my kid, I'd want assurances that he was being well cared for."

Chapter Twenty-Five

On the way back, Seven mentioned a meeting with Grey that I knew didn't involve me in any way, so he wouldn't be happy to see me. "Do you mind dropping me at home?" Which he did. If he knew what I was planning, those cuffs of his would magically appear.

I had him let me out in front of the building and, with a quick kiss, went upstairs. I needed some cash and a cold water. Needing backup and knowing Grey wasn't home, I picked the lock on Harper's door. "Hello," I yelled as soon as I stepped inside, dropping my bag in the entry. The patio was her preferred office space, and glancing in that direction, I saw that today was no different. She was waving. I went out and dropped into a chair next to her. "Raise your right hand."

"Just tell me. If this is about me needing to keep a secret, it's rude that you think I wouldn't," Harper huffed. "Is this about my author gig? Can't go without Rella, and she's got a meeting."

"Rella would lobby hard to talk me out of this idea." I told her about the Riggs Brennan case and meeting Cara earlier. "She avoided giving a straight answer to most of my questions, and when she talked about this woman, Evelyn, who has her kid, there was fear in her eyes."

"You want to go to the strip club?" Harper looked surprised.

"I want to go back to her apartment building, see if the kid who guarded Seven's car is still there, and pay him for more information. It's not the kind of neighborhood a woman wants to go to by herself, day or night."

"You're going to have to get out of the car." There was a *duh* in Harper's tone.

"Not if you drive. I roll down the window, conduct business, and we drive off. That's if we can find him."

"That scenario is likely to get you arrested on suspicion of peddling drugs."

"You know it's a good idea," I insisted.

"We'll take my SUV. If the neighborhood is as you say, your Porsche will attract even more unwanted eyes." Harper stood. "I've got to change."

As she went down the hallway, I went into the kitchen and helped myself to a cookie, knowing that she always had them around for Grey.

Harper was back within minutes, having swapped her sundress for a pair of jeans. We both grabbed our bags and headed down in the elevator. "When the guys find out, they're not going to be happy."

"If neither of us tells them—"

"Grey finds out about everything," Harper said with a knowing smile.

We got into her SUV, and she exited the garage and headed over to the highway while I programmed her GPS. With traffic on our side, it didn't take long before we were turning onto Cara's street. I grabbed money and a business card out of my pocket.

"It's the olive-green monstrosity up ahead." I nodded through the windshield. "We're looking for a skinny little smoker leaning up against the side of the neighboring commercial building."

"That's assuming he's not off buying more cigarettes with whatever Seven paid him. What's the going rate for making sure your car doesn't get boosted?"

"I should've asked, but Seven gets testy when I ask those kinds of questions. Good thing I didn't or I wouldn't have been allowed out of his sight. Not that he allows it anyway."

"You two are so cute."

"I think we're in like, but I could be reading it wrong."

"Do you even know what you're talking about?" Harper asked with amusement.

"There he is." I pointed to the kid, who'd moved down a building.

"Under no circumstances do you get out of this car." Harper pulled up parallel to the curb, stopping in front of him.

I rolled down the window. "Remember me from earlier?" No response. "My friend paid you to watch his SUV." He stared like I'd lost my mind. "I've got another job for you." I held up the cash.

"How old is he?" Harper hissed.

He walked over and stood about a foot back. "What kind of job?"

"You know Cara North? Stripper?"

He snorted. "Most of the girls here swing the pole. Cara mostly bartends."

"I want you to ask around about a woman named Evelyn connected to her and get a last name. I'll pay extra for an address."

"That's it?"

I nodded and held out the money.

He stepped forward and counted it. "So we're clear, no refunds if I can't deliver." He looked at my business card, then back at me, and pocketed both.

"There's more money for you for calling with a heads up if she decides to pack up and leave."

"The other guy offered a real job or a referral or something. What about you?"

"If you're willing to do grunt work to prove yourself, I can get you a job. Whether you keep it or not depends on whether you're a slacker. If you're interested, I'll ask my friend. After you assure me that I won't be wasting my time." He nodded. "You got a name?"

"Trace."

"Are you over eighteen and do you have ID to prove it?"

He grinned. "I'm nineteen, and yes."

"Call me tomorrow, and I'll have a number for you."

He turned and went back to holding up the building.

I rolled up the window.

Harper, who'd left the engine running, took off down the street. There were more men than before, and even a couple of women hanging out, and they stared as we drove by. "Nineteen. He reminds me of Dixon. First time I saw him show up at your office, I didn't think he was a day over twelve." She smirked. "You're planning to hit up Hugo on Trace's behalf, am I right?"

Hugo rented the first floor of the office building, using it to expand his maintenance company. He had hired a motley crew of hard workers and was always on the lookout for a new face. Not one of the guys that worked for him had a bad word to say about the man. They were like a boy's club and had each other's backs.

"Smartie. You know Hugo's always willing to take a chance on someone new, even one who probably doesn't have any references."

"As soon as Seven lays eyes on him—and it will happen working out of the same building—you're caught. You better start figuring out what you're going to say." Harper weaved out of a lane of backed-up cars. "This was kind of fun, even though I was just the driver."

"I appreciate not having to come by myself."

"And if Trace is able to get you Evelyn's full name?"

"Run a check on her. Verify the address. Riggs has already said he wants a relationship with his son, and knowing where his son's at is going to be his first question. Might as well have the answer."

Chapter Twenty-Six

I hadn't seen much of Seven in the last couple of days, though I knew he'd finished up the stakeout job and turned in a report on what he'd found. The owner had a couple of friends on the local police force, and he turned Seven's findings over to them. The detectives independently verified the information and set up a sting that resulted in the arrest of all the players and the seizure of a large quantity of cocaine that would otherwise have been distributed to local dealers.

I tried several times to contact Cara, but she didn't answer her phone or return my calls. The second day, she turned it off.

I was getting ready to meet Harper and Rella to check out Stella's neighborhood when my phone rang. Caller ID showed a number I didn't recognize.

"It's Trace," he said when I answered. "This morning, Cara left with a suitcase. I told her to have a nice trip, and she didn't say anything. Snapped a pic of the license plate of the car that picked her up. I'll text it to you."

So Cara'd split. Was it our questions that

made her pack her suitcase? Was she afraid of Riggs? I needed to know what'd happened to River and that he was better than okay. Riggs wasn't going to like that we'd found Cara but were now back to square one.

"Talked to one of her roommates," Trace continued. "Since she didn't give them a return date, they're renting out her bed so they don't get stuck on the rent. And nothing on any Evelyn. I did ask one of the roommates, and she didn't know what I was talking about. Don't think she was lying."

"I owe you and can drop it off tomorrow. Early."

"Give me the name of the guy hiring, and we'll call it even."

"I've got both the name and money for you. It's Hugo—he runs a full-service building maintenance company, and he's expecting your call. I'll text you the information. If you take the job, we'll be seeing each other around. Let's go with the friend of a friend explanation; acquaintance from the old neighborhood is another good one. That should put an end to nosey questions."

We hung up, and I texted him the info and received a shot of the license plate in return.

The front door opened, and Rella beckoned to me. I met her and Harper at the elevator.

Rella handed me a shopping bag; inside was a baseball hat and a pair of large sunglasses. "I know you're staying in the car, but it's better to make you harder to identify."

We got downstairs and climbed into Harper's SUV. She removed earbuds from her bag and handed them to me and Rella. We put them in, and she tested the sound. "You'll be able to hear everything that's said," Harper assured me. "And this—" She pointed to a flower pin on her shirt. "—is a camera. You'll be able to watch everything that happens on my phone." She handed it over the seat.

"What's the plan?" Rella asked.

"We'll cruise Stella's neighborhood, check it out." Harper drove out of the garage and out to the highway. "Then we're going to the two houses that have the best view of the comings and goings at Stella's house. I'll tell whoever answers the door that I'm writing a story about the murder and ask if they want to comment. Last time, I said I was writing a book; this time, I'm going to try to be a little more vague and hope I don't get pressed with questions."

"A stranger shows up at the door, and the person who answers just starts talking?" Rella asked with a note of disbelief.

"You'd be surprised what people will tell you." Harper grinned. "I doubt I'll even be asked for credentials, but I photoshopped a set just in case."

"What's my role?" Rella asked.

"Another thing I'll be surprised if we're asked,

but if we are, I'm going with my cousin, who's here visiting from... somewhere and came along to make sure I didn't get into any trouble."

Rella and I laughed.

"Somewhere?" Rella teased. "As usual, I was hesitant at first, not wanting us to get into any trouble. Now that I'm fairly certain we won't, I was hoping for a more exciting role."

"If there's an awkward lull in the conversation, you can step in and keep it going. If we get someone to answer the door, we need to keep them talking. 'How exciting to be interviewed for an article,'" Harper said in feigned surprise.

Rella flipped down the visor and eyed me in the mirror. "Is anyone living at Stella's?"

"Before she died, she lived there by herself. Her husband of forty years died a couple of years back."

Harper turned onto Stella's street and slowed as she cruised past the Cape Cod-style homes with their manicured lawns; without exception, they were all well taken care of.

"Rather than drawing attention by parking in front of Stella's, I'm going to park between the two houses. That way, if whoever we're talking to looks out, they'll see my SUV and know we didn't just appear out of nowhere." Harper pulled over to the curb and turned to me. "The windows are tinted, but scoot down anyway so there's no way you attract attention."

I turned and leaned back against the door, legs stretched out, with an unobstructed view of the front of both houses. "If either of you senses trouble, just leave."

Harper and Rella got out and trooped up the walkway of the house on the left. Harper had left a pair of binoculars on the floor in case something went wrong with the camera. So far, so good. They got to the door, and Harper knocked. "Testing," she whispered.

"Great connection," I said.

"Since I don't hear anyone sneaking up to the peephole, I'm going to ring the bell." After a pause, she said, "No one's home. On to the next house."

"Let's hope we have better luck at the next one," Rella said as they headed back down the walk and over to a beige-and-white house with a wide porch.

"Here's hoping someone answers," Harper said and knocked on the door.

The door was opened by an older woman in a floral sundress. "If you're selling something, I'm not interested." She gave them a friendly smile.

Before she could get the door closed, Harper went into her writer speech and asked if the woman had anything she wanted to contribute to the article.

The woman craned her head out the door and looked around, checking out the street, first one way and then other, before stepping back. "The

Bassett murder—that was quite something for this quiet neighborhood," she said in a hushed tone. "I wouldn't want word to get out that I talked to a reporter." She made a zip lip gesture, though her tone brimmed with excitement. "Do you have credentials?"

"I certainly do." Harper pulled them out of her bag. "You're smart to ask."

The woman beamed and barely gave them a glance. "You should come inside, that way we won't attract attention." She motioned them forward and closed the door. "I could answer a question or two, as long as you don't use my name." She led them into the living room and motioned to chairs in front of the almost floor-to-ceiling windows.

The interior was charming, the furniture oversized and comfortable-looking. Lots of family photos on the bookcases on both sides of the fireplace.

"This is very nice of you," Rella said, holding out her hand. "I'm Rachel, and this is my cousin, Brenda. I came along to watch her work. So exciting."

"Beverly Parnell. But no names." She made a shushing noise. "Where are my manners? Would you care for something to drink?"

"That's very sweet of you, but we just had coffee," Harper said.

"What did you want to know?" Beverly, who'd sat across from them on the couch, moved forward in her seat to peer out the window.

I could have told her that there was no one anywhere in sight.

"The night of the... that the cops found Stella, it was rumored that there was an eyewitness who claimed to have seen the murderer fleeing and was adamant that she could identify them," Harper said. "That story just disappeared. I figured that it would have to have been you or your neighbor, since you're the only two with unobstructed views of the house across the street."

"There were whispers about that story, and one of the neighbors confirmed that Arlene Hayes was the witness. The blue-trimmed house." Beverly pointed diagonally across the street. "But there's no way she could see anything—the tall hedge that runs down the property line prevents either neighbor from peering over at the other."

Harper and Rella both turned and looked out the window.

"Why would this Arlene woman insinuate herself into the case that way when a woman's life is on the line?" Harper asked.

"That's a good question. Like the rest of us, Arlene has lived in this neighborhood a number of years. She's always kept to herself and been a quiet neighbor." Beverly lowered her voice, forgetting she was inside. "The police had more than a few questions and showed up several times. I noticed that after the second time, Arlene stopped answering the door, even when I knew she was home."

"Which neighbor confirmed the story?" Harper asked.

"Amy lives down at the other end of the block. It's interesting that she knows so much about my neighbors, who keep to themselves. I get out every day and never know as much as she does, and because of it, I'm careful what I tell her." Beverly's brows went up. "If you're planning on talking to Amy, know that she'll tell everyone."

"And your next-door neighbors?" Rella asked.

"They weren't here when it happened. They'd just left to take the grandkids to Disney World and stayed for over a week." Beverly rolled her eyes. "All those rides that jerk back and forth aren't for me."

"Do you have grandchildren?" Rella asked.

Beverly stood and walked over to the mantle, taking down a framed photo of a large group of people of various ages—young to old. For the next several minutes, she pointed to each one and told Harper and Rella what they'd been up to. "Listen to me." She laughed. "Prattling on. This doesn't help your story one bit."

"Nonsense. You have a lovely family," Rella assured her.

Beverly replaced the picture and sat back down. "I honestly don't know anyone who would want to hurt Stella. She was part of our walking group and was always nice to everyone. I'm certain it wasn't anyone on this street. There's one or two that have their noses planted in the air, but not murder." She shook her head.

"Have you seen this woman around?" Harper asked, pulling my picture from her bag.

"Only on the news. I'll admit, I watched all the coverage, and when it stopped, I searched the internet. Oh, you mean, in the neighborhood? No. I'm a bit nosey, as we all are, and if I'd seen her, I'd have told the police. Are you going to interview her?" Beverly asked, excitement in her tone as she stared at my picture.

"I contacted her lawyer. He said, 'Absolutely not.' Then toned it down, saying, 'No lawyer would advise an interview when it's still an open case,'" Harper told her.

I almost laughed at the idea of Harper or anyone trying to get Cruz on the phone with such a request. Susie would hang up.

"That makes sense," Beverly said.

"You've been very nice to let us take up your time." Harper stood and stuck out her hand.

Beverly stood and shook Harper's and Rella's hands. "Nonsense. I can't wait to tell the ladies at bridge. But better not. I'll definitely tell my sister. Make sure I get a copy when the story comes out." She walked them to the door.

"I certainly will," Harper said.

Beverly walked the two outside.

Before they got to the sidewalk, I slid down

onto the floor to be on the safe side.

Harper and Rella got in, and Harper honked as she pulled away from the curb.

I waited until Rella said Beverly'd gone back inside before sliding back onto the seat. "The camera and earbuds were a great idea. I saw and heard everything."

"I think Beverly was excited to be interviewed," Rella said. "On the other hand, she certainly didn't want anyone to know of her involvement."

"At least now we know who fingered you." Harper cruised by Stella's house, going slow, her head turned. "What the heck. We're here, why not ask a few questions?" She got to the end of the block, hung a U-turn, and went back to park in front of Arlene's house.

"We're agreed that the guys are never going to find out, right?" I asked. Seven, my lawyer, the lot of them would flip.

"Agreed, since Grey would kill me. There's no way I could blame you; he'd know it was my idea."

Once again, Harper and Rella got out and I watched as they walked up to the door.

From what I could see before sliding down in the seat, it was clear that Arlene didn't have any kind of view of Stella's house. She'd had to have been standing on the sidewalk or in the street to see anything.

Harper rang the doorbell.

An older woman opened the door. "Can I help you?"

Harper gave her the same story she told Beverly. "Would you mind answering a few questions about Stella Bassett's murder?"

"I don't know a damn thing and don't come back here." She slammed the door in their faces.

As the two walked back to the car, the woman stood in her living room window and watched them.

"She's watching," I told them when they got in.

"We know she lied about IDing you. Why, we'll probably never know," Harper said.

"Maybe she wanted to be in the center of the excitement." Rella turned and scanned the front of the house, and the woman stepped out of view.

"As soon as I started my spiel, the color drained from her face and she all but stumbled back out of the doorway," Harper said. "Bet she wishes she'd minded her own business."

"I'm happy I didn't find a reason to play it safe and go to my office today." Rella turned to me. "I know we didn't uncover anything helpful, but I just know you're going to be found not guilty."

"Cruz's first choice is to get the case dismissed, and I hope he succeeds." My phone rang, and I looked at the screen and smiled at

Seven's picture. "Hello, dear," I said on answering.

"Now I'm suspicious." He growled a laugh.

"Once we've decided on a restaurant, I'm taking Harper and Rella to lunch. My vote is for tacos."

"I get hot dogs and they get tacos," he grumped.

"Just know that the offer still stands."

"Yeah, yeah." Seven laughed. "The reason for the call—were you able to get ahold of Cara?"

"She turned off her phone."

"At Riggs' request, the case is on hold, and if anything changes, I'll let you know."

I heard someone yelling his name in the background.

"We'll talk later." He hung up.

I stared at the phone and wondered why Riggs had made that decision.

"Everything okay?" Rella asked.

I nodded. "I didn't tell you this before," I said and told the two of them about trying to reach Cara and that she'd turned off her phone. "That was Seven telling me the case is now on hold."

Harper filled Rella in on our meeting with Trace. "Don't pout. You had a meeting that morning or we'd have dragged you along, even kicking and screaming."

"Just because of the neighborhood, I would've tried to talk you two out of that one."

"Why would Riggs put the investigation on

hold unless he'd made contact with Cara? And you know Seven has to know the reason, but not one word to me." I sighed out my impatience.

"Grey does like your work, but you're not an employee and he likes to micromanage. Seven's more laid-back, which is probably why they don't get on each other's nerves," Harper said. "There's something I'm not allowed to tell you. Not anyone actually."

Rella and I stared at her.

"I promised not to ever repeat any WD business that I overhear or that Grey tells me," Harper said.

"You need to give us a hint." Rella raised her brows.

I nodded from the back seat, though she couldn't see me.

"You need to ask Seven more questions," Harper advised me.

Rella turned to me. "Go to the office and hit them with one question after another. Irritate them enough, and they may let something slip. I'm not suggesting that you snoop around the office either," she told me in an admonishing tone.

"And don't use your lockpick anymore. Grey hates it when I do that," Harper said, although it was clear she liked the idea.

"I can't believe I'm the only one who doesn't know how to pick a lock," Rella lamented. "If I did, I could pass out business cards: 'Rella Cabot, lockpicker.' Can you imagine?"

The three of us laughed.

"We can't corrupt you too much. You need to be the good influence so we don't go totally off the rails."

I agreed with Harper. One of us needed to steer away from trouble. "Did Grey at least say whether the little boy, River, is okay?" I asked.

Harper shook her head.

"March into the office and threaten to call the client yourself if they don't answer your questions," Rella said, clearly liking her idea.

"I know that the guys are worried about safety, but I know the case well enough to ask the right questions; now all I need is you to come check out the strip club with me," I told Rella. "We'll leave Harper at home."

"Not fair." Harper hit her hand on the steering wheel.

Rella screwed up her nose. "We'll probably be the only women there besides the dancers, and we're certain to attract attention. But I'm in."

Chapter Twenty-Seven

I put on a pot of coffee and poured Seven a mug. I hadn't said a word about business, having already planned to be in the office this morning. Last night, Seven and I had watched a movie—I left the choice to him, and naturally, he chose an action flick. We'd stretched out on the couch, and it hadn't taken me long to fall asleep.

"What are you doing today?" Seven looked at me over the rim of his mug.

"I'm coming into the office later. Need to check in with Dixon, go through the mail." I smiled benignly.

"We've got a meeting with a new client this morning. I'll text you when we're finished, and if you're still around, I'll come down."

"Sounds good."

He gave me one of his penetrating stares, which I warded off. Not sucking information out of me today.

He downed another cup of coffee, kissed me, and left. I went back to my bedroom, showered, and changed into a casual dress and sandals. I sat on the bed and called Cara again. It only somewhat surprised me to find that the number had been disconnected. On purpose? Or lack of payment? I grabbed my bag and was out the door.

Plans are overrated, I thought on the way to the office; sometimes you just have to take it as it comes. I hoped that didn't come back to bite me.

I turned onto the one-way street to the office and found myself behind Anders' Mercedes, both of us headed to the office. Hmm... I'd thought his file was closed, but then again, no one had actually told me that. I let out a sigh, reminding myself I didn't work for WD. Regardless, instead of driving into the garage, I parked next to him and got out, waving. The poor man looked a wreck.

"I'm happy to see you, girl." He clapped me on the back, hard enough that I stumbled, and quickly caught me. "You okay?" He patted my shoulder.

"I'm fine." I smiled at him. "And you?"

"Has anyone told you how easy you are to talk to?"

"How about we go up to my office and I'll make you a cup of coffee?"

"That sounds good." Anders checked his watch. "I've got fifteen minutes."

I linked my arm in his and steered him towards the elevator. We got off at the second floor, and I unlocked the door to my office, not surprised to see Dixon there. I pointed to one of the chairs in front of my desk.

"Dixon, Mr. Anders," I introduced.

"Anders, please." The weight of the world came out in a sigh as he sat down.

"Coffee's coming right up." I went to the kitchen and, remembering his preference from before, chose a cup and inserted it into the machine.

"You need me to leave?" Dixon asked.

"Not on my account," Anders rasped.

Upon closer inspection, he appeared pale and out of sorts. I hoped he wasn't sick. Even Dixon gave him close scrutiny.

The coffee didn't take long to brew, and I handed him a mug. He took a long drink. "I went out of town for a couple of days, came back, and Sissy'd moved in. I called the cops like I said I would. Different ones showed up, and she had her proof of residence, saying she'd only been out of town on vacation. They told me a judge would have to decide."

"I thought you were going to get a court order," I said.

"My fault. I just wanted to bury my head in the sand, and mistakenly thought she was gone and wouldn't be back. I should've known that she was just getting her ducks lined up." Anders' hands trembled as he tried to hold the mug steady. "She's been driving me crazy, and I haven't had a moment's peace or privacy. Last night, she had a party. I don't know where all the people came from—didn't know any of them—and the music went on into the wee hours. I was tempted to call the cops on my own house, but the thought of getting hauled off scared me."

"What do you want to do?" I asked.

"I was planning to put the house on the market, but she'd make sure it doesn't sell. She mentioned a payoff, and I stormed out of the room before I heard the number." Anders downed his coffee. "Can you recommend a divorce lawyer? I'll let him or her deal with Sissy. One way or another, I'm going to have to pay to get rid of her. And after she thought she left me penniless, she'll want to make sure she doesn't miss a dime."

"Are you certain you want to move? I hate that you're feeling pressured."

"Since you invited me to the party at Morningside, I've made a couple of friends there and have been having a good time. Played a round of golf the other day; nice to be back on the course. Looking forward to doing more of it. Jean Winters got me an interview—it went really well, and I was approved to move in."

Leave it to Gram.

"You could turn the tables on this Sissy woman," Dixon said. "If you can swing it, you could move out and let someone move in that terrorizes her. Not in a bad way—music that she'd hate, people she'd stick her nose up at."

Anders chuckled. "Like that idea, except the

cops would throw them out. Or worse, they might get arrested, and I don't want that to happen."

"The end run around that would be to rent out your portion. Make it all legal-like by giving them a signed agreement," Dixon said.

I shot him a thumbs up. "I know a couple of guys you could hire to make sure she doesn't get a minute's peace. She won't think it's so funny when it's happening to her. If you really want to move, I suggest you pack up what you want and move out now."

"I noticed a couple of things missing and mentioned it to her, and she accused me of not remembering where I left them—a couple of watches for starters, which I kept in the top drawer of my dresser. I put the rest of my collection in the safe." Anders slumped. "I can move to Morningside in two weeks, when they have an available unit, but it'll take me a lot longer to get everything packed up."

Dixon caught my eye and surreptitiously pointed downstairs. I nodded.

"What if you hire a service, tell them what to pack, and have them haul it off either to storage or your new place? If the new place isn't ready yet, have it brought here. There's a storage room in the garage that runs the length of one wall, and it's not being used."

"I'm happy that I ran into you." Anders smiled at me, more color in his cheeks than when he arrived. "Is it possible to hire you to organize everything so all I have to do is pack a suitcase?"

"Are you certain you want to make the move?" Anders nodded. "It's just that Sissy shouldn't get to run you out of your home, one that was yours before you married."

"To be honest, I was thinking about the move before she invaded my life again. I'm looking forward to this new chapter. New friends."

"You need to make sure that Morningside is a done deal and you're not left without anywhere to go."

"I've got an appointment to sign the contract today. On the way home, I'll give you a call."

"Just want you to be aware that it'll take more than just me to orchestrate this move of yours. In the meantime, I've got a business contact who can make everything go smoother, supplying the needed muscle."

"You're something. You tell me what to do, and I'll do it."

"How soon do you want to get started?" I asked.

"ASAP." His phone rang, and he pulled it out of his shirt pocket, checking the screen, then his watch. He didn't answer the phone, pocketing it. "I'm late for my appointment." He pointed at the ceiling. "But now that I've hired you, there's no need to go. One of the first things you can do for me is tell them I changed my mind. Nice guys, but you're easier to work with."

My cheeks burned as I grimaced.

Dixon grinned and dropped his head.

"Your phone." I crooked my finger, and he handed it over without question. "I'm texting: 'Need to cancel.' That way, they won't wait on you." Awkward. I'd get Seven off by himself, explain everything, and ask him to tell Grey that I stole a client but to wait until I was miles away. I put my number into his phone and then called mine so I'd have his number, though I was pretty sure I had it already.

Anders stood. "I'm going to head on over to Morningside and sign the paperwork."

"If you have any problems, give Jean a call; she's never met a problem she can't handle." Steamroll, but that didn't sound nice.

"Jean's offered on more than one occasion to help me, and I'm taking her up on it. I'll be giving her a call once I'm in the car."

That was Gram—nosey to a fault. She'd love every minute of helping him. "While you're taking care of that, I'll get the rest organized." I stood. "I'll walk down with you." I hooked my arm around his and led him out to the elevator. While riding down, I said, "Everything is happening fast for you, and since moving is major, you might want to take some time and think about it."

"Not fast enough." Anders humphed. "I've been thinking about it ever since Sissy ripped me off. The only thing that stopped me was the money. But now that that's not an issue... Since you invited me to the party, I've known that's the place for me. Not sure I thanked you enough for including me." He gave me a side hug.

I patted his arm as we got off the elevator. "I'm happy that you met new people and have been having fun. You've got my number. Call anytime."

Who should open the door for us but Seven? The surprise that flitted across his face disappeared fast. I didn't have the nerve to make eye contact and suspected it'd get even more awkward when we started talking.

Not the least bit embarrassed, Anders said, "Sorry about the last-minute cancellation, but lucky me, I ran into Miss Avery again. This one's a gem." He gave me a big smile.

"Gem all right," Seven mumbled.

I walked Anders over to his car and waited until he got inside. "Talk soon." I waved.

With a deep breath, I fortified myself to turn around and face Seven. I knew darn well he'd be waiting. I continued to wave as Anders drove out. Finally, I turned and swallowed a groan, but barely. Behind Seven, the door opened again, and Hugo and Trace walked out. Seven did a double take and closed the space between them, and I couldn't hear what he said. Did I want to know?

I pasted a smile on my face and walked over.

"Just hired your friend Trace. Think he's going

to fit in around here." Hugo clapped him on the back.

"Congrats," I said. Trace held up his knuckles, and I reciprocated with a fist-bump. "If you ever need a ride, I'm on the second floor."

"Got my bike." He nodded across the parking lot to a motorcycle sitting under the tree.

"When's a good time for me to come to your office?" I asked Hugo.

"We're done here, so now's a good time." He motioned me to follow.

"Just one second." I pulled Trace aside and lowered my voice. "I owe you money. If you're not in a hurry and don't mind waiting upstairs, there's drinks and snacks. Just tell Dixon we're related."

Trace laughed. "The boyfriend, husband, whatever he is, knows something's up, so whatever story you feed him, let me know. It's embarrassing when they don't match." He headed up to the office.

"Is this a private discussion?" Hugo asked as Seven joined us.

"We don't keep secrets, do we, hon?" Seven asked. Even Hugo caught the sarcasm.

Ignoring him, I turned to Hugo. "If you want, we can talk right here. I've got a client that needs his mansion packed up. Is that a service you offer?"

Hugo nodded. "I don't see why not. We've done it for offices, so no problem."

I was happy when Seven's phone rang and he stepped back to take the call. "It's not a typical move." I went on to explain Anders' problem.

"You know my guys can handle any situation, and if they know they don't have to take any guff, it'll be that much easier."

"Anders will be there to direct them in what to pack. I'd appreciate your guys not letting Sissy anywhere near Anders unless it's what he wants, and I doubt he will." I hurriedly told him about my idea to contact Floyd, thinking his oversized self and maybe a couple of his like-sized friends would be the perfect temporary renters and a deterrent to any more problems.

"I'll pass along the message, but Floyd is working for WD this week."

Floyd did double duty, and Hugo was always willing to accommodate his WD schedule, knowing the young man wanted to build his career as a private investigator.

Seven walked up in time to hear the last part. "Floyd's got a bodyguarding job keeping rich teenagers out of trouble," he barked. "Leave him a message and he'll get back to you, I'm sure."

"I only need a couple days' notice to set the other up for you," Hugo said as one of his guys came around the front, calling for him. He waved and left.

"Appears we have a lot of secrets to share. You, anyway." Seven hadn't lost his grouchy tone.

"I'd love to chat—" I almost laughed at his *yeah, sure* expression, but better that I didn't. "—but I have someone waiting on me upstairs."

"Your *good friend* Trace." Seven snorted. "I wouldn't want to keep you." He grabbed my hand and led me inside.

"If I fall down trying to keep up with your long-legged stride, expect retribution."

Seven slowed but not much, dragging me up the stairs at a run. I hadn't climbed them that fast before and was out of breath at the top, where I opened my office door, preceding him inside.

Dixon and Trace were in a discussion about something, and both appeared to be enjoying whatever they were talking about. The nerd and the tough guy, an interesting combo. The only thing they appeared to have in common was looking considerably younger than their actual age.

"Have a seat." I pointed Seven to a chair—better than him looming over everyone, me in particular. Maybe he'd relax.

I opened a desk drawer, removed the envelope I'd put in the side pocket of my purse earlier, and handed it to Trace. "Thanks for your help."

He eyed the money. "More than I expected. I don't have anything new for you. You need anything else, you know where to find me. Thanks for the recommendation. You don't need to worry about me embarrassing you; I'm a hard worker." He nodded toward the door, and I walked with him. At the door, he reached into his pocket, pulling out a scrap of paper and handing it to me. I tucked it down my top, hoping that Seven hadn't seen and wasn't about to turn around and find out one way or the other.

I went back and sat behind my desk, and Seven and I stared at each other without a word.

"I'm leaving for the day." Dixon threw his stuff into his briefcase and beat it out the door.

"Nice job scaring him off."

"As it happens, I'm not the least bit sorry." Seven made a sad face. "I'll go first. You've sunk to client pilfering? How did Anders turn into your client?" His phone dinged with a text, and he took it out of his pocket. "I've got to go upstairs." He stood. "You're coming with me."

"I'm sure you won't mind if I wait here."

"Nice try. But I don't believe you'd be here when I got back." He walked around and pulled me up out of my chair. "You walking or am I carrying you?"

I stared at him, not coming to a decision quickly enough for him. He picked me up, threw me over his shoulder, and was out the door on one of my squeals and running up the stairs.

"You're such a show-off," I said when he set me down before opening his office door. He flexed his muscles with a grin and pushed me inside.

I took a seat at the reception desk, waving to

Grey, who waved back, his brows in his hairline.

"Took you long enough," he grouched at Seven.

Seven went over to his desk, opening his briefcase and pulling out a file. "It was sitting on the top; you couldn't find it on your own?" he said, handing it to Grey.

"What did you do to grouch him off?" Grey asked. I shot him a *Who me?* look. "He was in a decent mood when he went downstairs. What did Anders say?" he asked Seven. To me, he said, "We saw his car on the monitor and wondered if he was okay."

Seven turned to me, and we engaged in a stare-down. "Fine. I'll tell him." I told them about running into Anders and everything that'd transpired. "So you don't think I stole your client, as suggested by someone—" I glared at Seven. "—I'm going to bill Anders on one of your invoices, because it's the right thing to do and I don't want this to create a problem between us."

"Anders preferred you from the start," Grey said. "The ideas you laid out are good ones. Don't get directly involved with Sissy; you never know how she's going to react. If Hugo's guys run into a problem they can't deal with, let one of us know."

"What happened with Riggs Brennan's case? Were you able to locate Cara and her son?" I asked.

"Riggs asked us to put everything on hold. Said he was going to make contact with her himself and reassure her that he only wanted to help her and his son," Grey said.

"I gave her my word that I wouldn't share her information, and it happened anyway?" I wasn't one to go back on my word, and it didn't sit well with me.

"My fault," Seven said. "Forgot to tell Grey, and by the time it came up again, he'd already told Riggs."

"Do you know if he was able to make contact?"

Seven and Grey traded a look I couldn't decipher. "Don't know. Riggs said he'd get in touch if he needed further assistance," Grey said in a diplomatic tone. Not quite *none of your business*, but close.

"I hope that when you do hear, you'll let me know River's doing okay." I couldn't shake the feeling that there was something off about the boy's situation. Like where was he?

Grey nodded. "Heard that you, Harper, and Rella went out to lunch. What kind of trouble did you get into?"

"You'll have to ask your girlfriend about that one." I stood. "I've got another appointment. I'll see you later," I told Seven and jetted out the door. It didn't surprise me that he was right behind me.

He grabbed me before I reached the elevator

and turned me around. "You really have an appointment?"

I shook my head. "I just wanted out of there. I'm going to go home and walk on the beach."

"You know you can tell me anything. Even if I won't like it."

"How about I order dinner—I know your favorites by now—and we eat out on the patio?"

Seven pulled me into a kiss. "I'll walk you down."

Chapter Twenty-Eight

I'd gotten all the way home before remembering the piece of paper I'd stuffed down the front of my top. I pulled it out, and printed on it was Cara's name, with "work" and a phone number. I grabbed a cold drink, my laptop, and my phone and went out to the patio. I blocked my number and called.

A man answered, music blaring in the background. "Men's Club."

"Sorry, wrong number." I hung up. Another strip club?

I looked it up, and sure enough, it wasn't far from the other one Cara had worked at. A little more digging, and I found out that both clubs and a third were owned by the same corporation.

I set my laptop aside and grabbed Harper's door key. Each of us had a copy of the other's key. I rang the doorbell and unlocked the door, yelling, "Hope you're decent."

Harper waved me over to where she sat on the patio. "You're lucky Grey's not home."

"I knew that or I would've called, considering what I'm about to ask." I sat in the chair next to her and told her about the morning.

Harper laughed. "Anders really likes you and told Grey that fifty-five times. He could do what you're going to for the man, but I can assure you that he's happy to have it off his hands."

"The reason I'm here... I asked about the Riggs case and got a nice version of 'none of your business.'" I told her about the note Trace had passed me. "What I want to know—and you can just shake your head, so technically you didn't say anything—"

Harper snorted. "That's not something I'd like pulled on me."

"I know Grey gave Riggs contact information for Cara. When he went there, had she lit out already?" I gave Harper a wide-eyed stare.

She huffed. "The two did talk."

"She did it after that?"

Harper nodded.

"Riggs couldn't wait two seconds? After all the time he's already waited?" Oh to be a fly on the wall and know why she packed up afterwards and left...

Harper shrugged.

"I'm going to stop with the questions, knowing that I should've respected your request not to ask. So instead, I'm going to jump to my own conclusions. We both know that only works some of the time." If that.

"I'm afraid to ask what you've got planned."

"I know the hours that Cara worked at the other club, and I'm going to assume they're the same at the new one because they weren't the money shifts, and that's probably something you have to work up to. I'm going to show up, offer her help, and promise that this time, I'll be keeping my word, since I'm the only one who'll know what I'm doing." *Well?* in my tone.

"You can't go to a strip club by yourself."

"Rella already said she'd go, and that way, you can maintain deniability."

"You know—"

I cut Harper off. "I'm only going to offer Cara assistance—whatever she needs, and that's unknown at this time. I just want her to have an option or two. If she's not interested, then I'll leave."

"If you like Seven, and I'm assuming you do since he's been staying at your place this whole time, you should be honest with him. Especially after everything he's done for you," Harper scolded lightly. "If he's anything like Grey, the only thing he won't be happy about is if you put yourself in any kind of danger."

"A couple of people have hinted that Seven did something to help get me sprung from jail. I thought they meant getting Cruz to represent me, but now I'm beginning to suspect something else. You know, and I want you to tell me."

"You didn't hear this from me, as I eavesdropped, so no one knows that I know and I want it to stay that way."

I nodded, wondering what the heck.

"Turns out the judge on your case is a friend of Seven's. While you were awaiting your initial hearing, he casually ran into the man while getting a coffee or something and gave his word that if you got bail, you'd follow all the rules and not skate anywhere."

I hissed in a breath. "Isn't that illegal?"

Harper shook her head. "Seven just said it in passing and didn't offer to pay for the man's coffee."

"You know me and relationships. Short-lived. I want Seven to stick around."

"No worries with the way he looks at you. Quite frankly, I've caught you looking back with the same adoration a time or two. So don't mess it up by withholding stuff."

The door opened, and Grey came in, then stopped and stepped back out. "Avery's over here," he called down the hall.

"I forgot to order dinner," I said as Seven came in behind him.

"That's an easy fix. We all have to eat, so let's do it here," Grey offered. "The refrigerator is stocked with anything you'd want to drink."

We took a vote and it was unanimous, though it surprised me the guys wanted pizza. I ordered two different kinds and a large salad. Harper called Rella and ordered her to drop whatever she was doing and hurry on over.

Rella had good timing, arriving at the same time as the food.

By silent agreement, we didn't talk about business or my case.

We were finishing up when my phone rang. It was Anders. I was reluctant to take the call but felt like I ought to, so I walked away from everyone and answered.

"I wanted to let you know that I've signed a lease with Morningside. The unit is empty now, and I can move in at any time."

I could hear the relief in his voice. "That's great. When do you want to make the move?"

"As soon as I can make it happen."

"I'll work on getting everything organized and call you back tomorrow."

He thanked me profusely and hung up.

I walked back to the others, shoving my phone in my pocket. "That was Anders, and he's going to move right away. I told him I'd get everyone on board and call back with a timeline."

"I hope it's something he really wants to do and won't regret later," Harper said.

"He had a great time at Morningside—so much so that he's been back several times. Talked about playing more golf. Your Gram has become one of his besties, showing him around and introducing him to people."

"That sounds like Gram." Harper laughed. "She's had such great things to say about Morningside since she moved in, especially how it didn't take her long to make new friends." She gave Rella a quick rundown of what was going on.

"I meant it when I said that I'm happy you're taking over dealing with Anders," Grey said to me.

"I'll send you emails and keep you up-to-date on everything I'm doing," I promised.

Seven put his arm around me, squeezing my shoulders.

We all silently agreed no more work talk and went on to other topics.

Eventually, I slipped my hand in Seven's and squeezed, inclining my head.

He stood and pulled me to my feet. "Hate to break this up, but I've got an early meeting."

Grey's brows shot up—he knew it was a lie but didn't say anything.

I'd helped clean up and knew we weren't leaving a mess. "This was fun. Next time, my place."

Rella stood. "I'll come with you." We said our goodbyes and headed out. When we got to my door, Rella said to me, "We'll talk tomorrow."

Seven unlocked my door, then walked Rella to hers.

I waited in the doorway and, when he got back, said, "That was very sweet of you."

"Sweet, that's me." He picked me up and walked inside, kicking the door shut. He carried me into the living room, setting me down and sitting next to me. "Okay, out with it."

"How about a glass of wine?"

"If you're trying to get me drunk, it'll take more than that."

I laughed. "I want to say thank you for all you've done for me. I've said it before, but there was a part of me that held back, wanting to protect myself. I'd be more comfortable discussing a report entirely of numbers than telling you all the things I've been up to. I don't know why I didn't share it with you from the beginning, and I'm promising that it won't happen in the future."

"Do I want to know?"

"I'm pretty sure you do, since you're not one to shy away from anything. Where to start?"

"The beginning. Or, if you're not ready, I can wait."

"I was the one who put the money back in Anders' account. It didn't take long to track it down and snatch it out of Sissy's greedy fingers." His smirk told me he'd already guessed. "Your guy is so slow—it was hard to sit back and wait on him when I knew I could get it done quicker. I really wanted to boast to Grey and couldn't." Seven's smirk was fleeting. "I hoped he would hire me as the man's replacement, but now that I think about it, it's a violation of my terms of release. I want to tell you right now that I won't be tracking any more money transfers, but that would be a lie. I'm still looking into the Bassett accounts."

"Every time I've caught you down on the beach with your laptop, you've been doing something shifty, haven't you?"

"Pretty much."

"Grey and I came to the conclusion pretty quickly that it was you who returned Anders' money, but we didn't ask—plausible deniability and all. What it did do was make Grey and I realize that we need someone faster who isn't moving our files to the bottom of the stack in favor of a bigger client. You didn't hear this from me, but don't be surprised if, when your case is resolved, Grey offers you a job."

"I'd give your requests top priority."

"I already told Grey he'd be stupid if he didn't follow through."

I told him how I'd met with Trace and that he'd given me information on Cara's whereabouts, but I wasn't sharing it until I talked to her and she gave the okay. "If Riggs and Cara have already hooked back up, then I won't bother her further. But if not, and Riggs comes back wanting to rehire you, like I suspect he will, then we're going to have to try it my way."

"Couldn't believe my eyes when I ran into Trace. Rolled them in his face when Hugo introduced him as your family friend. I think he's going to fit in with that motley crew."

"There's one other thing... I checked out Stella's neighborhood, and before you have a fit, I didn't personally confront anyone. The only thing I learned is that the eyewitness was the neighbor to the right, Arlene. If she was standing on her property facing the house, there's no way she could have seen anything going on over at Stella's. The gossip is that Arlene backtracked on her story fairly early on, but then, we already knew that." I smiled at him. "That updates you on all of my transgressions, and should there be any in the future, I'll tell you sooner."

"How about I'm your first call before you do anything?"

"That's easy enough."

He didn't look convinced. "What's on tap for tomorrow?"

"I'm going to start the ball rolling for Anders, since he wants to move right away."

"When Grey said he was relieved not to be handling this drama, that was an understatement." Seven pulled me into his arms. "Does all this confessing mean you trust me now?"

"Truthfully, I've always trusted you. Just slow to show you. But no more."

He leaned into a kiss.

Chapter Twenty-Nine

It took me almost a week to get everything organized for Anders' move. I'd moved before, but that didn't prepare me for the prep work that went into packing up a mansion and making sure it arrived on the other end and was promptly unpacked. Floyd hopped on the faux-renter gig, and several phone calls later, he'd signed up a couple of friends. It was their job to make sure that Sissy didn't steal anything or interfere with any realtor showings when those started to happen. How they accomplished that, short of physical violence, Anders didn't care.

Anders' original plan had been to stay in his house until the furniture was moved. But Sissy, angrier than a hornet by what was happening — and all of it out of her control — cornered him when no one was around and scared the heck out of him. He packed his suitcases and bolted. She swore at him for stealing her money, conveniently forgetting that it was never hers in the first place. He denied getting the money back and told her that he was selling the mansion because he needed the money to move on. She shouted that she'd bleed every last dime from him in divorce court, then turned around and hired a lawyer with a sleazy reputation to file the papers and put a stop to the sale of the house.

Naively, I'd expected to coordinate everything by phone. Nowhere in my plan was I going to show up at the property and personally direct the comings and goings of the different companies, but Anders insisted. Since I wasn't comfortable using the key he'd given me, lest Sissy call the cops—and who knew how she'd use that to her advantage—I arranged for Floyd to let me in and made sure that he didn't have an appointment elsewhere that would result in him leaving me there by myself.

"Now you show up," Floyd said upon opening the massive front door. He grinned at me. "Where were you when I first arrived and all hell broke loose?"

"I apologize?" I said weakly.

"You should've been here… or maybe not." Floyd motioned me into the dining room, where packing boxes were stacked against the wall. "Sissy was here when me and my friends got here, suitcases in tow, and she charged us like a bull, screaming, 'Help!' You'd have thought the whole block would've turned out to see what was going on, but this place must be more soundproof than I'd thought. Nobody even stuck their head out the door, let alone called the cops." Floyd wasn't the least bit upset since he grinned all through the retelling.

I didn't remind him that I'd warned him his showing up would be a surprise, as Anders had already told me he hadn't told Sissy, fearing reaction.

"Given she thought we were burglars, or whatever, you'd think her first inclination would be to run or call the cops. But nope. She got up in our faces, not noticing or caring that any one of us could squash her with a thumb."

I grimaced at the thought, but still laughed. I wondered how the situation had resolved itself, since it was all quiet at the moment and I hadn't gotten any emergency calls. "How did it end?"

"Sissy's attempts to block us from claiming our bedrooms were laughable. I didn't think the woman could shriek any louder until we upended our suitcases. I explained to her about the rental agreement, and she called me a liar at least a dozen times."

"I need coffee." I'd already downed one cup, but that wouldn't be enough for this day.

"This way." Floyd headed to the kitchen, and I followed. He pointed to the machine on the counter and got out a mug, leaving the cupboard open so I could choose my own blend.

Espresso should get me hyped for the morning ahead.

"It took Sissy long enough, but eventually, she figured out we weren't going to leave just because she ordered us to, and many times over. I fetched the rental agreement, which she looked over, spitting anger, and ripped to shreds, then shrieked, 'This is the last time I'm going to tell you and your hoodlum friends to get out.' I thought she'd explode when I turned my back on her and made myself comfortable on the couch."

"It's hard to believe that she backed off." I knew she'd be difficult but...

Floyd waved me off. "Out of options, she made a show of taking out her phone and calling the cops. First thing out of her mouth when they came through the door was, 'I was afraid for my life.' Not sure how they kept a straight face. For someone terrified, she was still standing in the entry."

"I didn't get a call for bail money, so that's good?" I downed half my coffee.

"Thought Sissy would burst a vein when I handed one of the cops a duplicate copy of the rental agreement that she tore up. One cop took her aside, the other talked to me, and I assumed that she was told the same as me: 'It's a matter for a judge to decide.' Lucky me, the cops weren't impressed by her theatrics. Before the one talking to me left, he issued a warning: 'You might want to keep your bedroom door locked. The woman's a bit volatile.'"

"I'm going to make sure that you guys get bonus pay," I promised.

"None of us will turn that down; you're going to be a favorite among the guys." Floyd grinned at me. "If you haven't already guessed, Sissy was disappointed that we weren't hauled off to jail and, when that didn't happen, that she couldn't get us tossed out by the cops. That's when she got her court order limiting what we can pack up and cart out of here. I've talked to Anders and know what's important to him."

"Now that she's somewhat gotten her way, has it calmed down around here?"

"For the most part, Sissy keeps to her bedroom. When she does come out, it's to go the kitchen or the pool. We all avoid her so as not to provoke another scene. We don't want the cops getting called every five minutes. They'll run out of patience with us wasting their time and arrest us all."

I wondered if she was in her bedroom now but didn't get to ask since the doorbell rang and Floyd went to answer it. A few of Hugo's men trooped inside, and Floyd greeted each one by name. Trace came in last. I waved.

He walked over with a smile on his face. "One of the guys suggested I say hello to my 'aunt.'"

I laughed. "That's fun. I haven't been one of those yet. Everything going okay?"

"When I first met you, I thought you were a lot of things, crazy being one of them, but I'm happy I didn't tell you what I thought, since I got a job out of it and it's working out good. I'm the youngest on the crew, and everyone looks out for me. Nice for a change, but I don't take advantage." He got called away.

A stylish woman walked in the open door, and her eyes swept around the house. I recognized her as the moving consultant I'd hired to make sure everything got packed correctly. Turned out it was more than wrapping something in newspaper and tossing it in a box. I'd thrown out that description when we talked, despite knowing that the process entailed more than that, and thought she'd faint. She strolled over to the guys, and they had a short conversation, then got to work under her direction.

I climbed the stairs and stopped halfway, taking my phone out and snapping a couple of pictures to send to Anders, updating him that packing had begun and was in capable hands. I caught movement out of the corner of my eye and turned as Sissy, who I recognized from her picture, rushed down the stairs, stopping at my side.

"What do you think you're doing?" she hissed, flinging out her hand, hitting mine. My phone flew to the floor below, landing with a sharp crack.

Dismayed, I looked over the railing and stared down at what was left of my phone.

Her eyes followed mine. "Oh, so sorry," she said in the most saccharine tone. Her eyes spoke the truth, brimming with amusement.

I put two more steps between us, hanging onto the railing, just in case. "You absolute bitch!

You take one step in my direction, and I'll have you arrested."

"How dare you speak to me like that!" Sissy spit.

At least she stayed put. "Look, I don't want any trouble. I'm only here to supervise the move. I promise we'll make it quick."

"That's what you think. Thanks to my lawyer, I know my rights, and you can't move a damn thing out of here."

Should I tell her she has spit in the corners of her mouth? I noticed that one of Floyd's friends, Brand, had picked up my phone and turned it over, shaking his head.

"Ladies." The bulked-up cutie looked at the two of us. "I couldn't help overhearing. Before you do anything drastic..." He angled an eyebrow, not taking his eyes off Sissy. "Can we talk?"

Sissy nodded, shooting me a look of pure hate, and huffed her way down the stairs. Brand set my phone on a side table and met her at the bottom of the stairs, ushering her out the front door.

I retrieved my phone and groaned at the splintered screen. I ran my finger lightly over it, adding drops of blood to the cracked glass. I sucked on the end of my finger and headed to the kitchen to put my doctor skills to work, rinsing it off and placing a piece of damp paper towel over it. I was sliding onto a stool at the counter when Floyd entered.

"What happened?" he asked.

"Fair warning: Sissy just might be hot on the phone to the cops." I told him what had happened and how Sissy might spin it. She was determined that not one item leave the property.

Floyd chuckled, and the dark sound made my hair stand on end. "No worries. Sissy's not going to be a problem; Brand will make sure of it. They've got some yucky flirty thing going. Told him to be damn careful. The nutjobs can be fun… until your goods get threatened." He winced, conveying *been there, done that*.

"Brand does know that he can't put her in a shipping box and send her off to another location, right?"

"Good one." Floyd laughed. "He's got more finesse than that."

"I trust you." Mostly because I wanted to and hoped, however irrationally, that the rest of the day would go smoothly. "I'm going to grab my laptop. I'll be here in the kitchen if you need anything. When your guys are ready, I'll order lunch."

"You're spoiling the guys. They're going to want to come work for you full-time." He chuckled, this time less threateningly. "Back to work." He left with a wave.

I wrapped my phone in a paper towel, shoved it in my pocket, and went outside. I kept my eyes peeled for Sissy and Brand as I walked to my car.

There was no sign of either of them, and I wondered where they went. I grabbed my laptop, talked myself out of hiding in my car until needed, and went back inside.

It took most of the day to get everything Anders wanted packed up. It was amazing how fast and organized the guys were as they went room by room, loading the boxes and furniture onto the truck. I was happy not to have another showdown with Sissy, but wondered more than once where she and Brand had disappeared to and whether it would come back to bite Anders. When I saw that nothing more would be needed from me, I packed up my laptop, double-checked with Floyd, who assured me that everything was under control and the moving truck was on the way to its next stop, and didn't run out the door, but close.

Chapter Thirty

I got home with a giant headache, took a shower and some aspirin, and fell into bed. When Seven came in and sat next to me, I gave a rambling discourse on the day. The last thing I remembered him saying before I fell asleep was, "Don't worry, I'll take care of any problems."

Didn't he always? I needed to put more trust in the man. And one of these days, I needed to return the favor.

When I woke up, I felt like a human again. I wandered out to the kitchen and made a pot of coffee first thing. When Seven joined me, I set a mug down in front of him.

"You feeling better?" He smiled over the rim.

"So much so that I'm asking you out on a date. You available tonight?" I got the squint-eye I was getting used to and laughed. "This isn't some trick. I'll be knocking on my own door to whisk you away. You can drive, but I get to tell you where to go."

"Wouldn't miss it. I'll be ready."

"I'll be making reservations, so although it's a short drive, don't dally at the office."

"I'll be home early." He downed his mug and

refilled it. "Checked up on the Anders job. Sissy's fine and back at the mansion, although not happy. Showed back up with a sunburn and not a hair out of place, claiming to anyone who'll listen that she was kidnapped and held hostage on some island. She can't prove a word of it, but that's the story. One thing she didn't do was call the cops."

"There's so much more to that story, and I don't want to hear a word of it. I'm assuming that Brand also made it back okay?"

"I didn't hear anything to the contrary. I did tell Floyd—as he relayed the information, laughing—that he was full of BS and hung up."

I laughed and pointed at him. "Home early, and be ready when I knock."

"Gotcha." He leaned over and attempted to bite the tip of my finger off. I jerked it back.

* * *

I chose a black dress with a v-neck and a slit on one side and paired it with heels, confident that I wouldn't trip, even though it had been a while since I'd worn a pair, then pulled my hair up and pinned it in a twisty bun. I was right on time, standing in the hallway and beating on the door from the inside.

Seven came down the hall in dress pants and a button-down shirt that fit him perfectly. Instead of his usual messy finger-combed hair, he had it slicked back. He whistled.

I needed to fan my hot face.

He stopped in front of me, holding out his arm. "You look great." He led me out the door and down to the car.

I took out my new phone, which I'd picked up earlier, and inputted the address. "Head west until you get to Highway One," I said, fastening it to the dash mount.

"Where are we going exactly?"

"Not far."

"You really have me thinking that I need to brush up on my interrogation skills."

"That sounds fun."

The best part of this drive: it was all along the water, with a view of the Miami South Channel. He took the turn for Biscayne Bay but didn't have to go far before he turned onto another causeway, taking it to the end. He pulled up to the Rusty Anchor, an elegantly understated two-story restaurant, and handed the keys off to the valet.

We walked up the palm tree-lined stairs and into the restaurant. I had requested a table outside, which boasted one of the best views of the Downtown Miami skyline, and it delivered. We sat side by side at a table that faced the water, lights strung overhead and pelicans diving into the water a short distance away.

We ordered drinks, which arrive promptly. I picked mine up and held it out. "I want you to know that I appreciate you and all you've done." I clinked his glass with mine.

"Something about you when we first met— and not those big glasses either… I just knew that I wanted to get to know you, no matter how much you thought otherwise."

"I don't wear those anymore to stop you from complaining." I had gotten over wanting to hide away and put distance between me and people in general.

"I'm good for you."

It felt as though my cheeks caught fire. "Yes, you are. Very good."

He clasped my hand, kissing the back of it.

A blond-haired woman approached us with the intensity of a starving animal. I might not have noticed her but for her stare, focused solely on Seven. She was a woman that most men wouldn't ignore, as evidenced by the heads that turned. She slunk past nearby tables in a tight black dress that clung to her voluptuous body and showed off an impressive set of double D's. She paused, giving me a thorough head-to-toe once-over, letting it show in her eyes that she found me lacking.

"Seven, sweetheart." She swooped down and left a red smudge on the corner of his mouth. "She's your date?" she demanded.

"As a matter of fact, she is," Seven said in an even tone.

It surprised me that he didn't introduce either

one of us.

"Oh, Seven." She slapped his shoulder. "Rain." She held out her hand to me and then retracted it as I stuck mine out.

"Avery. Nice to meet you," I added, only because it sounded polite. Now I wanted her to leave.

Rain continued to stare at Seven, and whatever she was expecting, she didn't get — possibly the reason her cheeks turned red. "Dishwater whatever that is…" Indicating my hair. "She's not your type. Far from it."

I was tempted to tug a strand of hair free and take a better look. Dishwater, my ass.

"People change, grow up. I've done both," Seven said easily.

"She's dreary… and well, flat… skinny anyway." Rain shot me a dismissive look.

I'd had plenty of mean-girl experience, and I'd developed a shield. She was going to have to ramp it up to scare me off. I turned to Seven. "Would you like it if I got a boob job?"

He laughed. "Hell, no." He brushed my lips with his. "You're perfect just the way you are."

Rain glittered with anger but wasn't put off. "I wanted you to know that I've moved to the Miami area. We need to reconnect. I'm sure you've found out that what we had can't be duplicated. We were perfect in every way."

"We were just getting ready to order," Seven said flatly.

Apparently, she didn't hear it as a brush-off, like I did, because she didn't even blink. "I know you were hurt when I left," she purred.

"You were stupid enough to dump Seven?" I blurted.

"Who asked you to stick your nose into this conversation?" she snapped.

"Are you going to share the story?" Seven snapped back. "Rain claimed to be pregnant, and yes, I offered to marry her, but told her I wouldn't leave my job like she'd been nagging me to. Two minutes later, she had a miscarriage and left town. Then came the headline in the gossip section that she'd married billionaire Daniel Adams, and it lasted, what? A year?" he asked with an arched brow.

"I want to make amends for the hurt, the misunderstanding, and want you to know I regret my choices." Rain let out a sigh that made her breasts heave. "But trying to make me jealous with this… Trust me, we can get past everything and move forward."

I snorted.

Seven shot me a smile.

"I wasn't talking to you," Rain said, her voice rising several decibels.

The people at the tables on both sides turned and stared.

"Rain, listen to me," Seven said, in a low, intense voice. "The past has been over and dead for a long time. Now, if you wouldn't mind, we'd like to get back to our dinner. One other thing — I never want to have this or any discussion with you again."

A tear ran down her cheek. I wondered if she'd somehow faked it, as there didn't appear to be any emotion other than anger.

"I just can't believe..." She made a sweeping gesture towards me.

"Apparently, I wasn't clear enough. Avery is the one for me. I love her, and we're making a life together."

The one? Loves me? My mouth formed an O, and I licked my lips, then blinked several times, lost for words.

Rain sucked in a breath, tears glittering in her eyes. About the time I was starting to feel sorry for her, her gaze flickered and all emotion left her face. Good actress, I'd give her that.

Seven tightened his fingers in mine and placed our hands on top of the table.

She smiled, cold as an iceberg. "You'll change your mind, and it might be too late." She turned, hips swaying, and disappeared inside the restaurant.

His lips brushed mine. "It was years ago. I haven't seen her since and have no interest in rekindling anything."

I leaned forward, wrapping my arms around his neck and brushing a kiss across his lips. "Our pasts don't matter. You've proven to be pretty damn amazing."

He took my face in his hands. "I meant every word of what I said. You're it. No one else holds the slightest bit of interest for me."

"I'm a very lucky woman."

The waiter appeared and took our order.

We held hands until the food arrived. During dinner, we talked about anything and everything—our families, mutual friends, sharing tidbits about ourselves that we hadn't previously. No talk of business or my case.

"Sorry about earlier."

"Since you're what's known as a catch, I don't blame the woman for wanting you back." I winked at him.

"It's not the way I wanted to share my feelings with you—blurting it out that way."

"I must be wearing off on you; it's something I would do." I chuckled.

"Even if I hadn't met you, there's no way I'd ever hook up with Rain again. She showed up at the station and expressed her dissatisfaction about me being a detective, saying a real man would show some ambition."

Ouch!

"I was about to tell her to go to hell, and the sooner the better, when she blurted out she was pregnant. And only thinking of Seven Jr. or Sevenette, I asked her to marry me."

"I'm thinking your daughter, a little mini-you, would prefer just Seven." I grinned at him.

He grinned back, liking that idea.

"Rain didn't acknowledge my impromptu proposal, only wanting to be assured that I could give her the life she craved—glitz and glamor. I didn't hear from her again until she texted me that she miscarried."

That's cold. "I'm sorry."

"Two weeks later, she was married."

"What a bitch."

"Plenty of what-ifs about my son or daughter, but not a single regret about her. In a way, I feel like I got lucky."

"You're going to make a great father." I could imagine the Sevens and Sevenettes bringing down the house with their laughter and antics.

"How do you feel about five or ten?"

Ten Sevens? I covered my face and laughed.

Chapter Thirty-One

The next morning, Seven left for the office, and I took my laptop outside, curled up in a chair overlooking the water, and waited while it downloaded my email, then sorted through it, and mass-deleted the junk mail. I'd run at full speed organizing Anders' move—now it was quiet again, and I didn't like it. Busy worked better for me. My phone rang, and I flipped it over. It surprised me to see Seven's name on the screen.

"Hi, hon," he said when I answered.

I groaned. We both used that term of endearment when we were up to something, and I hadn't missed the smirk in his tone.

"I know you didn't hang up."

"Am I going to regret asking what you're up to?"

"Grey would like you to come to the office for a meeting, and I volunteered to call, figuring I could use my influence."

"Do I get a hint?"

"There's no fun in that."

"Be there in a few." If only out of curiosity. I

gathered my stuff together and took it inside, then put everything in my briefcase and set it next to the door. I went and changed into a short-sleeve a-line dress in various shades of blue and sandals and pulled my hair up into a high ponytail.

It was a short drive to the office. When I pulled around the back and into the garage, Trace was dumping trash, and I waited until he caught up to me.

"Your boyfriend tried to hit me up about what I knew about Cara," he told me when he got closer. "Dude was on a fishing expedition, and I pled ignorance. He claimed to know that I'd shared information with you and said he'd like to hear it from me. Told him he wasn't family and to shove off."

I laughed.

"Lucky for me, Hugo appeared and heard the last part of the conversation, and he also laughed," Trace continued. "With that eye-twitch thing he does, he let Seven know that I was under his protection. I shouldn't have, but I smirked and followed Hugo into the building."

"Not sure what came over me…" I said. Ah yes, my feelings for the man. "I thought it was time to fess up to all my sneaking around." Trace laughed. "I kind of, mostly anyway, told him everything. I should've added a contingency that if I forgot anything, I'd catch him up later."

"Got a number for that Evelyn woman—

wormed it out of one of Cara's mattress mates." Trace pulled a scrap of paper out of his pocket. "She mentioned that Cara was afraid of the woman, but she didn't know why, as Cara refused to talk about it."

I opened my purse and pulled out my wallet.

Trace waved my hand away. "I'm in a bit of trouble, and I was thinking that since you work upstairs, you'd have a fix for me. If not, that's fine, but I'd appreciate your not telling anyone."

"The police after you?"

He shook his head. "Thank goodness for that."

"I've got to run upstairs for a meeting. When I'm done, I'll stop by Hugo's."

"I'll be out back, scrubbing out one of the work trucks." Trace pointed.

I rode up in the elevator, getting off at the third floor. I didn't bother with a knock, instead opening the door, dropping my stuff on the reception desk, and grabbing my bottled iced tea out of my bag.

"Have a seat." Grey waved to a chair in front of his desk.

I sat down next to Seven, who leaned over and kissed me.

"Thanks again for taking over the Anders file and making sure everything got done without incident," Grey said. "Neither Seven nor I would've had the patience. So you know, Anders has been effusive in his praise."

"I'm just happy that he's put distance between

him and Sissy and that I was able to get a promise out of him that he wouldn't be leaving a forwarding. Also told him to give me a call when he starts seeing someone new—if Gram doesn't know the woman well enough to give her approval, I'll run a background check free of charge." I took a long drink of my tea.

Grey and Seven nodded. "We're good with that," Grey said. "The reason I had Seven get you here today… I wanted to call but he insisted." He grinned. "Riggs is back. He made contact with Cara and came on a little strong, not happy about her current living situation or refusal to answer his questions regarding their son."

So that's why she took off.

"Riggs would like her found, and this time promises a far more low-key approach, trying not to overwhelm her," Grey continued.

"As you can imagine, he'd like to know that his son is safe and being cared for, since it's clear that Cara's not doing it," Seven said.

"And you want me to…"

"It's rumored you know where Cara can be found," Grey said, *True?* on his face.

"As I'm sure you know, Seven and I were able to find out where she lived, then drove her to work at a nearby strip club. But I heard that she packed up and can't be found at either place." I didn't flinch from his stare. "Cara's skittish, and you can't just move in like a steamroller. I'd suggest that, if there's another reunion between her and Riggs, she be prepared ahead of time."

"If we can get the two of them together, I'm sure he'll be willing to take the slow approach," Seven said.

"Cara's supposedly working at another strip club, but I haven't been able to verify that," I told them. "Riggs goes barreling in, and she'll bolt again. Your best bet is to find out if she's amenable to meeting with him and take it from there."

"That's why Seven and I thought you'd be the perfect person to smooth the way—feel Cara out and find out if she's willing to sit down again."

"It was my idea," Seven grumbled. I bit back a laugh. "I don't want you hanging around strip clubs, so I'm making myself available for any field trips. That's what a partner would do."

"It's sidekick," I reminded him. "How about I make a few phone calls and see what I can find out?" Grey nodded, and I got a squint-eye from Seven. "I'll need an agreement from the two of you—no leaning on any of my informants."

"What informant?" Seven demanded. "That little squirt downstairs?"

"Is this true love I'm watching unfold?" Grey laughed at us. "This reminds me of Harper and I, and you're not going to win, buddy." This time, his laughter was directed at Seven.

Grey's computer beeped, which I recognized as a tone for a meeting about to start. "If we're through here?" I stood. "I need to check in at my own office, and then I have a client I need to meet."

"What kind of client?" Seven demanded.

"A new one that I didn't pinch off you two. As for Cara, I'll make some calls and get back to you." I shot them both my cheesiest smile.

Seven stood, ready to follow. "Our next meeting is about to start," Grey reminded him, and he gave me a quick kiss, looking disappointed that he couldn't follow me.

Chapter Thirty-Two

I went down to my office and sorted through the mail. Nothing exciting, and I junked most of it. Dixon had left a couple of files on my desk, which I double-checked, signed off on, and left on his desk. I grabbed my briefcase and went down to the garage, put everything in my car, and walked out to where Trace had just finished working and was putting his supplies in a bucket.

"Did you want to go inside?" I asked, realizing there was no place to sit except for the bench that Hugo'd installed for smokers.

Trace opened the side door of the van he'd just cleaned and motioned for me to sit next to him. We had an unobstructed view of the street, and as usual, there was no traffic zooming by.

"Word has it that you're the building manager." Trace raised his brow. "Is that true?"

I chuckled. "It's not an official title, but yes. I wanted the job and insinuated myself into it. Loved the building at first sight and didn't want to share it with just anyone, so it was my way of making sure some cretin didn't move in. Other than getting the building cleaned, painted, and the floors rented, nothing has come up. If any repairs are needed, Hugo is the man."

Trace took a deep breath. "I know there's a fourth floor—checked it out, actually—and I'd like to rent it for a couple of months. I can't pay much, and you'd have to take weekly payments. But I'd be happy to do any jobs that need to be done."

I didn't like that request one bit... I gave him the same intense stare Seven often gave me, but learned nothing. "What the heck is going on?" I asked, a little gruffer than I meant too.

"Is that a maybe?"

"Being a very detailed-oriented person, I can tell there's quite a few details you're leaving out, and I don't make decisions without all the facts. If you're worried that I'm going to repeat anything you tell me, I won't, not without your permission."

"The manager at that pee-hole building I live in is blackmailing me," Trace blurted out. "I just need a place for a couple of months where he can't find me. After that, he won't have anything to hang over my head."

That was the last thing I expected him to say. Not sure what the first was.

"Where are your parents?" I was careful to soften my tone.

"Dead."

"Both of them?"

Trace nodded. "We were living in the building

when they got into a car accident. My mom was killed instantly; my dad died a few days later. Ringer, the manager, let us move into the storage room, and in return, I did all the odd jobs."

"We?" Storage room? What a dick!

"My brother. He graduates from high school in two months. He can easily get a bus to school from here—I checked it out."

"Why is Ringer throwing you out?"

"He's not. He's mad because I got a job and wants me to turn over my paycheck. If I don't, he's going to call the cops and report my brother to Social Services." Trace blew out an exasperated breath. "If my bro misses the last couple months of school, then he might not get to graduate, and he's worked really hard. Better student than me."

"I'm not saying I won't help you, so hear me out." He didn't look convinced. "The fourth floor is a storage room. To use a bathroom, you'd have to come downstairs to one of the offices."

"That wouldn't be much worse than what we've got going on now."

"If Ringer knows where your brother goes to school, he can still carry through with his threat," I said, wiping the hopeful look off Trace's face. "You need a better plan—one that gets you two away from Ringer—and better accommodations than a storage room."

Trace covered his face with his hands. "I had to ask."

I pushed his hands down. "I've got this friend — we call her a do-gooder behind her back, and sometimes to her face because it makes her laugh. Anyway... she works with various charities, and one of them deals with children and single moms. Before you interrupt..." I held up my hand. "How about I call her and see what she suggests? I promise we're going to figure this out."

"You don't have to mention my name, do you?"

"No worries there," I assured him. "Hugo pays you guys on Fridays, right? And that's when Ringer is going to have his hand out?"

Trace nodded.

"I see another issue. As soon as he sees that you've packed up and are heading out, he's going to call the cops."

"That's why I planned for my brother and I to leave in the middle of the night."

"Moving your personal belonging on a motorcycle? I don't know what time you're talking, but buses are scarce and that's not a much better option."

"We don't have much, and when Anders decided not to use the storage area in the garage, I snuck in a few items. I had the key and so... well..."

"Gotcha. Anyone asks, you have my permission, but chances of anyone asking are slim, as everyone minds their own business. I feel a better idea coming on." That got a half-laugh out of Trace. "Pack up and move out right under Ringer's nose, using Floyd's muscle and his truck. And while at the property, Floyd can have a chat with Ringer about blackmailing one of his friends. Do that knuckle-cracking trick of his." At Trace's surprised look, I added, "He owes me a favor, and it's a good way to get it off the books." Trace didn't need to know that I'd pay Floyd on the side. "That ensures that you don't have to look over your shoulder for Ringer creeping out of the bushes."

"It's just that I work with him, and he might say—"

"No worries there—Floyd's tight-lipped." He'd better be, and if not, he would be this time. "Can I call my friend? I'm telling you that she's a chick who snaps her fingers and makes things happen. She's also really nice, and people love to say yes to her. If you won't do it for you, then do it for your bro, because he deserves better digs than a storage room."

"No cops, right?"

"Promise. Your current living situation, what's that like?" I asked.

"We've got a toilet, sink, and a microwave."

"Ringer should be in jail. I'm tempted to tell Floyd to rip his nose off and shove it somewhere or hand it back in pieces."

Trace laughed. "You don't know how many times I've thought about doing just that."

I got out my phone and called Rella, getting her assistant. "Tell her it's Avery."

"You never call the office, so it must be important," Rella said when she answered.

I repeated the story that Trace had told me.

After a slight pause, she said, "I know just the woman. Not only is she a good friend, but she's feeling the effects of her empty nest—her sons are grown and living on their own. I'll ask as long as you can assure me that your friend and his brother aren't trouble. If he's there, I have a few questions."

"Rella Cabot, meet Trace Wyatt," I said, handing him the phone.

I didn't set out to eavesdrop, but it was hard not to when I sat less than a foot away. I was impressed that Trace answered all Rella's questions—straightforward and not a single hedge. Turned out, his brother, Matt, was an honor student. Whatever Rella was pitching, he asked, "Are you sure about this?" After a few more answers, he handed me back the phone.

"We've got two days to make this happen," I said.

"I'm going to hang up and set up a meeting for him now, then give him a call back."

We hung up.

"Rella's got some woman maybe willing to house a couple of boys for a short time," Trace shared. "It would be good for my brother, as long as she's not psycho."

"There's no way that Rella would hook you up with someone like that. To make sure, though, I'll come with you."

"You don't have—"

"I'll borrow Seven's SUV, so there'll be plenty of room when we pick up your brother," I continued, as though I hadn't interrupted him. "That way, the two of you can meet the woman together and make a mutual decision about what you want to do. The initial meeting will still be a bit weird, but less so with both of you there," I responded to Trace's raised eyebrows. "Just know that Rella is never full of it. If this woman is as a nice as she says, any awkwardness will evaporate in a second. If you think for any reason that it won't work, make a face at me, and I'll get us out of there."

"I really didn't expect—"

"One of these times, I'm going to let you finish a sentence." I enjoyed his laugh. "You probably know a little of my story—it's hard for people not to gossip about something so salacious. Working on your problem will keep me out of trouble… well, maybe anyway."

Chapter Thirty-Three

It didn't take long for Rella to call back. The woman, Rosa Carlo, was excited to meet the boys and help out in any way she could. We decided on a local burger joint because it had a play area that was seldom used and we could grab a table for privacy.

"Do you want me to pick you and your bro up at the apartments?" I asked.

"Oh heck no. It wouldn't go unnoticed and would be hot gossip in a minute."

It was decided that I would pick them up at the office, and further decided that after initial introductions, I'd sit at a nearby table. And that we could be out of there fast for any reason at all.

I called Floyd on the way home. "I've got a job for you, and it pays extra if you don't ask a single question of the client." Other than casual guy talk, whatever that consisted of.

He readily agreed.

"It's a moving job. There won't be much in the way of personal belongings, and your truck will handle everything. So basically, muscle and transportation. The move will happen no later than Friday. It's just a matter of figuring out the destination, and that decision will be made soon."

"Sounds easy enough. I agree to the terms."

"There is one part that I didn't mention." Floyd's growly laugh told me he'd known something else was coming. I filled him in on Ringer's attempt to blackmail Trace and said that, in addition to helping them move, I wanted him to have a conversation with Ringer and scare him into minding his own business.

"What a hole and a half. No worries—Ringer won't be flapping his gums to anyone, much less the police, unless he wants them removed," Floyd growled, no trace of laughter. "Trace could've come to me. He probably doesn't know that yet, but he will. No worries about me embarrassing him in any way."

I told him about the meet-and-greet and that I'd be giving him a call to firm up the time for the move.

"Talk soon, then." And we hung up.

I weaved my way through traffic and finally got home, wanting a drink, but that would have to wait until later. You'd think trading rides with the guy you're living with would be easy, since my Porsche wasn't a beater, and even if it was… but nope. I'd called him on the way home, and he'd hemmed and hawed. Realizing that was his way of saying no without saying it, I made an excuse to get off the phone. It surprised me to see him on the balcony, feet kicked up, and I wondered if he'd been home all along. I grabbed an iced tea and joined him.

"Do you have a good reason for why I can't borrow your truck tonight?" I asked, sitting down. "I'll swap you keys, in case you have a hot date." Oops, he didn't think that was funny.

He shot questions at me—who, what, why, and on and on. Some, I just shook my head, as though that was an answer, but that didn't slow him down.

Finally, I asked, "Did you have an irritating day and decided to take it out on me?"

Seven took a page from my playbook and didn't answer. "I'm coming with you, and I'll be driving."

"Under the condition that you don't ask any questions." I raised my right hand as though he would mimic me but nope.

"Maybe."

"Nooo. Agree or I'll ditch you and sneak out of here. I know the exits better than you." That was a stupid threat, since there was only one. Vaulting over the balcony wasn't an option.

"At least a hint."

"The client that I teased about kind of did become one, of sorts. I'm definitely helping to find a solution. One more thing—client confidentiality and all, so you won't be blabbing a scintilla of info to anyone." I guess an eyeroll was a response—kind of. Suspecting that we were at the end of our one-sided conversation, I jumped up and ran down the hall to change. Tonight called for jeans to fit in with the burger-eaters at the fast food joint. I called and told Trace about the glitch known as Seven. "There's no ditching him. But I did wangle promises out of him." Admittedly, wasn't sure that he'd agreed.

"No problem. Floyd called, and like you said, he didn't ask any questions, just said to call when I had a time and date."

"Let's meet an hour early, and I'll treat you and Matt to the burger deluxe meal. They've got pinball and a couple of other machines if we've got time."

"You more excited by the food or the games?" He laughed.

"I'm a game girl."

We agreed on a time and hung up.

* * *

Seven's brows shot up when I said, "First stop, the office."

It didn't take long to get over there. He pulled into the parking lot and saw Trace and Matt at the same time I did, sitting on the bench in the front. They were totally cute lookalikes in jeans and t-shirts, one leg crossed over the opposite knee.

"Make a u-turn, babes." I rolled down my

window and unlocked the door, waving them over.

Trace opened the back door, got in first, and made the introductions.

"Next stop, Hank's," I told Seven.

It was a quiet drive but not totally weird.

We got out, went inside, and got in line. "I expect you two to eat like growing boys and not girls," I whispered to Trace.

"I'll pass it along," he said with a laugh.

While waiting on our order, I chose a table large enough to seat ten inside the play area; since it was empty, there wasn't anyone to care where we sat. Rather than sit through an awkward silence while we ate, I asked Matt about school and Trace about work.

"It's nice of you to hook us up with this woman," Matt said. "Have you met her, checked her out?"

"All of us here at the table are meeting Mrs. Carlo for the first time." I smiled at the brothers. "She's a friend of my friend, Rella, who wouldn't have set up this meeting unless she felt certain that it could work out. If it turns out she's a freak-job, like I told your bro, make a face, and I'll get us out of here." Trace flashed a face at his brother, and they laughed. "If necessary, we'll come up with another option or go back to the original one." I squirmed at the idea of them living on the fourth floor. To change the subject, I said, "Hear you like numbers. Me too."

"I love numbers," Matt said in awe.

"Anytime you want to talk the subject to death, I'm your girl," I said with a big smile. "You should introduce your brother to Dixon," I told Trace. "He's a numbers nerd, his own label."

We continued to trade easy banter until Rella showed up with Rosa Carlo in tow. They ordered cold drinks before coming to the table. I made the introductions.

Rosa nodded to Seven as though they'd met before.

"We'll be over here." I nudged Seven and indicated another table, giving Trace a nod.

"What the hell is going on?" Seven demanded.

"Tone down the grouchiness." I looked over my shoulder, but no one had heard.

"They both look twelve, and they ate like they hadn't had a meal in a month."

"Trace is nineteen and Matt is seventeen, graduating high school in June. I promised that I wouldn't air their laundry. But I can say that they need a safe place to live for a few months."

"They couldn't find a better place than with Rosa. She's used to riding herd on boys, having had five of her own, and they adore the ground she walks on."

"So you two know each other?" I thought I'd misinterpreted the look.

"Yep. And another thing—she's a damn fine cook. She'll fatten those two up."

"Sounds like you're giving the Seven thumbs

up on Rosa?"

"I can vouch for the woman. The other two better not be little turds or I'll wring their necks, and I'll be sure to tell them that. If they mess up, they'll also have to answer to Floyd or the other four brothers, and that won't be pretty."

"Floyd?"

"I guess you didn't know—Rosa's his mother."

"Whatever reservations I might have had are now gone. I really want this to work out for Trace and Matt."

Seven and I went over to the machines. He wanted to wager, but I was smart enough to nix that one because he was way too eager. I tried to ace him in basketball but didn't come close, and didn't fare much better on the pinball machine.

The four talked for a long time and finally wrapped it up.

I hugged Rella and whispered, "You're the best."

"Small world," she said. "Once Trace found out that Rosa is Floyd's mother, the weight dropped off his shoulders and he was far more open to the idea."

Rosa hugged both boys and told them she was looking forward to their arrival. "Not to worry. We're going to get along," she reassured them both.

They didn't look like they were being led to their deaths, so that made me happy.

When we got in the SUV, Matt—definitely happy—said, "Rosa said we could come tomorrow, that a day sooner was nothing." He was definitely happy.

"She assured us that she had the room and would enjoy the company," Trace said. "I promised we wouldn't be any trouble and that I would be handy around the house."

I'd called Floyd again before we left the restaurant and now turned in my seat. "When he's moving you, Floyd will also take care of the Ringer problem. I expect you to come up to my office and check in once in a while."

"I asked Avery what was going on, but she kept your secret. You mind telling me a little about it?" Seven asked.

The brothers looked at one another and exchanged some kind of silent code.

Matt shrugged. "Fine with me."

Trace filled Seven in, his jaw clenching a couple of times during the telling. It mirrored pretty much what he'd told me.

"You see this Ringer guy around, let me or Floyd know." Seven had started out in a gruff tone but calmed down. "Don't open yourself up to trouble by confronting him yourself."

"Once Floyd's done talking with Ringer, if he's not dumber than a stump, he'll cross the street should he see you boys out somewhere. I doubt that will happen, since you're not going to be anywhere close to your old neighborhood."

The boys nodded at me.

Seven got back to the office and pulled around the back. Trace had parked his bike in the garage.

I rolled down my window and stuck my head out. "Nice meeting you, Matt."

"I want to thank you for everything," Trace said.

"It was fun. Not that you had a problem, but that I could be useful."

"You delivered big time." Trace waved, and we watched as the two went into the garage and got on his motorcycle, cruising out to the road ahead of us.

"I'm going to find Trace tomorrow and remind him to keep us updated," Seven said.

I brushed a kiss on his cheek.

Chapter Thirty-Four

Early the next morning, Seven and I were having coffee on the balcony, and he was tormenting Arco with a feathered string that reeked of catnip, sending him into whirling frenzy. Eventually, he collapsed on the footrest for a nap.

My phone rang, and I held the screen up so Seven could see that it was Floyd.

"Got the guys moved last night," Floyd rumbled through the phone, loud enough for anyone within several feet to hear.

"I thought that was tonight." I made a face at Seven, who nodded.

"Not when Mama Rosa snaps her fingers and wants it done now. Dare anyone to say no to the woman. You have about a minute to change your mind if you know what's good for you." Floyd laughed.

"Trace and Matt were fine with the change?"

"They were overwhelmed when I showed up. What a stinkhole. I helped get them packed up. Didn't like it when that Ringer dude came out of his hole and tried to intimidate them."

"Ringer didn't call the cops, did he?" Seven's

jaw tightened when I asked the question.

"I told Trace and Matt that it would only take me a minute to deal with Ringer. That little worm caved fast. I asked him if he knew how long it would take him to die from his bones getting broken one at a time. Which was what would happen if I heard his name again. Then cracked my knuckles because someone told me it's a nice sound effect." He laughed.

I blushed. "But you left him in one piece?"

"Never touched him."

"Trace and Matt are doing okay at your mom's?" I asked.

"As expected, they were nervous, but Mom smothered them with hugs and food, her typical, and all awkwardness evaporated. She made sure Matt got to school, so that worked out."

"Your mom's amazing, opening her home to them. I'm thankful for the people that came together for those two. Now they'll have a couple months to breathe and figure out what they're going to do next."

"Another thing—now that the guys are family, I won't be taking any money. Wouldn't be right."

"Anytime you need anything, hop up the stairs, or call if I'm not around." I took his grunt to mean he would.

We hung up.

"What's on your agenda today?" Seven asked.

"Harper thinks I need to get out and do something fun. She knows I'd never say no to ice cream, so the three of us are going to take a couple of hours and girl chat."

"I'm meeting with a client this morning, and then I'll be at the office." He got up and went inside.

The black ball of fluff rolled over and wrapped himself around my feet.

I pulled my laptop off the table, putting it in my lap. Back to my personal case, I checked for any new articles.

* * *

When I got the "meet at the elevator" text, I grabbed my purse, and the three of us rode down together and got into Harper's SUV. She pulled out of the garage and took the road that hugged the water. It was a beautiful day for a drive along the ocean, the blue water lapping the white sand.

Our favorite ice cream shop had outside seating and was a prime place for people watching, as there were a variety of stores that lined the block in each direction. We ordered our favorites and grabbed a table on the small patio within spitting distance of the sidewalk.

I tried to thank Rella again for helping Trace and Matt, but she waved me off.

"It was fun to be hands-on," she said. "I'm usually behind the scenes. It's a testament to those boys' inner strength that they survived in squalid conditions for so long. I'm going to continue to check in on them, make sure they're doing okay."

"Grey suspects that we ran the writer con, as he calls it." Harper blushed. "He sent a guy out to ask around Stella's neighborhood and found out about the two writers that showed up asking questions. The descriptions were too vague for him to be sure which of you was with me, and not wanting to lie, I diverted his attention with kisses and other things."

"You should've just fessed up," I said, and Rella nodded in agreement. "Let him grouch at you and get over it. I'm surprised he didn't want to know if I was one of the writers."

"Trust me, it would've come up if... you know." Harper's cheeks burned.

Rella and I laughed.

"If Grey suspects, then Seven will be asking more questions. I did tell him that we cruised the neighborhood, and he's going to remember that he didn't ask enough questions and have more. I'll also be telling him that we're not going back. There's no reason, since we didn't find out anything that would necessitate a second trip."

A woman walked past the table, then backed up, staring at the three of us. I didn't recognize her, but Harper and Rella obviously did. "I knew you two were full of it, showing up at my house asking questions." Now I recognized Stella's neighbor, Arlene. "And here you sit with the murderer herself. I bet the police would love to know that you've been harassing me, a witness, at my home. They'd send you back to jail where you belong."

The neighboring tables had filled up, and the people sitting at them didn't bother to hide that they were hanging on every word.

"I don't know what you're talking about," I said.

"Yeah, sure," Arlene sneered.

"Go ahead and call the police," Harper said. "Apparently, you haven't noticed that this isn't your house and we're nowhere near your neighborhood. You'll just reinforce that you're a crackpot."

"You two can explain why you're here with her after showing up at my door. That should be entertaining." Arlene fumbled around in her pocket.

Another woman skidded up and patted her back. I recognized this woman immediately and swallowed a groan. This jaunt for an ice cream fix just kept getting better. Next time, I'd get it to go.

"Do you honestly think Seven's going to forget about me?" Rain demanded shrilly, her nose in the air. "You're so pedestrian."

I was done rolling over to mean girls. "Seven forgot you a long time ago. Accept the fact that he's moved on, and with me, whether you like it or not."

Rain jabbed a finger at me. "Stay away if you

know what's good for you. Seven is mine. We'll get past this misunderstanding and get back together, and you'll be the diversion sitting on the curb."

"You don't listen very well. Seven's spelled out very clearly that he was done with you a long time ago. If he wanted you back, he could've packed up and left after the last time we ran into you."

Arlene Hayes patted Rain's shoulder. "What you and Seven had was love, and he'll be back. Her… it's just sex. Besides, that one is going to prison for the rest of her life. Why she isn't there now is mystifying. But she'll be back behind bars once I file a report."

"Prison?" Rain smirked.

Didn't the older woman know any other tone except loud and nerve-grating? As I watched the two women interact, I started noticing similarities—I'd guess mother and daughter.

Rain whispered something to her mother.

"Avery English murdered Stella Basset in cold blood," Arlene yelled, loud enough that people on the sidewalk stopped. Every one of them produced phones in a nanosecond. "All for greed. She managed her finances—what a crook; what she did was clean out her accounts."

I wanted to shrink away. Whatever good that would do. At least eight people had captured the drama on video. I'd be back in the headlines in an hour. All it would take is for one of them to post it on social media.

"When the story I'm working on comes out, everyone will know you for the shrew you are." Harper hiked her nose higher than the other two women combined.

The owner of the ice cream shop came skidding out the glass door. "You two need to leave or I'll have to call the cops," he said to Arlene and Rain.

"You're choosing to serve a murderer over law-abiding folks?" Arlene screamed in an ear-splitting tone. "I'll never set foot in your store again, and you can bet I'll be telling my friends."

I doubted that she'd ever eaten here. I knew I wouldn't be coming back.

"You'd think, being Stella's good friend, you'd want the real murderer in jail, and that isn't me," I felt compelled to say in my defense, even if no one believed me.

"Liar," Arlene spit.

Rain hooked her arm in her mother's and stepped over to the sidewalk.

"As long as Avery English is roaming the streets, good people aren't safe," she yelled before walking away.

"If you ladies wouldn't mind…" The manager pointed to the street.

I stood and dropped the rest of my ice cream in the trash, although it pained me. My stomach in a hard knot, I couldn't handle another bite.

Harper and Rella stood and flanked me,

making sure that anyone still filming wouldn't be getting any good footage of me.

Harper handed Rella the keys. "Once you exit, go south and circle back. I'm sure that all eyes will stay on us. We'll continue up to the first side street and hopefully blend into the neighborhood."

It didn't take long before Rella coasted up alongside us. The doors were barely closed before she took off. I kicked back in the backseat and let out a huge sigh of relief to no longer be the center of attention.

Harper turned in her seat. "I take it that was Seven's ex."

"Rain accosted us on the night I asked him out on a date. The restaurant, the view, the food was unbelievable, and then her. Honestly, I thought the evening was over once she opened her mouth and went on and on about how much she still wanted him. Turned out that we got closer than ever that night."

"So what happened between the two of them?"

"None of your business, Harper," Rella said.

"What's important is that they're over and I believed Seven when he said he had no interest in rekindling the relationship. I'm the woman he wants, and he isn't going anywhere." I smirked.

"At least he's not stupid," Rella said with a smile.

"If you're about to ask, I like him too. A lot." I grinned.

"Duh," the two said, almost in unison.

Laughing felt good.

I sobered quickly when Harper confirmed what I'd figured out. "In my background search, I learned that Arlene had two daughters—didn't realize… there was any connection to Seven, though. Now I wonder if she lied so her daughter and Seven could get back together. I won't be asking her for an interview."

"We shelved that gig," Rella reminded her.

"Do you think I'm going to be hearing from the cops about today?" I asked.

"They've got better things to do than chase down the ramblings of a lunatic, especially when you weren't within miles of her house," Harper assured me.

Chapter Thirty-Five

Harper decreed that dinner would be at her place and we'd better show up. We took a vote, and it was unanimous for Mexican food. My contribution—the bottle of chilled tequila I had in the refrigerator. I went home, scooped up Arco, and took a nap.

An hour later, I rolled out of bed, took a shower, and slipped into a t-shirt dress, tempted to go barefoot, since Harper lived next door. I went out to the patio, taking my laptop, and searched websites for any mention of today's fiasco. I didn't find anything... yet. The upside was there weren't any videos of me doing anything embarrassing.

Seven came through the door. "I hear dinner's at Harper's. No excuses."

I nodded, and he disappeared down the hall and changed into shorts and a shirt. We were cutting it close by the time he was ready. I slid into a pair of sandals that I'd left by the door. Remembering the tequila, I ran and got it, then met Seven at the door. "I should give you a heads up—today was a bit of train wreck. Your ex was front and center in the ensuing drama.

She wants you back, or so she says. I think she doesn't like to lose."

Seven's jaw tightened, and he shook his head. "If there was no you, I still wouldn't get back together with her. I flat-ass don't trust her and will tell her so if I ever catch her so much as looking at you again, much less saying anything. I'll sic the cops on her for harassment."

"Do you have friends on the force down here?" I grinned at him.

"A couple. I'll suggest they pull her over for a traffic violation and make sure she sits there all day."

I laughed, thinking about her reaction as the minutes began to tick by and she was just sitting there with no end to the wait.

Seven wrapped his hand around mine as we walked next door. He was about to knock when I reached out and turned the knob. "Harper's expecting us."

"Just because she does that doesn't mean you should do it."

"Yes, sir."

Harper waved us to where she'd set up a mini-bar on the patio. Rella had already arrived and was lining up the shot glasses. Grey and Seven opted for beer and laughed at us as we tossed a couple back.

Max two, I told myself. No need to make a drunken spectacle of myself. If Harper didn't stop, she'd be the entertainment. I leaned up against the railing; the view of the water from this high up never got old.

The conversation was light while we devoured the food. I built my own taco and loved every bite. Then Rella and I cleared the dishes, despite Harper's objections that Grey could do it.

"I wouldn't want to deprive the ladies of any fun," he said, and he and Seven laughed at that one.

Harper herded us to the other end of the balcony and offered refills on drinks. I'd had enough with the first go-round and sat back in my chair, feet up. Rella joined me in switching to water. Harper was showing signs of bursting if she didn't get to tell the guys about the ice cream trip. So much like her Gram. Rella and I traded knowing smirks.

"So, we were minding our own business..." Harper threw out her arms with a theatrical flair.

Seven side-eyed me, and I nodded.

Harper launched into the details. Who needed video with her remembering every bit of minutia? When she got to where Rain showed up, Rella cut in and mimicked the woman.

Seven grimaced. "That just gave me chills."

All of us laughed.

"You know, dude, no one liked that chick," Grey told him with a grin. "We hoped you'd get tired of whatever she was doing that had your attention and dump her."

"I apologize for all the embarrassment she

caused, turning your outing into a sideshow," Seven said with a shake of his head.

"Her mother was the one to really amp up the drama," I said.

"Mother?" Seven looked at me. "That's quite the twist."

Harper cut in and told him about how they were Stella's neighbors.

"When I sent my guy out there, he said that Arlene was the least friendly on the block, shutting the door in his face," Grey told us. "Most weren't interested in answering any questions but were at least nice about it."

"She acted the same way when we were there," I said. Oops!

"I knew it." Grey slammed his hand down.

"Could you dial down the dramatics? You knew from the beginning, unless you're dumber than a stump, and I haven't heard anyone mention that," I said.

Harper laughed and side-hugged Grey. "I know, I know, I shouldn't have, but we took precautions and Avery didn't get out of the car." She tossed down another shot and gave the guys her rendition of that day's events. "We didn't hit up every house on the block, like your guy did. We stuck to the two who had an unobstructed view of Stella's property, and only one was home and answering the door."

"Several of the neighbors knew you interviewed her, so she must've spread the news," Grey said, voice full of sarcasm.

"Must have been too good a tidbit not to share," I said. "And you know that with every retelling, something was added."

"Today, Arlene came uncorked," Rella said. "I honestly thought she was going to call the cops. Not certain why she didn't follow through. Maybe Rain talked her out of it."

"Interesting. When I dated Rain, she rarely mentioned her family, saying they lived out of state," Seven told us.

"You'll be happy to know the writing gig is retired again." Harper giggled.

Grey gave her the evil eye, and she laughed more. He turned to me. "Wanted you to know that we hired a new forensic computer investigator who promises he can turn around our jobs faster than the old guy. First up, he's looking into Stella's accounts."

I'd also been looking and needed to do more research. Maybe this guy could find out where the money had been funneled to and who owned those accounts.

Grey brought up Cara, wanting to know if I'd found out anything new.

I'd made a couple of calls since we talked. "I know that she's a fill-in bartender and goes to whatever location needs her. But no one's been willing to give out information over the phone as to when she'll be showing up, and it's unclear if they even know."

"Riggs has been beating the streets and not coming up with anything," Grey said. "He's tried bribing the neighbors and found the information to be worthless, which has him frustrated. He thinks they're doing it on purpose."

"I've got a new plan if anyone would like to hear it." Grey and Seven stared at me, *well?* on their faces. Maybe I should have prefaced that with *it's in the preliminary stages*. "The club Cara works for has three locations. I thought I'd take Harper and/or Rella, whoever's free and wants to go, and hit up one club at a time. In the past, she's worked opening shift, and I thought I'd start there."

"And once you get there?" Harper asked.

"If Cara isn't behind the bar, then I'll leave. Maybe sit down and have a drink first. That should give her enough time to show up if she's on the schedule."

"I'll go." Seven pointed to himself.

"I think it's better if it's just us girls. That way, I can reassure her that we're there to help." I tried to ignore Seven's glare. "In all the drama about Trace, I almost forgot that I got a number for the Evelyn woman. Ran a check, and it's a burner, so wasn't able to get an address. I did get a call record but haven't had time to check the numbers out."

The conversation got off work and stayed there until it was time to go home.

Seven stood. "I have an announcement. I'm

going to be the one backing Avery up. It makes sense since she's my girlfriend and it's WD's case. If anyone has an objection—tough."

Harper and Rella grinned at him.

Grey saluted.

Seven hooked one arm through mine and the other around Rella and walked us out. He dropped me off first.

"You can forget doing anything reckless," he said when he came back. "That includes making the rounds of strip clubs."

"Did some thinking while you were walking Rella to her door?" I was happy Seven had volunteered and would feel safer if he was close by. "The day the three of us went to Stella's neighborhood, we mic'd up so I could hear every word, since I really did sit in the car. In addition, Harper wore a camera pin on her clothing so I could watch what was happening on her phone. I'll call in the morning and ask to borrow all that stuff."

"Hold off on that until you hear what I've got." He gave me a crafty smile. "I've got these pens that are cameras and mics in one. They record everything and store it on a memory card, and you don't need to worry that the camera's noticeable. All you need to do is wear a blouse that has a front pocket." Seven went into the kitchen, where he'd left his briefcase on the island. I followed. He opened the lid, withdrew the pens, still in their original packaging, and handed me one.

I flipped it over and read the directions. "This looks like it would work for what we want. You don't mind waiting in the car?"

"As long as we stay hooked up and I can hear and see everything going on. If for some reason, the connection goes south or there's trouble, which I doubt, I'm coming in."

Seven removed the pens from the packaging and inserted the batteries. He hooked one to the neckline of my dress and opened his computer, installing the app. We spent a while playing with them, until we were comfortable with how they worked.

I leaned in and kissed him. "Happy we're doing this together."

Chapter Thirty-Six

The club opened at eleven, and I timed it for us to get there right as they opened so I could ask a couple of questions before customers arrived. No clue what to wear, so I chose a sundress—the only one I had with a pocket on the bodice—and sandals, and spent a few minutes adjusting the pen in the mirror.

Once we were in the car and headed out, I inputted the address on Seven's phone and hung it in the holder.

"Did you call and make sure Cara's going to be at one of these locations today?" Seven asked.

"They don't answer before they open. Doesn't matter anyway because when I tried various ways of finding out if she worked there, the first time, I was told, 'Personal calls not allowed.' I waited and called back, asking for the bar on the pretext I'd left my wallet, and that time, the person went and checked, apologized that it wasn't turned in, and refused to tell me anything about Cara. I tried all three locations, and not one of them would even verify that she was employed there."

"They're protective of their employees. We

could get lucky and Cara will be behind the bar. If not, take cash. Oftentimes, it's easy to tell if someone will be receptive. Know that it gets billed back to Riggs." He handed me his wallet. "Take a couple of hundreds. One alone should get you something, and if it's good info and you need more, then add to the pot."

"You got any tips for me?"

"You're a good judge of character... if you sense trouble of any kind—though I don't expect there to be any, as these clubs don't allow it—say my name, and I'll be in in a second."

The drive took longer than anticipated. I'd expected some seedy area, but it was on a busy street in a commercial zone, surrounded by a variety of other businesses. He turned into the driveway of the purple-and-white building, a neon woman lounging on her side taking up a corner of the roof, and had to pull around the back to park.

Seven pulled me closer and kissed me. "Remember the code word: Seven."

"I think I can remember." I got out and walked through the open double glass doors, instantly hit by the blaring music. It was a wide-open space, the circular stage in the middle empty at the moment. Except for one man at the bar nursing a beer, there were no other customers. The bartender wasn't Cara but another scantily clad young woman. I walked to the opposite end of the bar.

The bartender placed a cocktail napkin in front of me, a practiced smile on her face, "What can I get you?"

I already had one of the bills from Seven in my hand and held it out. "I'm Cara's sister and wanted to know when her next shift is."

She took the money and pocketed it. "She got fired yesterday. Boss man doesn't like it when you show up drunk."

I imagined not. "I've been trying to track her down because I know she's been having a hard time and I want to help."

The bartender snorted at "hard time." She shrugged and was about to step away.

In my ear, Seven said, "Ask if she knows where Cara lives."

"Wait." I held out another bill. "You got a forwarding for Cara?"

"You're not going to like it," she said, pocketing the bill. "There's a trailer park down the road." She pointed to the north. "She's shacked up with Billy Ed, who's old and creepy but known for paying the bills. He likes them young." She made a face. "His *relationships* don't usually last long."

A man walked behind the bar, a big box in his hands, and set it down. She turned her attention to him, and I slipped out the door.

"Would love to know what happened between Cara and Riggs that she won't even talk to him," I said, getting into the car. "I had a few more questions for the bartender, but the guy showing up ended that opportunity."

"We'll get our own answers." Seven merged back into traffic, staying to the right, both of us on the lookout for the trailer park. "If it weren't for the mystery over the whereabouts of the kid, Grey and I would've told Riggs to take his business elsewhere. This one's messy."

You had to be on the lookout or you'd miss the wooden "Trailer Court" sign hanging from a chain-link fence, the arrow underneath pointing north. Thanks to one more sign, we made a right and continued down the street, turning at the dilapidated guard shack and weathered welcome sign that signaled the entrance.

A large bulletin board in front of the office showed street after street of mobile homes, and based on what we'd seen so far, you could stick your hand out the door and touch the one next to you.

Seven parked, leaving the engine running. "I'm going to run in and ask which way to Billy Ed's." He got out and tucked his head back inside. "Keep it locked."

I didn't get his code word. If he said my name, did I run in or call 911? I didn't have long to think on it, as he was back in two minutes.

"I got a freebie." He slid behind the wheel. "Down to the end, turn right, and next to the outhouses."

The place was quiet, the road free of cars and

pedestrians. The trailers differed in size and condition, and there didn't appear to be a rule about how much junk you could cram into the small strip that ran along one side of each trailer.

Seven parked in front of a pool area with the water drained and the gate chained. "This place has plenty of potential; not sure why the owner doesn't spruce it up."

"My guess is that it brings a great return on investment as-is, so the mindset is generally why spend the money? I've had a few clients with real estate investments, and you can't convince them that a few bucks spent would bring bigger returns."

"I'm sorry that you've had to put a hold on what you like to do."

"I didn't think anything could surpass my love of numbers, but these outings with you have me rethinking what I want to do." Of late, I'd been giving thought to juggling both, but it was too early to share that. "Here I go." I reached for the door handle.

Seven tugged me back. "Not so fast. I don't want Billy Ed getting an eyeful of you and thinking you're next for his harem."

"You can escort me as long as you lose the scary face and stand back. Let me do the talking."

We walked up the driveway to the lime-green aluminum trailer. I guessed it to be damn old and no larger than a postage stamp, the overhang that covered the driveway larger than the home itself. We both halted and gawked at the silver Lamborghini parked in front.

"I'm thinking it's stolen."

I smacked Seven's arm. "I don't understand. If you can afford…" I pointed to the car. "Then why…?" I stared at the trailer.

"Priorities." Seven smirked.

"Remember…" I turned up the corners of my mouth.

"Got it." He gave me a peck on the lips.

I continued across the gravel and checked out the solid metal door with two small windows at the top. I knocked, the door reverberating under my knuckles, and stepped back so it wouldn't hit me in the face when it opened. Good thing, since it flew open.

Even though it was going on afternoon, Cara was clad in a silk shortie robe and appeared confused, resting up against the door jamb.

"I don't know if you remember me or not." I wished now that I'd given more thought to what I'd say.

"This really isn't a good time." Cara rubbed the sleep from her unfocused eyes, entirely too pale.

"If you'd give me a few minutes, I won't bother you again. I promise that whatever is said will be kept confidential."

Cara looked over her shoulder, stepped outside, and closed the door so softly, it barely made a click. She slid into a pair of flip-flops next to the door and trudged to the front, sitting on an empty planter box.

"Who's he?" Cara motioned to Seven, who'd backed up to the end of the driveway.

"Husband." I heard him laugh in my ear and shifted slightly so he'd have a close-up of Cara. "I don't know what happened between you and Riggs—"

"My fault." Cara covered her face with her hands and took a breath. "I'm always promising myself to make better decisions, and I always fall short," she said on a sigh. "I thought he wanted to take River away from me, and I have enough problems on that front. I trusted him once, but now? I don't know him, and I'm pretty sure he wouldn't like the new me."

"Riggs would like to make sure that you and River are doing okay and wants to get to know his son. If you're moving forward with Mr. Ed here…" I nodded toward the louvered window.

"It's Billy Ed Perry. He prefers Billy."

Got it.

"Billy knows nothing about River and would toss me out if I suggested bringing my kid here, even if I could get him back. In case you haven't guessed, my life is a hot mess, and there's no fixing it, at least anytime soon." Cara clasped her shaking hands. "Everything didn't fall apart at once; it happened gradually, and then I couldn't put it back together."

"I really would like to help you."

"Why?"

"I see the sadness when you mention your son. If it's possible, I'd like to help reunite the two of you. Is he with family?"

"I wish. They disowned me a long time ago. I called once, my mom answered, and I didn't have the nerve to say, 'Hey, my life's a mess.' I chickened out and hung up."

"Last time we talked, you mentioned a woman named Evelyn. Is she the one that has River?" I asked.

"I thought Evelyn was a friend. She offered to look after River while I worked. I got it together for a while and then went off on a bender, and after that, she refused to give him back. On the one hand, I don't blame her; on the other, I hate her. I always managed to hold my life together when River was my focus, no matter how bad it got. Without him, I just don't give a damn. When Riggs finds out… That's more hate that I can't deal with." Cara started to cry.

Seven came over and handed her a wad of Kleenex, which she took, and stepped back.

I waited for her to pull herself together. "Does Evelyn have a legal right to River? Did you sign anything?"

"No way. She used the threat of calling Social Services to keep me from trying to take him back. Then it's anyone's guess where he'd end up, and I for sure wouldn't see him again. She reminded me constantly that unfit mothers don't get custody."

"What does Evelyn have on you that she could ensure you lose your son? Even if she did call, it's their job to reunite kids with their parents."

"When I got arrested, she cut me off, threatening to call Social Services if I tried to contact my son. It was the proof she needed that I'm a drunk, and that's not far from the truth. I tell myself I can give it up but find an excuse to drink every day."

"Is it worth it to you to get sober to get River back?"

"Evelyn would still call Social Services, and I can't bear to have him end up in foster care. He'd hate me."

Seven made the short trek from the end of the driveway, standing in front of Cara. "Do you love your son?" Not waiting for an answer, he continued in a gentler tone, "You need to step up and take all the help that's offered before your son is lost to you forever. I don't know what Evelyn's game is, but it can't be good."

"She can't have kids of her own, and I know she loves River. She has a girl that she calls her daughter living with her, whose mother shows up for a visit every other weekend. She lets people believe that the girl is her biological child. I never did get the whole story."

"If you want River back, you need to start by getting sober. That would be a good start to showing you're a fit parent." I rubbed her shoulder.

"Riggs could be your biggest asset in getting River back," Seven said. "He'd be by your side no matter who came after you, shielding you both. A judge would look favorably on giving custody to the biological father, and I know he'd never keep your son from you."

"I'd need to get out of here. Billy's been nice to me, not asking questions, but we drink all day and night." The ravages of alcohol showed in her eyes and on her face.

"Let me make a call," I said and stepped away, calling Rella. I lucked out, and she wasn't in a meeting and took my call. I explained about Cara.

"Depending on the degree of her dependency, going cold turkey isn't good on the body. It can cause other health issues, and some of them are life-threatening."

"What do you suggest?" I asked.

"I'll text you a phone number to give Cara. When she's serious and ready to get sober, have her call, and they'll get her into a sober living program. Treatment can take thirty to ninety days. After that, she should think about joining a support program for the times she needs someone to listen to her and tell her when she's full of it."

"You're amazing."

"Well, look at you." Rella humphed. "Keep me

in the loop on Cara's response, and I'll let you know if she calls. Remember: she's the one who has to make the call."

We hung up, and I went over to the car. I fished a notepad out of my purse, ripped off a sheet, and scribbled down the number Rella sent. I walked back over to Seven and Cara, knowing from my earpiece that they hadn't talked while I was gone.

I handed Cara the paper. "When you're ready to get sober, call this number, and they'll help you. For health reasons, it's not recommended that you go cold turkey."

Cara stared at the paper, then folded it up and stuck it in her pocket. "A year ago, I was accepted into a sober home up north that took kids and made the bad decision not to follow through."

"You have another opportunity here to turn your life around," I said. "I'd like to run a background check on Evelyn, find out more about her. That could help you avoid any problems she tries to throw at you." I opened my phone, asking for the woman's full name and address.

"I'm afraid of her," Cara whimpered after telling me.

"She's not going to know what I'm doing," I assured her and handed her my business card. "My cell number is on the back."

"What do you want to do about Riggs?" Seven asked. "He's very worried about you and River."

"If you want, we'll help you set up another get-together with him at a neutral place. Also know that I'll keep my promise not to say anything if that's what you prefer," I reminded her.

"What I've done hasn't been fair to Riggs. I didn't have the guts to confess all the ways I'd screwed up." Tears dripped down her cheeks, and she swatted them away.

"You need to conserve your energy to move forward, so let the recriminations go and focus on that," I said.

A man's voice called "Cara" several times from inside the trailer.

Cara stood. "I need time to think. I'll get back to you. I've got to go inside." She scrubbed her face on her sleeve and headed inside without a backward glance.

"Fifty-fifty whether we hear from her." Seven held out his hand to me, and we walked back to his SUV. "You know I didn't make the same promises you did. You check out this Evelyn broad, but if it's bad news, I'm not sitting on my hands."

"Just give Cara a few days to call. That's my advice and Rella's." I stared out the windshield, unable to wait for a view of the water. I needed a walk on the beach to blow the emotional day out of my head.

Chapter Thirty-Seven

Seven and I rode home in silence. I told him I needed to walk on the beach, and we both changed into shorts and went down to the sand together. We took a long hike up the beach to a hotel with an outside bar and, after perusing the menu, stayed for dinner. Neither of us wanted to walk back, so we climbed into a taxi that was dropping someone off.

We decided over coffee the next morning that we each had things to do at the office and would take separate cars. On my way in, Dixon called, his voice low. "There's a Stacy Davis here who wants to talk to you. Claims you didn't return her calls."

"That's because she didn't," a female voice yelled.

"She's right there, sounds like." I shook my head.

"Uh-huh."

"Tell Ms. Davis that I should be there in about ten minutes. Anything else you want to tell me, save it until after she's left. Which will be quick once I tell her I'm not taking any new clients."

After another vague response that I couldn't

make out, Dixon hung up. A minute later, my phone dinged with an incoming text from Dixon: *I think she broke in.*

One way to know for sure. I'll check the security tapes.

I got to the office and rode up in the elevator, thinking, *What if she did? Do I call the police?* I suppose that depended on whether she stole anything. If I hadn't had pending legal issues, I would've called whether she did or not. I threw the door open and saw that Stacy Davis had made herself comfortable in my chair. Dixon appeared overwhelmed, his brows permanently in his hairline. "I'm Avery English. We didn't have an appointment or I'd have been here." So much for professional and friendly.

"No we didn't, but since you didn't return my calls, I didn't know how else to get a meeting with you."

That was a lie because I always returned calls. "I'm sorry, but I'm not taking new clients." I pointed to my chair, and she took her time moving to the one in front of my desk. "I don't know what services you're looking for, but Dixon might be able to help you." He shook his head behind her back. Okay then.

"You obviously don't recognize me." She stared as though she wanted me to contradict her, but she was right—I knew I hadn't met her before.

"I'm one of Arlene's daughters. I'd like to start

off by apologizing for her behavior at the ice cream shop."

Arlene had two daughters? Stacy and Rain.

"You need to cut her some slack. Mom's grieving heavily over the death of her best friend, Stella."

No actually, I don't. Grief didn't mean you got to scream *murderer* at someone in public when they hadn't been tried and convicted.

"Stella was the most amazing woman, and everyone that knew her loved her. There isn't anyone that wasn't hit hard by her death."

"She was quite the woman." I smiled fondly.

"The reason I'm here is that I know you managed her money, and I was hoping that you could go over my portfolio and give me suggestions." Stacy took a folder from her purse and pushed it across the desk.

I eyed it cautiously before ignoring it. "How did you get into the office?"

"The door was unlocked." Stacy flashed a practiced smile. "I came in, figuring you were in the bathroom, or close by, and made myself a cup of coffee." She tittered, as though her actions were reasonable.

Dixon was shaking his head again. Both of us knew she was a liar, as neither of us left the door unlocked when we weren't in the building.

"Your mother accused me in front of witnesses of murdering Stella. I'm surprised that you'd come here. If she found out, I'm certain it would upset her greatly."

"That's just nonsense. I'm sure you'll be found not guilty," Stella said, her voice ringing with insincerity.

"You're probably not aware that the court has barred me from working on client accounts, so I won't be able to offer my services."

Stacy shoved the folder closer. "How about a couple of tips on the side? I mean, who would know? There's just the three of us here. I won't tell, and I'm sure your son wouldn't say anything."

I quickly did the math. If I'd gotten knocked up when I was four, then maybe I could be Dixon's mother. Clearly, this woman didn't give a thought to what came out of her mouth. I pasted on a smile that strained at the sides to stay in place. "I'm not going to violate the terms of my bail," I said firmly.

Stacy turned to Dixon, and he cut her off. "I don't have my license, so it's illegal for me to handle client money. My mom can easily refer you to someone else."

I could see the amusement dancing in his eyes, but still, I'd so get him back for that one.

"My mother told me about some friend of yours wanting to write an article or something about Stella. If you'd give me her number, I'd be happy to make myself available for questions. And a byline of course."

Of course. "When your mother confronted me

at the ice cream shop, the reporter was attempting to interview me, but due to my pending case, I wasn't able to be that helpful. As for her number, she tracked me down, and it was a waste of her time."

Stacy made some kind of mewing sound that had Dixon and me staring. Maybe she meant it to sound supportive. It didn't.

"I did have her card, but I think I threw it out. If you give me your number, I'll check and, if I find it, text it to you later." I picked up a pen, waiting for her to rattle off her number. She just stared. "Your number?"

"It's an old-school house phone. You'll have to leave a message." She grabbed another pen and my pad, wrote it down, and passed it back.

A landline? I suppose there were still a few of those around. "I'm sorry that we couldn't be of any help." *Take the hint and leave now.*

"Mom," Dixon piped up, "the contractor's going to be here in five minutes. Did you print out the list you need to give him?"

"Thanks for the reminder, hon."

Dixon grinned and stood, striding over to Stacy and handing her his business card. "If you have any financial questions, I'd be happy to check into referring you to someone else. I'll escort you to the elevator."

Caught off guard, Stacy finally stood, grabbing her folder. "Be sure to call. We should have lunch." She moved slowly to the door.

Dixon escorted her out, and from the length of time it took him to get back, he must have ridden down in the elevator with her.

"Well played, dude." I clapped as he came back into the office.

"I'd have never even thought of that maneuver if I hadn't seen it on TV. I didn't quite carry it off in the same fierce fashion as the actor, but it got her out of here." Dixon laughed. "I didn't believe her story about wanting financial advice. I wonder what her game really was."

I had my laptop open, busy banging on the keys. "According to the security video, a locksmith met her out front and got her into the building and this office, where she snooped through the drawers in your desk and mine. She only took a seat about a minute before you arrived." I flipped the screen around for Dixon.

"I wondered why the door was cracked open—probably so she could hear the elevator doors open." Dixon restarted the footage. "It doesn't look like she stole anything."

"I'd like to know what she was looking for." I picked up my phone and searched for a number for the locksmith Stacy used. The name had been clearly visible on the side of the van, so it didn't take me long to find and call the number. I introduced myself, then said, "You sent a serviceman to my office building this morning, and I'd like to speak to the man."

"That was me, Miss Avery. My name's Hank.

How can I help you?"

I told him that a woman had apparently impersonated me to gain entry to the building and my office.

"Been in business twenty years, and this is a first. She had identification, and the picture matched."

"Do you mind if I ask how she paid you?" I asked.

"Cash. I didn't find that odd either."

"I appreciate you answering my questions. Should she call back, call the cops on her."

"Might I suggest that instead of using a key, you put in a security pad with each of the tenants of the building getting their own code?"

"That's a great idea." Especially since we all used the garage entrance. It would keep anyone from doing this again. "There are two other tenants here. Let me run it by them, and I'll get back to you."

"One more thing—I made her a key. So you need to get the locks changed ASAP." Hank assured me once again that he'd thought it was a straight-up job, adding, "You can bet I'll be more careful in the future," before he hung up.

I repeated the conversation to Dixon while reviewing the footage. Then I moved forward to when Stacy left the parking lot and zoomed in on her license plate, writing down the number. "Hank would be easy to put something over on—he didn't know who he was talking to but just took my word and was free with information."

"You should call the cops," Dixon said.

"I'd probably already be on the phone if her mother weren't the so-called eyewitness, no matter that her story hasn't held up. Get this, Stacy's sister is Seven's ex. I'm not going to do anything until I talk to Seven. I'd do it now, but they had a meeting this morning."

"If she comes back when you're not here, what do you want me to do?" Dixon asked.

"My guess is Stacy will be sure to come back when no one is here, because she has a key and doesn't know that we know. Maybe instead of getting the locks changed today, we should let her come back and find out what she wants."

"Not sure there's anything left for her to snoop through." Dixon had reviewed the tapes a couple of times.

"It takes big ones to do what she did, not to mention criminal tendencies, and that scares me. I say we call it a day and work from home until we get this figured out."

We both picked up our briefcases and rode down in the elevator.

Chapter Thirty-Eight

I drove straight home. The whole morning had creeped me out. I'd felt safe knowing that no one could just show up at my office, and never thought about them breaking in. Changes were needed at the office—currently, in order to gain access, you needed to ring the bell. All of us had access to the front door camera, making it easy to buzz in a client. None of us had ever considered the possibility of someone going to the lengths Stacy had to break in. How to prevent this from happening in the future? I needed to talk to a locksmith and figure out the options. It wouldn't be Hank.

I rode the elevator upstairs, headed straight to my bedroom and changed into a t-shirt dress, then grabbed my laptop out of my briefcase and headed out to the balcony, where Arco launched himself onto the footstool and curled up around my feet. My fingers raced across the keyboard, easily finding out that Stacy's older model Toyota was registered to her mother's address. It didn't take much more digging to come up with the information needed to run a complete background check. That also showed her address to be her mother's, and I wondered if she lived there or was just having her mail sent there. She didn't have much in the way of credit, and what she did have was low-rated. No criminal record. What did she want with me?

Curious to know if Rain also lived there, I ran a check on her. Then looked up her address, since I wasn't familiar with the area, and it was a mailbox drop. Who knows where she actually lived.

Scrolling through my phone, I typed in the information that Cara gave me on Evelyn Dibbs and discovered that she'd been a widow for a few years. Not a lot in the way of outstanding debts—her house was paid off, and her score high enough she could get a signature loan. And no criminal record. It was possible that Evelyn wanting River had to do with her genuinely caring about the boy.

I picked up my phone and called Seven. "If you want in on the latest, you'll need to get home early for dinner. I'm thinking pizza and having the rest of our guests bring their own drinks."

"I'm on my way now."

"Issue the same invite to Grey, and I'll call Harper and Rella." We hung up, and I called them both. They accepted but wanted a hint as to what was going on, which I didn't give them.

I ordered two different kinds of pizza, covering our favorites, and a large antipasto salad from our favorite Italian restaurant not far down the beach, then set the table outside—nothing like an enjoyable view. I knew I'd be needing my laptop for show-and-tell and stuffed it into my carry bag, setting it on a chair inside.

Seven came through the door, set down his briefcase, and headed straight to me, picking me up and whirling me around, then setting me down with a kiss. "You sounded stressed?"

"How about a beer?"

He groaned. "That bad? I'm not one to turn down a cold one." He took my hand, and we went into the kitchen together.

"I'll hold off until everyone's here… and after a shot or six." I slid onto a stool. "You've got choices, since I know you want answers—the slimmed-down version now, or wait for our guests and get the details. Better yet, you tell me about the new client and whether they signed on the dotted line."

"It's an old client that moved their business north; now they're back and want an upgrade to their security system. They also had a few personnel issues that they wanted to discuss. We took them to lunch and pitched them a plan that they signed off on."

I leaned forward and kissed him.

"The phone rang a few times today with referrals, so business is only getting better."

The doorbell rang.

"Must be Rella. Harper would pick the lock," Seven said.

"Rella has a key."

The door opened, and I shot Seven a *told you so* look as they all trooped in at once.

Not long after that, the food arrived. We laughed, drank, and ate. By mutual silent agreement, we didn't stir up the drama until we were finished.

Once finished, Seven and I cleared the table while the others joked about how domestic we looked. We stayed at the table but adjusted our chairs to enjoy the sky darkening over the water.

Eventually, I got up and retrieved my laptop, setting it on the table. "Any word on Cara?" I asked Rella.

"According to my counselor friend, it can take time for someone to come around and accept that they need help."

"A little bit of good news—I ran a background check on Evelyn, and no red flags," I said.

"I talked with my legal counsel and got a handle on what would be required going forward," Rella said. "There are several options, depending on what Cara decides."

"Let's hope she gets in touch soon," Seven grouched.

"Big news of the day…" I shot Seven a phony smile that had him doing a double take and probably wishing he'd gotten details upfront. "Dixon called this morning, frantic that a woman had, as it turned out, broken into the office and was waiting to speak to me about my services.

You'll never guess who she turned out to be—Stacy Davis." That didn't register with any of them. I launched into a more thorough rundown of events.

The anger radiated off Seven like he wanted to strangle someone, thankfully not me. "A sister? How long did I date Rain? Months. Turns out I didn't know much about her."

"Time to upgrade the security," Grey growled.

"My dad didn't think it was a necessary expense," Harper said, and shifted her gaze to Grey. "As I recall, you didn't tell him he was full of it because you were hot for his daughter and trying to impress him. Even though I told you I was a sure thing and it wasn't necessary."

Grey gave her a quick kiss.

"I'm authorizing it." At everyone's raised eyebrows, I added, "I'm the building manager, and if you need proof, I have it in writing. I prepared a document, pointed out the advantages of having someone on site, and badgered Harper's dad to sign or I'd hound the hell out of him. He and I both knew he didn't want to be bothered with pesky calls. Every time I see him, I remind him that I want to buy the building, and he gives me that *but you're a girl* look. Wait until he finds out I'm a mom." I told them about Stacy's bitchy comment, and everyone laughed. "Dixon was quite amused." I filled them in on her background check, which didn't raise any red flags except for bad credit.

"It did surprise me that she uses her mother's address. No way of knowing if she actually lives there."

"Maybe this is where I resurrect my writer persona and call to set up an interview," Harper suggested. "It would be interesting to see if this Stacy actually has any useful information on Stella's murder, which I doubt or she'd have gone to the cops. So what does she want? Just the byline?"

Grey leveled a glare at Harper, expressing what he thought of the idea. She winked at him and got a head-shake in return.

Rella said, "If we're going to do this—"

Seven snorted. "You've all lost your minds."

She ignored him. "I suggest we meet at a coffee place. Who passes up a free cup, especially if it's overpriced?"

"Stacy struck me as being caught up in the excitement of being in the middle of a murder investigation," I said. "If she thought I was the one to pull the trigger, she didn't say, unlike her mother."

"Stacy belongs in jail," Seven barked. "And just so you know, it's not too late to put her there. A copy of the tape to the cops is all it would take. The locksmith backs up the story."

I shook my head at him.

"How about we—" Harper wiggled her finger between herself and Rella. "—interview her ASAP. Then you can turn the tape over to the cops or have Floyd pay her a call and scare the devil out of her. He seems to enjoy that kind of work."

"That reminds me," I said. "I need to check in with Trace and make sure everything's going good for him and Matt."

"I know." Rella raised her hand. "Talked to Rosa yesterday, and first thing she said was, 'They're such sweet boys.'"

"That's good to hear," I said. "I didn't want them moving from one storage room to another. I'd have brought them here first."

"What have we decided?" Harper asked.

"We haven't," Grey snapped. "I don't like the idea of you confronting Stacy. She went to a lot of trouble and expense to break into the office. Who knows what she'll do next. And what about her sister, Rain? They're a pack of trouble."

"I agree with Grey," Seven said. "But if you're going to do this interview—and I'm not convinced it's worth wasting your time—I'll make myself available to sit at a nearby table at the coffee shop. Under no circumstances do you leave with Stacy, or anyone else who contacts you saying whatever to get an interview, no matter what their story is."

"I'm going," I said, "and will once again stay hunkered down in the back seat. You two need to wear these cool pens of Seven's."

Seven told them about the pens and how they worked. Not surprisingly, Harper and Rella both wanted one.

The guys weren't happy about it, but we agreed that Harper and Rella would do the interview. I took out my phone and texted Harper the contact information. She'd get back to Rella and me with a time and date, and we'd all ride together.

Chapter Thirty-Nine

It took a few days for Harper to set up a meeting with Stacy, who didn't hesitate when it came to getting together at The Grinder, a favorite coffee spot across from the beach.

As it turned out, it was going to be a busy day. We had the meeting with Stacy in the afternoon, and Riggs had requested a meeting in the morning. He'd told Grey it was about River and that he was moving forward with getting custody.

"Does this mean that he and Cara have talked?" I asked.

"It was a short conversation, as Riggs was at work and couldn't talk."

"If not, I'm not comfortable breaking my promise unless something's changed."

"Come to the meeting. We'll find out what's going on, and then we can figure out what course of action to take."

I couldn't shake the feeling that I should've handled the situation differently. Better, somehow.

I drove myself to WD and arrived after everyone else. I bypassed my office, knowing that Dixon was talking to a new client and didn't need me checking on him.

Riggs nodded when I walked in, so he knew I'd been invited to the meeting.

I sat on the other side of Seven, not wanting to insinuate myself into whatever was about to unfold.

"Cara finally contacted me," Riggs told us. "We ended up meeting and spent several hours over two days talking, sharing everything, some good and some not so much. After a lot of discussion, she made the decision to check into rehab and has made a commitment to getting sober. I told her I'd stand by her."

"That's good news." Grey smiled encouragingly.

"Thanks to Rella Cabot, we met with a lawyer and a social worker and worked out the legal issues. Rella's an amazing woman. I'm told that you're all friends."

I nodded and sighed inwardly, happy to hear that Rella was involved—she'd make sure they got good advice. Her foundation was totally equipped to handle this kind of situation.

"I was proud of Cara when she came totally clean about her situation to the lawyer and social worker," Riggs said. "Though it was hard listening to it a second time. I can't imagine what she went through living it."

"What about River?" I asked.

"Legal papers were drawn up and signed;

we're doing everything by the book. I don't want any mistakes that could end up taking River away from us," Riggs said adamantly. "It's the social worker's recommendation that I start by arranging regular visits with River, giving him a chance to get to know me so he won't think he's being taken away by a stranger. Although we could go that route. I'd like to meet Evelyn before deciding, since Cara didn't have anything nice to say about her. I'm just hoping that she doesn't take off with my son. I'd like her house watched until I'm certain that she's going to be agreeable to the process."

"I don't know that Evelyn can just run away," I interjected. "She has stable roots in the community and a girl she considers a daughter in junior high school."

"Cara seems convinced that she'll do just that," Riggs insisted.

"If that's the case, then you should do an immediate transfer," Grey advised.

"I don't have legal authority… yet. I do have an upcoming court date, and it's up in the air as to what might happen. The social worker couldn't guarantee anything, since it won't be her case."

"I'm certain that Evelyn's going to be upset that the biological father is now on the scene, but would she risk going to jail when she has another child to care for?" Seven mused.

"If you want round-the-clock surveillance, I've

got a couple of men I can assign to watch the house," Grey said.

"If Evelyn does decide to pack up and leave, I'd expect you to inform the cops immediately and let them handle it," Riggs said.

If that happened, then River would go into foster care until his living situation had been sorted out. I didn't see an easy solution, and my stomach pounded in agreement as I hoped that Evelyn would make the transition an easy one. There wasn't any reason I needed to be part of this discussion, and I was happy when my phone dinged with a message. It was Dixon letting me know he'd be out of the office for a couple hours.

I stood. "I'm sorry, something's come up. It was nice seeing you again. Hope everything works out," I directed to Riggs. I ignored Seven's questioning glance and picked up my briefcase, not sure where I was going when I went out the door. I ended up in my office, putting my head on the desk.

My phone rang. I took it out and groaned at the screen, seeing it was Cruz's office. I didn't want to, but answered anyway.

"This is Mr. Campion's assistant, Susie. The court has set a date for jury selection." She told me the date and time.

I reluctantly wrote down the information and squeezed my eyes shut.

"Cruz will need you to come in that morning, and he'll go over a few things. Be sure to dress professionally. I'll be sending you an email."

After she hung up, I wondered if she'd noticed that I hadn't said anything after hello. So much for the case getting dismissed. I'd looked up the percentages for getting a not-guilty verdict, and they were slim. Juries were prone to think you were guilty just because charges had been brought. I hid out in my office until it was time to meet Harper and Rella.

Chapter Forty

We'd decided that I'd park close to the coffee shop and stay in my car. It was easy to find a parking space that afforded a view of the outside patio, which was where Harper and Rella planned to sit. The door opened, and they came out, coffee in hand, Stacy behind them, and sat at a table that bordered the sidewalk.

Trusting in my hat and dark glasses to conceal my identity, I didn't bother ducking out of sight. As it happened, I wouldn't have needed to anyway, since Stacy didn't look around. Her voice came clearly through the earpiece.

She couldn't contain her excitement over being interviewed. "My mom and I both believe that Avery English did it, and anything we can do to help you prove it, we will. Mom's been devastated by her best friend's death. It would crush her if that woman walked away after all the pain she's caused."

I leaned back against the seat, shaking my head. I'd bet that Rain was on the same team, though her name hadn't been mentioned. She'd see my incarceration as clearing the path to Seven.

"You sound so convinced. Why is that?" Harper asked.

"It was my mom who saw Avery bolting from Stella's house the morning she was found. I can't imagine walking into that kind of scene."

"I heard that she retracted her story and refused to cooperate with the prosecutor's office," Rella said.

"Poor Mom was so distraught that when she talked to the prosecutor, she collapsed under the pressure."

"If she wasn't able to answer their questions, I imagine that anything she'd have to say going forward would be discounted," Harper said.

"My mom would never say anything untruthful when someone's life is on the line. She may have mixed up a detail or two, but that happens." *No big deal* in her tone.

"It's my understanding that your mother wasn't able to identify Avery in a lineup," Harper said in a testy tone.

"When we're done here, I'm calling and suggesting another lineup. Mom's calmed down considerably, and there shouldn't be any problem picking her out now."

I groaned.

"Since you were the one who suggested this meeting, do you have any actual evidence as to who committed the crime?" Harper asked.

"Besides the information you gave us about your mom," Rella added tactfully.

"We all know who did it, now to make sure she's found guilty. Anything I can do to help with that, I'm available."

"It would be illegal for any of us to interfere in the case," Rella cautioned.

"That's no fun." Stacy giggled.

"I have another appointment." Harper stood abruptly. "My advice would be not to do anything that could land you in jail."

"Would you mind keeping me up to date on your story?"

"One or the other of us will give you call when it's ready to be published," Rella said diplomatically.

Stacy left with a wave, turning into the parking lot. Harper and Rella stepped behind a couple of potted plants and waited for her to leave.

"I was about ready to strangle her," Harper said. "People like her who decide something is true with no evidence scare me. Let's hope she never gets on a jury."

"Stacy's pulled to the end of the parking lot," I told them. "The honk you just heard was the car behind her telling to her to get going." I waited until they were back in the car, then pulled out behind them. "See you back at home."

Chapter Forty-One

It had been a quiet couple of days. For me anyway. I had nothing to do except worry over my upcoming court appearance. That morning, Seven had left early — another new client — and rather than sit around at home and sulk, I decided to go to the office and do it there. On the way, I decided to go through the coffee drive-thru — a shot of espresso was just what I needed to get my edge back and ward off tiredness from lack of sleep.

At the last minute, I decided to go inside and easily found a place to park. I placed my order and went out, sitting on the patio. It didn't take me long to get bored with people-watching, and I hurriedly downed the rest of my coffee, tossing the cup in the trash.

Rather than go to the office and do nothing, I decided to go back home and walk on the beach. I was uncertain how long the trial would last — who knew when I would be able to do it again.

Back in the parking lot, I reached for the door handle of my Porsche and was pushed against the side panel, my face smooshed against the glass. I managed to whirl back around at least partially and found myself staring into the face of a grinning woman who'd covered her eyes with large dark sunglasses. Her arm flew back and swung down, something glittering in her hand. I attempted to wiggle away, but there was a sudden sharp pain in my neck and my legs went weak. I opened my mouth to scream but nothing came out, and my attempts to kick at the woman were weak and didn't connect.

I was vaguely aware of her opening the back door to the car parked next to mine. Balling her hand in my top, she half-dragged me the foot or so and threw me into the back seat. A cloth bag dropped over my head, and she dragged my hands behind my back and tied them tightly. The whole time, I attempted to fight her, but my attempts were futile as I grew weaker. Whatever she'd drugged me with was making it harder and harder to move.

I shook my head back and forth in an attempt to get the bag off. My breath caught in my throat, I kicked out, but only connected with the back seat.

"Stop struggling!" She jerked my head back and slugged me so hard my head flew back. "Make this easy on yourself. One more stupid move on your part, and I will shoot you. And trust me, you won't enjoy bleeding to death."

I felt something cold pressed against the side of my neck and clamped my mouth shut, since I doubted that anyone could hear my cries and didn't want to risk a bullet. I nodded weakly. A moment later, I was given a hard shove off the seat onto the floor and lay face down, the hard hump on the floor poking me in the stomach.

First one door slammed, then another, followed by a clicking noise. "Always thought these kid safety locks were a pain until now." She started the car and backed out.

Kidnapped? Why? What was this all about? I spit out the fabric that had gotten caught in my mouth, trying for a calming breath in an attempt to clear my head. That didn't work, but at least there was enough air that I didn't pass out completely.

I squirmed from side to side, trying to find a comfortable position, but the small space made it impossible. I decided that I'd take any opportunity to get free of this woman, even if it meant one of us ended up dead. Preferably her. Though that would make it even harder to convince a jury that I wasn't a murderer.

I had no idea how much time passed. If I had to guess, I'd say we stayed somewhere in the Miami area, but that covered a lot of real estate. She certainly wasn't a speed demon, cruising the streets in a cautious fashion, probably knowing that if she got pulled over, there was no reasonable explanation for having someone tied up on the floor.

Eventually, she cut the engine and got out, slamming the door and hitting the locks.

I waited for my door to open... and nothing. Wherever we were, it was quiet. If she was meeting up with someone, I couldn't hear voices. I was back to twisting around, the drug having begun to wear off.

The door opened, and a hand wrapped around my ankle and dragged me out, my face taking a beating. I cried out every time it made contact with the floor. My toes hit the ground. "Do what you're told, or I'll wrap a rope around you and drag you through the dirt. Now stand." Another tug on the back of my shirt. The back of my head made contact with the door frame, and I yelped in pain.

She led me forward a few steps, then gave me a hard shove. I tumbled backward, screaming, and landed hard on something metal. She planted her hands on my chest, thrust me back, and spread my legs over the sides of a flat platform. "I suggest you use those muscles of yours to keep from falling off. If not, I'll have to drag you through the weeds and rocks, and that will take a while."

It was a bumpy ride to wherever she was taking me. A couple of times, she hit obstacles and had to back up and go around, swearing the whole time. She hit a big bump that jarred every bone in my body, and then the ride smoothed out. It surprised me that I hadn't tumbled off. She stopped suddenly and backed up, then pushed forward several times, slamming into something hard. Then, pushing forward again, she came to a sudden stop, unhooked my legs, and shoved me off. I screamed again as I hit cement and rolled over into a shallow space, lying at an odd angle in the tight area, metal jutting into my back. I became aware I'd lost my shoes somewhere along the line. The bag was ripped off my head. Disoriented, I shook my head.

Chapter Forty-Two

I'd been pushed into a narrow trough that at one time might have held water. Now it held dirt and unidentified objects. I wasn't going to look too closely for fear of bugs. They'd have a feast in this place. The empty, filthy building might have been a processing plant at one time. Dirt and weeds covered the floor from wall to wall, and from the smell, it was clear no one had set foot in here in a long time. Accordion pipes jutted out from one of the walls and hung precariously into the center of the room. Overhead, they crisscrossed the ceiling, and it was clear that some were only still attached by a breath. The windows had been boarded over, the only opening in the far corner where a small glint of sunshine came through a three-foot wide rollup door rusted in the up position, giving a view of trees and more weeds.

The trough ran through the middle of the room and was barely a foot wide. I managed to just barely get into a sitting position, my hands still tied. Making a run for it would likely get me shot, if indeed the woman had a gun.

She reappeared, walking under the rollup door, and headed straight for me. I struggled not to flinch. Almost on top of me, she leaned down into my face and removed her sunglasses.

I stared into Stacy Davis's hard brown eyes. I made a dive for her in an attempted headbutt, but she was too quick and I got a fist to my right eye for my trouble. Anticipating that I'd make another move, she shoved me hard against the steel pipe that ran along one side of the trough.

Patience, I told myself, but it was hard, as my eye throbbed.

"Let's make these match." She drew back her fist and hit my other eye. "That was fun." She sucked in a deep breath. "Can't forget I need this to look like suicide. Case closed on the criminal charges. You think anyone will be boo-hooing over your death? Fat chance."

I wanted to scream, but it came out as a rasping sound. I mentally called her every obscenity I could think of. If looks could kill, I was certain she'd be dead. "I don't understand. I've never done anything to you. Is this some weird payback for Stella's death? You've got the wrong person. You will be caught, you know, because I've got friends who won't give up until they find you and make sure you rot in jail. Trust me, you won't like it there."

Stacy's dark eyes spit fire as she loomed over me, a muscle twitching in her jaw. "You done with your pitiful tirade?"

"Go f— yourself." I braced for physical retaliation and was surprised when she laughed instead.

"Get comfortable. You're going to be here a while. When I'm ready, I'll dump you out in the weeds. With any luck, you'll have been at least partially eaten before you're found, if you're ever found. As far as your threat about your friends goes, they'll never know what happened to you."

"Do I least get to know why?"

"When I'm damn good and ready." Stacy turned and crossed the room, going out the door.

I waited a long time for her to return. Eventually, I began to wonder if she'd left, but I hadn't heard a car starting. So I didn't know what the heck she was doing. Time passed—I didn't know how much. I couldn't hear a sound. I kept my eyes peeled for her return. Finally, I decided I had to at least try to escape. If death was imminent, having it happen sooner might be better. I managed to stagger to my feet, stumbling a couple times during the effort, and hobbled across the room, my feet scratched and bleeding. Finally, I made a leap through the door, the sunshine blinding.

For the first time that morning, luck was with me, as I was able to duck before Stacy bashed me in the head with a 2x4, which ended up grazing me instead. Still, it hurt like the devil.

"Back up and into your hole or I'll beat your

brains all over this warehouse." She wagged the board in my face.

I shuffled sideways and back into the building as quickly as I could while still managing to stay on my feet. The last thing I wanted was to go down in front of her. I stepped gingerly into the hole and sank down.

"Do that again, and the party's over." Stacy laughed, unamused. "I knew you'd make an attempt to escape. You made me wait long enough. Even if you were to get out of here, there's nowhere to go. There is a road, but far enough away that good luck getting there."

I hoped that when the end came, it was quick. But judging by the sheer hate in her eyes, probably not. I didn't know any certifiable people, but I'd bet I was looking into the eyes of one now.

She stared at me suspiciously as she stepped back and leaned against the wall.

I wasn't going to admit to her that she'd won my cooperation by sheer fear.

"Where are we?" I asked, biting back a wince at the pain in various parts of my body.

"You live in the Miami area long enough, you learn about all the fun places. This building was once a thriving company, but they went bankrupt. Apparently, no one was interested in picking up the land for a song, since it's rather remote."

"At least tell me why we're here." I'd never

experienced violence before and didn't know what I was supposed to be doing.

"The cops had you locked up; how is it you made bail, and for murder? I'd hoped for a speedy trial. A greedy woman, her older client — no jury would let you walk."

"You're doing this to avenge Stella's death?" I guess she didn't believe me when I'd told her a half-dozen times that I was innocent. "This is the wrong way to go about it."

"You really are stupid," Stacy drawled nastily. "I was tired of the news coverage, stories continuously popping up. Reporters, your friends nosing around the neighborhood asking questions… I know you three are friends, and I'm willing to bet you were somewhere close by while they were asking me questions. I made sure it was a waste of all our time." Her brown eyes shot sparks.

I sighed heavily. "You do know that my trial is starting in a couple of days? If you're right about it being an automatic guilty, why not wait? One-woman vigilante and you'll be the next to go to trial."

Stacy crossed her arms and glared. "I couldn't wait. I had to assure myself of the outcome."

"Why?" I stared at her formidable expression. "Did you kill Stella?"

"Ding, ding." She mimed ringing a bell. "Stupid girl gets a prize."

"Is that why your mother lied?" I asked in

disbelief. "And your sister, Rain, is she in on this too?"

"If you were a mother, you'd do anything for your children. We're very close and she doesn't want to lose me."

I wouldn't cover up murder.

"As for Rain, she doesn't care how she gets Seven back." Her smile slowly turned into a smirk.

In my searching, I hadn't found a link between Stacy and Stella. Her mother, on the other hand... I thought more than a few times that she might've been the one to pull the trigger but couldn't come up with a motive. "Do I get to hear why you killed Stella and framed me? We don't even know one another."

"Stella was getting older and having a hard time keeping her books up-to-date, and I fast-talked my way into coming over a few days a week to keep everything in order. Not my ideal job, but when you need the money... Thank goodness she didn't balk when I asked to be paid in cash, so when the cops came snooping around, there was no link to me," Stacy gloated.

"Needed money? You a shopper? What?"

"Gambling issues." Stacy made a sad face, looking anything but. "I ran up a rather large tab with Bene, and he was getting impatient. A girl does what she has to do."

"How are you paying back the money now, since you're still gambling?" I could guess, and I knew I was right from the hard glint in her eye.

"It's my responsibility to make sure his little friend is kept happy and satisfied." She'd begun to pace. "I'm basically on call."

So basically, you're ho-ing yourself out, I thought, but kept that to myself. Not wanting to venture farther down this road, I changed the subject back to Stella. "I'm guessing that you fleeced Stella and she caught on?"

"I knew something was up when she called, ordering me to come to her house, and now. My spidey senses kicked into overdrive, and without thinking about it, I pocketed a small handgun I'd stolen off her. That and a few other trinkets." Stacy appeared to be in a trance, reliving that night. "I was barely in the door when she confronted me, calling me a filthy thief and saying she was going to put me in jail and make sure I stayed there. She'd gotten her hands on a statement that came in the mail. The ones that came before that, I'd managed to photoshop in changes before showing them to her. The shortage on the new report was glaring. I sobbed and put on the show of a lifetime, but it didn't pierce her cold heart." Stacy dramatically wiped her dry eyes.

I struggled mightily to keep my disgust from showing.

"Funny, I thought I had all my bases covered, but Stella wasn't fooled for a second. I hated the old bag in that moment. I threw myself on her mercy, confiding that I had an addiction, which wasn't true, and needed help, anything but jail, thinking it would garner me sympathy. It takes time to overcome one's urges." Again, wiping her dry eyes. "Even reminded her that Mom was her good friend and that she couldn't do that to her. That didn't seem to register either. She reached for the phone to call the police, and I shot her. What else could I do? I couldn't go to jail."

I sighed for Stella. Had I known that she planned to confront the woman, I'd have told her to turn it over to the police, and if she had to confront her, then have them sitting in her office.

"Shot with her own gun, but I don't think she had time to realize it, as it happened so fast." Stacy smiled.

My back was killing me, but I didn't dare move an inch. The unhinged look in her eyes scared me. "Why me?"

"Why not you? Stella's financial adviser, who she thought was the second coming with all the money you made her? It set my teeth on edge to hear her going on about you. So when Bene started pressuring me for payment or else... I mean, who better than you to set up? Another good decision, as it turned out—I needed someone to frame for the murder and the embezzler seemed the logical choice."

There was no way I was getting out alive. She couldn't let that happen.

"It's Stella's fault that she's dead. I gave her every opportunity not to make the call."

"The person your mother saw leaving Stella's was you?"

Stella shook her head. "Another good idea of mine. I convinced my mother that I'd seen you leaving but was up for a big job and couldn't be the one to identify you. Part of it was true. I did get a job—signed on to be Bene's errand girl to keep the interest on what I owed from skyrocketing, since I knew I wouldn't be getting my hands on any more cash. At least, not anytime soon."

"How did you find me today?" I asked.

"Paid for a background check and found out what kind of car you drove. It was easy to spot. Your office building was a piece of cake, but that building where you live is another story. Never figured out a way inside. Didn't matter. Every few days, I'd park on the street, waiting for you to leave. Not the best plan, but I got lucky this morning. Didn't have to wait long either."

Happy I didn't inconvenience you much.

"People are stupid. You think you're so smart, but you're no different. Were you paying attention walking to your car? Heck no. I got lucky on that parking space, so I knew it was fated—dragging you across the pavement would've attracted attention."

"I'm betting we can make a deal that's mutually beneficial."

Stacy eyed me speculatively. "There may be a way to prolong your existence… for a few anyway."

I'd bet whatever was on her pea-sized mind was illegal. "As smart as you are—" Sort of anyway. "—why not turn your talents to something legal?"

"Gambling is legal," Stacy said with a shrug.

I groaned inwardly. "Can't wait to hear your idea."

"I need money. You tell me how to get it, and a lot of it, and I'll leave you out here to fend for yourself—tied up, of course. That'll give me time to catch a boat to Mexico."

I didn't tell her that the Caribbean was closer and contained the only countries without extradition treaties she'd want to set foot in. I'd done my research. But then I fell for Seven and knew it would cause him endless trouble and he wouldn't come with me, so decided against it. A tear slid down my face at the thought that I'd never get to say good-bye.

"I've got money. I'll transfer it all to you." I didn't want to go down like this, but I'd weighed my options and there were none. The cash wasn't going to do me any good dead. She was the last person I wanted to have a nickel of it, but if it bought me time… And if I got out of here and made it back home and she hadn't squandered it, I'd re-appropriate it. Was it stealing if it originally belonged to me? No, and I'd enjoy every minute, only wishing I could see her face when she saw the zero balance.

The woman knew how to secure a rope. I'd rubbed my wrists bloody but hadn't been able to loosen it up. She stared at me for the longest time, and it was hard to know what she was thinking. Probably wondering if I could make good on my offer. If I got access to a computer, I'd figure out a way to send a message, for all the good it would do when I didn't know where I was.

Chapter Forty-Three

Stacy glared, shaking her head. My fear ratcheted up even higher, which I hadn't thought possible, as I waited for her to say something.

"I don't believe a word out of your mouth." She spit, wiping her mouth on her sleeve. "I thought shooting you would be the best option—one bullet and..." She made a sound effect that made me flinch. "But should you be found, don't want the cops looking for a murderer. So, suicide." *Da-da-dah!* in her voice.

I struggled not to flinch and refused to think about what she had in mind.

"Giving it more thought..." Stacy tapped her temple. "A terrible fire. A big enough blaze that there won't be anything left to identify." She produced a lighter from her pocket and flicked it, holding it out. "All options, as leaving you alive isn't one of them. Good thing I came prepared." She flicked the lighter, staring at the flame. Definitely the face of crazy.

Breathe, I told myself. *No hyperventilating.*

"Can anyone join this party?" Seven walked under the rollup, gun drawn and aimed at Stacy. "Go ahead and do something, anything. It would be my pleasure to shoot you. Just remember you were warned."

Grey was behind him and armed.

Stacy hissed in a breath and attempted to draw her own weapon, which barely made it out of her pocket before Seven shot it out of her hand. She screamed like she was dying, her blood mingling with the dirt.

"You might want to take your top off, staunch the flow before you bleed out." Seven sounded like he preferred the latter, reholstering his gun as he made his way over to me.

Grey continued to stand in the doorway, his gun pointed at Stacy, daring her to move. His fierce stare let her know he didn't have a problem with shooting her.

"Try not to kill her," I said, thinking that no one would believe what had gone down just based on my word. Even with her alive, I could see it easily becoming a she said/she said. Dead—who would believe me? Seven. I smiled up at the man.

Cars skidded in the dirt outside. Seconds later, four of Miami's finest trooped through the door with weapons drawn. One nodded at Grey, who reholstered his gun and stepped back.

"You know, darlin', you've got to marry me now." Seven grinned down at me.

"So happy to see you," I choked out as the tears ran like a river down my cheeks.

Seven reached out and wiped my tears with

the tail of his shirt. "You gotta stop. Men sissy out on tears."

Another cop showed up at Seven's shoulder, handing over a knife. He took it and stepped into the trough, gently cutting the ropes. As soon as I was free, I leaned forward and buried my face in his chest.

Seven held up his shirt again. "Best I can do."

My cheeks burned as I blew my nose. "I'll buy you a new one."

Seven cupped my face in his hands, turning it from side to side. "Bitch over there do this?" At my wordless agreement, he nodded. "I don't hit women but could easily make an exception."

"I'd rather do it myself."

Stacy went into a screaming, ranting frenzy, claiming to be my victim and that she'd just turned the tables and was about to escape and call the cops.

The cops hauled her to her feet, fighting them the whole time. They cuffed her, blood and all, and bagged her gun.

I hoped that meant they didn't believe a word out of her.

Stacy continued her tirade, not making a word of sense at some points.

"Fresh air," I whispered to Seven.

He lifted me out of the hole and carried me outside. "You going to be okay to stand?"

I nodded into his shoulder. When my feet were on the ground, I leaned into him and took a good look around. There was a road in the distance, but it would be a hike to cross the intervening acres, the weeds and overgrowth tearing at your legs and rocks ripping the skin off your feet. This being Florida, you could bank on bugs, and big ones, every step of the way.

Seven eyed my feet, then scooped me up again and carried me over to his SUV, opening the tailgate and setting me down with my feet hanging over the back bumper.

"How did you find me?" I asked, hoping he could hear the relief in my voice.

"Wanted to talk to you—I had something to share. I called and you didn't answer, which almost never happens, and then you didn't call back." Seven made a face. "I tried a couple of times, and then looked first at the tracker on your car, which said you were at a coffee shop. Then checked your phone, and it said you were in the weeds. I knew immediately something was wrong."

"I didn't know about the one on my car."

"A guy's got to keep a few tricks to himself."

I leaned my head against his shoulder. "After today, you can embed one under my skin."

A different cop showed up and asked me what happened. I told him everything in precise detail, starting with the fact that I was out on bail for murder, then skipped ahead to stopping for coffee and everything that Stacy had said and done. I remembered it all, her words seared into my brain.

Seven growled several times during my story. I scooted closer to him.

"We got a report back from our forensic accountant, showing that Stacy set up the phony accounts and moved the money out of Stella's accounts," Seven told us. "Just got it this morning," he answered my raised eyebrow. "We had a well-respected firm compile the evidence — they haven't had their evidence in a single case discredited or thrown out of court."

Two ambulances rolled across the dirt, and medics got out, grabbing their bags. Two went inside the building, and two came over to me. They checked me over, and it was decided, in part due to the firm insistence of Seven, that I be carted off to the hospital. I wouldn't have gone if he hadn't ridden with me. To my embarrassment, I had a panic attack as they lifted me into the ambulance. A medic gave me oxygen, Seven grasped my hand, and off we went to the hospital.

I didn't ask after Stacy because I didn't care as long as they didn't release her. From the grim look on the cop's face as I relayed what had happened, I suspected that at the very least, she wouldn't be released until they'd thoroughly investigated.

The ambulance rolled up to the emergency entrance, and I was taken to a room. Seven never left my side, and surprisingly, the doctor didn't ask him to wait outside, for which I was grateful. Never having been to the hospital, I found the experience unnerving.

Later, Grey showed with Harper and Rella. They'd brought me a change of clothes since my skirt and top had been trashed from rolling on the ground. They didn't stay long, having primarily come to drop off Seven's SUV.

"I want to go home and sit on the beach. I feel too beat-up for a walk."

Seven growled. "I'm going to make sure that you don't go anywhere until you're feeling one hundred percent."

"Kiss me." I smiled.

Chapter Forty-Four

Jury selection had been put on hold. The forensic accountant testified that Stacy Davis had stolen the money from Stella Bassett, and that despite the fact that she'd transferred the money into different accounts, it had been easy to track. They'd found no link between Stacy and me. In addition, they audited all of AE Financials' records and found no irregularities—everything in compliance with laws and regulations.

Stacy's attorney told the court that after recovering from surgery, her ramblings had escalated until she didn't have a single lucid moment and had been transferred to a mental hospital. The judge ruled that she'd be held until she was deemed fit to stand trial.

He then asked the prosecution about Arlene Hayes. The woman looked disgusted as she responded, "The mother's under a doctor's care, and her other daughter has moved her to California. Her lawyer promises full cooperation once her doctor releases her."

Another month and a day went by, and it felt surreal to hear the judge announce that the charges had been dropped against me. Cruz's huge grin and hug made it all sink in.

"Seven's going to be disappointed not to get the chance to kick your butt," I whispered.

Cruz threw his head back and laughed. "You heard that conversation, did you?"

"You better hustle those Italian loafers of yours and get this damn case wrapped up." Seven barked.

He had no idea that I'd passed the open door, heard him on the phone, and now stood in the doorway to eavesdrop.

"If you don't, I'll kick your overpriced butt into the next century."

I laughed, thankfully remembering to cover my mouth.

Seven turned with a glower and shook his finger at me.

It didn't have the effect he desired, as I dissolved into more laughter, mouth covered, and sank to the floor.

"My friend is crazy about you," Cruz said.

"I kind of like him too," I said as Seven pulled me into his arms.

* * *

"Just a hint."

"Patience."

I pouted as Seven drove along the coastal waters, then pulled over suddenly and wrapped a black strip of cloth over my eyes.

"We're not going somewhere creepy, are we?" I smoothed my hands down the front of my tropical dress to keep my nerves at bay.

"That's no way to impress my girl." He unleashed a growly laugh. "The only hint you get is that we'll be there in five minutes."

I sighed dramatically.

Seven chuckled.

His SUV came to another stop, and he cut the engine. I didn't move until I heard the door open. Seven hadn't said that I couldn't take off the blindfold, but I'd wait for him to do it. I didn't have to wait long. His hand touched my arm, and I felt the warmth of the sun on my face as he helped me out.

I could hear the water, taste the salt air. A ship whistled in the distance.

He removed the blindfold with a kiss, then turned me slowly until I faced the most luxurious yacht I'd ever laid eyes on.

"It's beautiful." I eyed every inch of the three-story white yacht and couldn't help but wonder what was going on.

"This is one of the luxury yachts my family owns and rents out for parties and special occasions. I told my brother that I'd let him decide which one we'd be using but that it better wow you."

I stood on my tiptoes and kissed him. "This is so awesome. I can't believe it."

"We're meeting our friends for dinner." He linked his arm in mine and led me forward.

"You've totally outdone yourself."

I was a hot commodity, and everyone wanted me to come for dinner. Maybe after I'd sat on the beach for a week. Harper had stepped up and offered to be the mean one but, unbeknownst to me, had party ideas of her own. And that was how the five of us ended up on a yacht cruising Biscayne Bay.

Seven led me up an outside set of stairs that took us to the pool area, where we found Rella, Harper, and Grey seated at the bar. The unobstructed view of the water was amazing.

Behind the bar, Grey filled our glasses, knowing what everyone liked. He raised his glass. "To friendship."

"I want to thank all of you for everything you did to keep me from going to jail." I still shuddered at the thought. "And I apologize for invading your office. My only excuse is that I didn't know what to do with myself." I winked at Grey.

"You were great with Anders, and if you weren't married to Seven, he'd be wanting a date."

Seven growled. The rest of us laughed.

"I feel bad that I haven't stayed in touch with the man. Sissy's probably driving him crazy." I made a mental note to call him.

"Your call to Cruz got him to recommend a shark of a divorce lawyer, which is more than he'd do for me." Grey snorted. "Great news on that front—Sissy signed the divorce papers, which stipulated no settlement, and moved out. In return, Anders didn't press charges."

"What all did you have on her?" Rella asked.

"It took some digging," Grey said. "But the forensic accountant had a friend who was willing to do shadier things than he was and uncovered proof of several underhanded deals. She'd fleeced more than one of her exes."

"What happened with Charles—the man that originally had Anders' account?" I asked.

"The company investigated and didn't find any collusion, just stupidity, which Anders was happy to hear," Grey told us.

"Anders is happy with how everything worked out and having a great time at Morningside," Seven said.

"I'm afraid to ask about River Brennan, since his mother was reluctant to give straight answers." Though if it was bad, I'd have heard already.

"I have good news there," Rella said. "My social worker friend, Margie, volunteered to go along with Riggs in an unofficial capacity when he introduced himself to Evelyn. They showed up unannounced and were completely honest with the woman. She invited them in, and they sat and talked for a couple of hours. Evelyn confessed to threatening Cara if she took River from her house, but did it because she feared for the boy, knowing Cara was a drunk."

"And what's happening with River?" I asked.

"He's still living with Evelyn, but Riggs sees him all the time. Evelyn has made it easy." Rella smiled. "Riggs got full custody from a judge, and to celebrate, he took River for the weekend. When River makes the final move, Riggs has already worked a deal with Evelyn for childcare while he's at work."

"What about the mother?" Harper asked.

Just what I was wondering.

"Cara's still in rehab and doing everything asked of her. Hopefully it'll work out," Rella said.

"You eager to get back to work?" Harper asked me.

"Getting my case thrown out has been good for business, as the phone has rung off the hook. I've brought Dixon on full-time. He's going to maintain the client accounts, except for family and friends — those I'll do myself."

"Will that be enough to keep you busy?" Rella asked.

"I think so. This is probably a good time to announce that I'm going to branch out into computer investigations. I found out I really enjoy snooping around online and want to do more. But I draw the line at chasing people down and will refer those jobs to WD."

"We'll send work your way, since we already know you do a great job," Grey said. "But we'll expect a discount."

"The first few are going to be freebies, until

I'm certain that I'm getting you all the information you need."

"I have no doubt you'll do an excellent job." Seven hugged me.

"I've got news of my own," Rella said. "I'm going to the Bahamas this weekend. One of my big donors needs a plus-one for a wedding."

"How is it this is the first we're hearing about your trip? Is the big donor a man?" Harper demanded.

"It's a she, and normally I would've told her no, but she called when I was feeling down about being the boring one in this trio. So I decided why not? A couple of times, I've wanted to pick up the phone and bail, but I can't do that to her, knowing she'll feel awkward showing up by herself."

"Great way to meet someone," Harper encouraged.

"I'm going for fun and sun, not hooking up with someone in a different country. Dating would be awkward."

"I hope you have a great time," I said with a smile. Everyone nodded.

A man in white pants and shirt came out on the deck and announced, "Dinner is ready."

Seven stood, wrapping his arm around me. He flashed that smile that made me all tingly. I moved in closer, knowing this was the man for me.

~*~

Preview the next in the series

Excerpt from *Jilted*

South Florida. Mimosas, quickie marriages and...Miranda rights?

Chapter One

A picture-perfect Florida day. Fluffy white clouds floated in the brilliant blue skies. The temperature hadn't warmed up enough to singe your skin off... yet. I was contemplating my third cup of coffee, planning to take it out to the balcony and watch the waves lap the white sand of the southernmost tip of South Beach.

I barely made it off my stool at the kitchen island, steps from the coffee pot, when the front door flew open. I sighed and sat back down to wait, knowing it would only be seconds before the invaders made their appearance. I'd known that they couldn't be held off by my choice to ignore their incessant pounding. I'd better have a good reason to accompany my emphatic "No" to whatever they were planning. I leaned back and caught my two best friends, Harper Finn and Avery English, glancing around the living room/dining room before heading down the hall toward my bedroom. Not sure what they thought I'd still be doing in bed.

The three of us had met at the University of Miami and become fast friends, the friendship only getting stronger after graduation. Now we each owned a condo unit on the forty-first floor of a building I owned.

It took them less than a minute to figure out that they only had two locations left to check—the kitchen and the balcony. They barreled back down the hall and soon had me in their sights. I waved, checking out their colorful flowing spaghetti-strap sundresses, perfect for the Miami heat.

"Rella! You're just sitting there watching us look for you without saying a word?" Harper's tone conveyed that she wasn't quite sure whether to be upset or not. "I suggested that we kick your door down." She pointed to her strappy sandal. "Not the right kind of shoes. So I reluctantly decided to knock politely, and where did that get me? I know you heard us."

"I told Harper not to risk breaking her foot when I had a lockpick." Avery brandished one from her pocket. "You should be proud of your star pupil." She beamed at Harper, who'd taught her how to use it.

Harper had several sneaky tricks in her repertoire, none of them legal, and Avery wanted to learn every one of them. I had to admit that even I had learning them on my to-do list, but I hadn't made the time yet.

"The only practice I get is picking the locks at WD." Avery made a face.

Grey Walker and Seven Donnelly, Harper's and Avery's boyfriends, who'd partnered in opening WD Consulting, a private investigation firm, wouldn't be happy to hear that she picked their locks to hone her skills.

"And who listens to the endless grouching every time you do that, or any of your other sneaky tricks?" Harper pointed to herself. But if asked, she'd have to admit that she was the last to be opposed to a little drama. "I'm not sure where Grey got the idea that you were the fragile sort." She eyed Avery. "When he said that, I laughed at him and told him to tell you to knock it off."

"You need to stop with all the noise and banging on the door. What will the neighbors think? You two were loud enough for the residents on the next floor down to hear," I said in a faux huff, knowing that the building was well-constructed and noises didn't travel; plus, we were the only residents on this floor. "You're lucky I didn't call the cops and report a break-in."

"Idle threat." Harper blew it off with a toss of her head and signaled to Avery. The two ran up to me, each grabbing an arm, and pulled me off the stool. "You're coming with us. Slip into a pair of those uncomfortable heels you love, and we'll get out of here."

My Saint Bernard, Bruno, who'd been lying at my feet, didn't bat an eyelash at either their manhandling or the fact that I'd barely managed to step over his massive body without landing on him.

I looked down at my silk ankle pants and bare manicured feet. Out of habit, I always dressed as though at any minute, weekend or not, the office would call and I'd drop everything to go in. Too many times, I went with the thought that I'd only stay for a few minutes, but it always turned into hours. I knew that if I went to the office today, it would be one of those days. "I can't. I need to check in at the office after being away, and I've got a file on my desk that needs my immediate attention." Okay, lame excuse. Even they knew there was no reason to go in on the weekend except for my obsessive need for control.

The Cabot Foundation was started by my parents. After they died when their private plane went down, I stepped in as CEO and poured my energy into helping women's and children's charities. I was determined that it would continue to be a success, even if it meant long hours.

"Fibber," Avery said, hands on her hips. "You're too young to be married to your job." I wondered if she noticed my flinch. "Saturday breakfast is a ritual. You've already missed one week for that wedding in the Bahamas, and we've yet to hear detail one. I'm betting that nothing earth-shattering happened at the foundation while you were gone and anything you need to do will still be there tomorrow."

"We're not going to take no for an answer," Harper said, a finger-shake in her tone.

Excerpt from *Jilted*

"Can't we—"

"No excuses," Harper cut me off. "If you force us, we *will* drag you out of here, and then how will *the* Rella Cabot explain being barefoot?" She made an expression of faux shock.

"I'm taking my own car," I yelled as I headed down the hallway toward my bedroom.

"And give us the slip? Don't think so," Avery yelled back.

We know each other so well. I laughed, having thought of doing just that. I slid into a pair of my favorite heels, ran a brush through my shoulder-length blond hair, and grabbed my purse. How am I going to tell them? I know it'll have to be sooner or later, but I'm really pushing for later. Much later. I met them at the front door, and they both laughed, thoroughly amused with themselves for pulling off their coup.

The three of us chatted as we rode down in the elevator to the garage and climbed into Harper's SUV.

It was a short drive to the Cat House Café on Washington Boulevard, and as usual, there were a dozen people lined up on one side of the front patio, a few spilling out onto the sidewalk. All of the outside tables were filled, which meant that the inside would be crowded.

Today, the owner, Prissy Mayes, was manning the front door, greeting guests, and she waved us right in. She was rocking an ankle-length fuchsia boho tunic dress, an army of bracelets up both arms, and her signature look, a flower—this one a gardenia—clipped in her bright-red hair, holding it back.

I had a few personal projects of my own that I backed, and this restaurant was one of my favorites. I'd invested in it, loving the addition that had been built onto the back patio—an enclosed area that acted as a playroom for cats available for adoption. I exchanged cheek kisses with Prissy.

"Business is great," she whispered in my ear.

"As evidenced by the line I see out front every time I drive by." I smiled back.

Prissy escorted to us our regular corner table on the back patio, which faced the glassed-in room for the cats. The kittens were active today, running up and down the scratching posts and leaping back and forth. There were two older cats cuddled up together, asleep in one of the overstuffed chairs.

Harper stopped at the bar on the way in and ordered a round of mimosas, which arrived not long after we sat down. "Best friends," she toasted. We raised our glasses.

"We've barely seen you since you got back from the wedding last weekend." Avery made a sad face. "Tell us that you didn't have a terrible time."

One of my biggest donors, Marcella, had been invited to the wedding of a friend of hers in the Bahamas and needed a plus one. It did sound fun when she first pitched the idea, and I didn't blame her for not wanting to go by herself. "It was hectic, and the time flew by." I felt my cheeks grow warm, more than a few memories vivid in my mind. "You two insisted that I have a good time, and I did. The warm waters rival ours here in Florida." I downed the rest of my mimosa, wanting another.

"We're eager for the details." Harper held up her hand, silently ordering another round of drinks.

Mind reader. I smiled.

"Better yet, did you manage to take pictures?" Avery asked, excited to see whatever I'd snapped.

I didn't want to break it to her that the thought never occurred to me.

"The wedding…"

A breeze blew across the water and cooled down the day. The sun was setting, and fingers of color splashed across most of the sky. They were still bright but would soon fade, settling into dark-blue tones that filled the sky as it turned to night.

Marcella and I were among the first guests to arrive. All the seating was on one side of the aisle, and we were shown to seats in the second row of chairs in front of the flower-draped altar, within feet of where the blue-green water lapped the shore. The rest of the guests trickled in by ones and twos and made their way down the wooden walkway over the white sand. The crowd turned out to be small and intimate, all smiling and a number of them barefoot.

A woman seated herself at the baby grand piano and started playing. At the same time, fireworks shot into the air, bursting overhead and showering the sky with bright flashes of color.

The first to make an appearance was the groom, a well-dressed thirty-something, his black hair slicked back, in well-tailored white slacks and a dress shirt with a white rose pinned to it. Behind him was his best man, dressed the same except he wore a red rose. They moved up the petal-strewn aisle to where the pastor stood, their friends calling out greetings.

The groom-to-be and best man turned and stared down the aisle. They leaned towards each other, and the best man said something that made them both laugh. Then they waited. And waited.

It was at least fifteen minutes before a woman in a strapless sea-green dress came down the aisle and stopped in front of the groom, the best man stepping to his side. It was a short conversation, and then she left, an uncomfortable smile on her face. The groom talked to the pastor, who patted him on the shoulder.

Taking the microphone, the groom turned to the assembled guests. You could have heard a pin drop. "My bride has changed her mind, and there won't be a wedding. I want to thank all of you for coming. There's an open bar and plenty to eat."

"What?" Harper and Avery shrieked.

"Wasn't Marcella friends with the bride? What did she say?" Harper demanded.

"Marcella…" I laughed. "Realizing that the groom, Pryce Thornton, was now a free man, she ran after him with a proposal of her own. Her parting words to me were, 'I'll offer my condolences and my phone number.' By then, I needed a drink and went to the beach bar."

"I'm assuming the woman who broke the news wasn't the bride-to-be?" Avery asked, and Harper nodded, also wanting to know. "How awful, and to wait until the groom was already at the altar…"

"I ended up mingling with a few of Pryce's friends at the bar and found out that the woman who broke the news was a friend of the bride and the maid of honor," I said. "They talked about placing a bet about whether she'd volunteered to be the bearer of the news, but no one knew her well enough to ask."

"You partied with the groom's friends?" Harper asked, sounding excited.

"Before you start with a hundred questions, 'partied' is grossly overstating it. What I did was order a drink, sip slowly, and listen to their conversations. The consensus was 'Good riddance.' And before one of you asks—because I know what's coming next—no, I never met the bride or any of her other friends. Just a brief glance at the one who delivered the 'It's off,' message. Not sure what I would've said after the usual pleasantries, had I been introduced. I'm not very pushy when it comes to things that are none of my business. And to answer your next question, the groom didn't come to the party."

"Then you smiled politely, went back to your

room, and read a book," Avery said with a knowing nod.

I shot them both a faux glare. "I'll have you know, I got another drink and walked along the shoreline. Ran into this gorgeous stranger, and well… we hooked up." *So there* in my tone.

They both gasped.

Not entirely true — he wasn't a complete stranger, as I *did* recognize him, though we hadn't been formally introduced. "We spent the rest of the weekend together."

Not sure who laughed first, but they were both laughing, neither believing a word.

"When have you ever known me to lie? Or even engage in half-truths? Unless it's for a favor I'm doing for one of you." I maintained eye contact with them, not flinching. "You two are always encouraging me to do something a bit wild, and when I do, you stare at me like I made everything up. Now that's annoying."

It took them a minute, but they both came around to believing that I was telling the truth.

"Details." Avery snapped her fingers. Harper grinned. "You're smiling, which is good and can only mean you had a good time. Like a really good one." She tapped her finger impatiently on the table top. "Name, social security number, and I'll run a background check on the man." Avery, an established financial consultant, had ventured off into doing background investigations and now split her time between finance and investigation, working exclusively for WD on the latter.

"I'll admit that he and I may have tipped a few — an open bar is hard to resist. A drink or two, and we ended up spending the rest of the weekend on a yacht, talking about everything and nothing."

They both shrieked.

"Keep your voices down before we get kicked out." I tossed a glance over my shoulder. "People are staring." I froze in my chair, looking up into familiar deep-blue eyes.

"Are you going to introduce your husband to your friends?"

~*~

Other Titles by Deborah Brown

BISCAYNE BAY SERIES
Hired Killer
Not Guilty
Jilted (October 2021)

PARADISE SERIES
Crazy in Paradise
Deception in Paradise
Trouble in Paradise
Murder in Paradise
Greed in Paradise
Revenge in Paradise
Kidnapped in Paradise
Swindled in Paradise
Executed in Paradise
Hurricane in Paradise
Lottery in Paradise
Ambushed in Paradise
Christmas in Paradise
Blownup in Paradise
Psycho in Paradise
Overdose in Paradise
Initiation in Paradise
Jealous in Paradise
Wronged in Paradise
Vanished in Paradise
Fraud in Paradise
Naive in Paradise
Bodies in Paradise
Accused in Paradise

Deborah's books are available on Amazon
amazon.com/Deborah-Brown/e/B0059MAIKQ

About the Author

Deborah Brown is an Amazon bestselling author of the Paradise series. She lives on the Gulf of Mexico, with her ungrateful animals, where Mother Nature takes out her bad attitude in the form of hurricanes.

For a free short story, sign up for my newsletter. It will also keep you up-to-date with new releases and special promotions:
www.deborahbrownbooks.com

Follow on FaceBook:
facebook.com/DeborahBrownAuthor

You can contact her at Wildcurls@hotmail.com

Deborah's books are available on Amazon
amazon.com/Deborah-Brown/e/B0059MAIKQ

Made in United States
Orlando, FL
25 July 2024